Caught Up

Also by Amir Abrams

Crazy Love

The Girl of His Dreams

Hollywood High series (with Ni-Ni Simone)

Hollywood High

Get Ready for War

Put Your Diamonds Up

Lights, Love & Lip Gloss

Published by Kensington Publishing Corp.

Caught Up

AMIR ABRAMS

Dafina KTeen Books
KENSINGTON PUBLISHING CORP.
www.kensingtonbooks.com

DAFINA KTEEN BOOKS are published by

Kensington Publishing Corp.
119 West 40th Street
New York, NY 10018

All Kensington titles, imprints, and distributed lines are available at special quantity discounts for bulk purchases for sales promotion, premiums, fund-raising, and educational or institutional use.

Special book excerpts or customized printings can also be created to fit specific needs. For details, write or phone the office of the Kensington Special Sales Manager: Kensington Publishing Corp., 119 West 40th Street, New York, NY 10018. Attn. Special Sales Department. Phone: 1-800-221-2647.

KTeen logo Reg. U.S. Pat. & TM Off.
Sunburst logo Reg. U.S. Pat. & TM Off.

ISBN-13: 978-0-7582-9478-4
ISBN-10: 0-7582-9478-6
First Kensington Trade Paperback Printing: December 2014

eISBN-13: 978-0-7582-9479-1
eISBN-10: 0-7582-9479-4
First Kensington Electronic Edition: December 2014

10 9 8 7 6 5 4 3 2 1

Printed in the United States of America

This book is dedicated to every young girl who has ever found herself caught up looking for love and excitement in all the wrong places and faces.

1

Swaggerlicious. That's the word that comes to mind to describe this dark-skinned cutie-pie standing in front of me with the gold fronts in his mouth, pierced ears, and an arm covered in intricately designed tattoos trying to get his rap on. Swag plus delicious equals *swaggerlicious*. Not that *that's* a real word found in Webster's dictionary or anything. No. It's found in the hood. It oozes out of the music. It jumps out at you in the videos. It's splattered all over the pages of *Vibe* and *XXL* and every other hip hop magazine there is. It's flooded in the pages of every urban fiction novel I've coveted over the last two years. It airs on *Love & Hip Hop* and *BET*. Okay, okay, maybe there's more ratchetness than swaggerlicousness on those TV shows. Still...it's there. That hood swag.

And it's my guilty craving. It's my dirty secret.

I want it.

Swag.

I ache to know what it's like to be caught up in the excitement of the fast-paced street life found across the other side of town—right smack in the heart of the hood, where I am not ever allowed to be. Where the streets are hot and alive and full of excitement.

God, my parents would have a full-fledged heart attack if they knew I was saying this, that I'm attracted to the hood life. Fascinated and intrigued by it.

See. I'm from the suburbs. Live in a gated community. And swag doesn't exist here. Not in my eyes. Not in my opinion. And definitely not in the way it lives and breathes in the hood. Or in the *ghetto,* as my mom would call it.

But I personally don't think there's anything *ghetto* about the hood. I think ghetto is a state of mind as well as a state of being. And I definitely don't think everyone who lives in the hood is ghetto. But of course, my parents, particularly my mom, would beg to differ. Whatever.

Anyway, back to my quest for swag. I attend an all-girls private school. And trust me, swag definitely isn't there, either. Nope. I'm surrounded by girls whose only focuses are cotillions, prom gowns, graduations, sleepovers, shopping sprees, dating boys with promising futures, while preparing for the SATs.

Can you say *borrrrrriiiing.*

My life is swagless!

Don't get me wrong. I dress nice. *Cute* is more like it. Okay, maybe a little preppy. Still, I have nice things. And I am always nicely dressed nonetheless. However, sometimes I feel like a fashion loser—even though I *know* it's all in my head—when I see a clique of girls stylishly dressed in all the hottest designer labels, strutting through the mall, yapping it up, catching the eyes of boys with a whole lot of hood swag.

That's the girl I want to be—the girl with the sexy strut and a whole lot of sass. Not that there's anything wrong with who I am now. It's just that... I mean. I'm a cutie and all. And I have a nice body, from what I'm told. And lots of guys try to talk to me. Still... for the most part, I am a really basic girl. No lipstick. No eyeliner. Not a lot of fuss with my crinkly hair. Not much time spent in the mirror. Basically, I'm what my mother calls "low maintenance."

Translation: Plain Jane. Nothing special. Ordinary looking.

Yup, that's me. Plain ole, ordinary-looking Kennedy, with nothing special going on in her life. Well, guess what? School is out. It's the start of summer. And if I have my way, a change is about to come. Soon.

"So, what's good witchu, ma?" Mr. Swag says, reaching out and touching my left cheek. He's about five-ten with a slim but muscular build. He kind of reminds me of a sprinter. Lean and trim. "You real sexy, babe."

I smile. "Thanks."

"You make me wanna do some thangs to you; real spit, ma. Who you out here wit'? I been checkin' for you for a minute."

I blush. Tell him I'm here with my friend Jordan. This is like the fourth time I've *run* into him at the mall. The first time was a few weeks back. He was with a crew of guys all dressed in different color POLO sweat suits with matching snapback hats and limited-edition Nikes. They were all looking like they should be on the cover of the latest *Hip Hop* magazine. And when he called me over to him, I felt my nervousness give way to excitement, like right now.

"Oh word? That's wassup. So how 'bout you 'n' me go grab a bite to eat real quick so we can get better acquainted while ya peeps do what they do?"

I glance at my watch. "I can't. I have to find my friend then get ready to go." It's a bold-faced lie. Truth is, I don't date much. I mean, I do. But I only date guys who are parent-approved. And this fine boy right here is definitely, unequivocally, not someone my parents would ever allow me to go off anywhere with, let alone date—even if it is only up to the next level of the mall to get something to eat. Not that it's a date. Not that he's even asking me out on one or anything like that. Although I wish like heck he would. Then again, maybe I don't.

I eye the thick chain hanging from his neck, wondering if it's silver, stainless steel, or white gold and if the diamonds in the cross dangling from it are real. My gaze shifts down to his half-laced Timberlands, then back up. I swallow. My mouth waters at the way his sagging jeans hang off his narrow hips, showing the waistband of his POLO boxers. He has on a Gucci belt.

Swaggerlicious. Hmmm. Yes, that's him. The expression used to describe someone who has lots of swag and loads of confidence. It's in the way someone walks, and talks, and carries himself. And it's a word I would never, ever, be caught dead using in front of my besties—or worse, my parents.

They'd die.

No scratch that. They'd kill *me* first. Then die.

How dare I want to use such street slang? How dare I want to toss away thousands and thousands of dollars' worth of my parents' hard-earned money they've spent to send me to the best private schools in order to shield me from such atrocities. I'd be damned to hell for eternity, roasting a hundred deaths, for shaming them.

Okay, okay. I'm being facetious.

I'm overexaggerating; just a little.

Still…they'd probably want to lock me away until my twenty-first birthday if they even thought I was standing here contemplating ditching my bestie to go off with this guy who I've only been talking to for—I glance at my watch—seventeen minutes and thirty-six seconds. He could be a stalker. Or worse.

A hoodlum.

A thug.

I want to laugh at the absurdity.

Rule number one: No hoodlums allowed. Rule number two: No profanity. Rule number three: No street slang.

And already I'm breaking two of the three parent-enforced rules. Standing here cavorting with the likes of a potential hoodlum and allowing the word swagger-licious—*gasp*—to enter my mind. Oh, this is grounds for a long, drawn-out lecture on how irresponsible it is to keep company with someone like Mr. Swag. And how catastrophic using such vernacular is. How unfitting it is. How improper it is. How unladylike it is. Blah, blah, blah.

Well, guess what?

I don't see anything wrong with it. Swaggerlicious. Swaggerlicious. Swag. Ger. Licious. There. I've said it.

And this guy right here reeks of it. Okay, along with the marijuana I'm sure he's smoked right before coming into the mall. I glance up at his ear and notice he has a Black & Mild cigar tucked behind it. But that's neither here nor there.

Point is, I'm tired of fitting into everyone else's box of expectations. I'm tired of being proper and polite—*all* the time. Why must I use proper English all the time? Why can't I take a leave of absence from *talking* and *sounding* white, just once?

I want a sabbatical from my life, just for the summer. Is there anything wrong with wanting a change of pace? No. I don't think so.

I'm sick of being everything everyone else wants, expects, me to be—*all* the time. The sixteen-year-old, college-bound, soon-to-be junior who gets straight A's in school; the high school varsity cheerleader who executes every floor routine with precision; the daughter who always listens to her parents and never breaks any of their rules—no matter how ridiculous I think most of them are; the little sister who has had to constantly live in the shadows of her three overprotective, overachieving, academically and athletically gifted brothers.

"You have some sexy lips, ma. I just wanna lean in 'n' kiss 'em."

I blink Mr. Swag back into view.

Wait.

Did he just say what I think he did?

I ask him to repeat himself. He does. "I wanna kiss you. Word is bond."

"You don't even know me like that." I try to stay cool about it and act like having some random guy telling me he wants to kiss me is an everyday occurrence when it's more like a once-in-a-lifetime opportunity that I am about to blow.

"Yeah, but I can *get* to know you like that." He steps in closer. "If you let me."

I am feeling light-headed. And right now. Here's my dilemma: I've never, ever gone against my parents. I'm the perfect daughter, the perfect friend, and the perfect little Miss Goody Two-shoes.

In a nutshell, my life is *predictable*. And *boring*.

But, like I said already, the school year is officially over. It's the start of the summer. And I want to have fun. I want to do something exciting. I want to live on the edge a little. Be daring. Be adventurous.

Instead of living vicariously through the characters in some of the hood—oops, I mean, urban—books I read, I want to be the girl exploring the world outside of the one my parents have given me. I want a little taste of the wild side.

A little slice of the hood pie.

Just a little.

I glance over my shoulder quickly to see if anyone's looking over at us. Then look up into his smoldering brown eyes, stepping closer into him.

One kiss won't hurt. Will it?

2

"*Ohmygod!*" Jordan shrieks the minute we step out of the mall and walk into the bright sun toward the parking lot where her parents' silver 2013 Mercedes is parked. She slides her Ray-Bans on, shaking her head. "I know *you*. Were. *Not*. About to *kiss* that boy, were you? Please, *please* tell me I was imagining things."

Uh, noooo! You weren't imagining anything. I was about to lock lips with him until you came along and ruined my chance at having a private tongue-dance moment with him.

I eye my bestie. Take in her smooth mocha-colored complexion. Her bouncy, shoulder-length hair is done to perfection. Everything about Jordan is always, always perrrrrfect. She has on a short white denim skirt with a yellow camisole and a pair of yellow Minnetonka Ashleys. Her hips swing as she walks. She doesn't walk. She sways.

"Girl, relax," I say, running my hand through my hair. "We were only talking."

She stops in her tracks. Peers over the rim of her shades and says, *"Talking?* Is that what they're calling that these days?"

As we approach her car, she aims the remote in the car's direction, disarming the alarm and unlocking the doors.

"Is that what they're calling what?" I feign ignorance as I open the rear passenger-side door, tossing my bags on the seat.

"Oh, don't even try to play me. You know exactly what I'm talking about. All that googly-eyeballing the two of you were doing. Looked to me like there wasn't much talking going on. Oh, wait. I get it. It's called mental telepathy. Was he telepathically telling you how much he wanted to shove his tongue down into your throat?"

I laugh as she opens the trunk and tosses her bags inside. "Whatever."

"Whatever nothing." She slams the trunk shut, pulling out her ringing cell. She glances at the screen, then rolls her eyes. "Ohmygod! Why does this boy keep calling me? He's such a frickin' loser."

She's referring to her boyfriend...um, *ex*-boyfriend—for today, that is. Howard. The very corny, very nerdy, six foot three, Harvard University–bound, aspiring neurosurgeon she's been dating since eighth grade. But lately, they've been breaking up like every other week over ridiculousness. Their most recent break-up was over onion rings. Onion rings! Can you believe that? He reached over and ate the last of her onion rings off her plate and it became a major catastrophic event. "He's so selfish and inconsiderate. And I'm sick of it," she'd said as she prattled on and on about how she could never spend her life with someone like that. "I'm done with him."

I roll my eyes at her, opening the passenger door. "Uh-huh. Girl, who are you fooling? We both know you are far from done with Mister Howard. You love that boy."

"Well…" She pops her lips. "That's beside the point." She opens the driver's-side door and slides behind the wheel, then fastens her seat belt. "He's doing too much. I mean, really. He needs to give me a chance to miss him."

I shake my head. "And this is all over what again?" I ask, pretending to have forgotten.

She sticks the key into the ignition, then starts the engine. "It's over his lack of consideration for my feelings, Kennedy. Geesh. How many times do I have to tell you this? I thought you of all people would understand that. I can't date anyone who can't be sensitive to my needs."

I blink. "Ohhhhkay. So because he ate the last of your onion rings that makes him inconsiderate and insensitive?"

"Yes." She backs out of the parking space and drives away. "And thoughtless. Wait. I thought you didn't remember why we'd broke up."

"Oh, how I've tried," I say sarcastically.

"Whatever. I know you think it's silly. But it's the principle. He had no right eating food off of my plate without asking me first. How did he know I was finished? He didn't ask."

"Well, were you finished?"

She gives me an incredulous look as if I've asked a trick question. "Yeah. But he didn't know that."

I give her a blank stare.

"Oh, save it. Don't give me that look. Today's it's onion rings. Tomorrow it's him telling me what I can and cannot wear, going through my cell phone, and deleting my Twitter and Facebook accounts. I will not have my boundaries violated by any boy. Not even one I'm madly in love with."

I wave her on, shaking my head. "Girl, please. That makes that boy greedy. Not thoughtless or insensitive. Maybe you're being just a little too hard on him. If you ask me, I think you're blowing this whole thing out of proportion."

She shoots me an incredulous look as we approach a red light. "Ohmygod! Whose side are you on here?"

"Yours, of course. When you're right, that is. Right now, however, I think you might be overexaggerating things, just a tad. I know I tease you about him being a cornball. But underneath all of his doofiness I kind of like him for you. He's a really nice guy, Jordan."

She smiles, driving off. "And he's really cute, too."

Yeah, I guess. If you go for guys with the light skin and green eyes. Howard sort of reminds me of a Corbin Bleu look-alike without the brown eyes, just taller and more muscled. Me, personally, I prefer guys with some color to them. Rich mahogany brown. Dark chocolate. Mmmhmmm... delicious.

"And he's really nice," I repeat, ignoring her "he's really cute, too" comment.

"Well, that's true too. He has his moments. But this isn't about Howard. Or me. Or any of his annoying ways that get under my skin. This is about *you,* so don't even think I've forgotten how you were practically ready to get lost in a lip lock with some random hoodlum."

I roll my eyes. "He's not a *hoodlum.*"

"Coulda fooled me. That boy reeked of marijuana and roach spray."

I crack up laughing. "Ohmygod. He did not. That is so

not nice. Just because he's from the hood, that doesn't automatically make him a hoodlum. He's actually a nice guy."

"Mmmph. And how do you know that?"

"Well, I don't. Not really. I mean. He seemed nice. And he didn't come off like a *hoodlum*, as you say."

"Well, he *looked* like one to me. And you know what they say, if he walks like a thug and talks like a thug, then…"

I shake my head. Any boy who wears Timberlands, hoodies, a do-rag, or sagging pants and isn't in a pair of khakis and a polo shirt, or doesn't play lacrosse, is her definition of a hoodlum.

"I know you're familiar with the expression 'you shouldn't judge a book by its cover,' right? Maybe you should free your mind and try it."

She takes her eyes off the road, glancing over at me. "My mind is free. And I'm not judging him. I'm merely stating an observation."

"Yeah, an observation based on opinion. Not fact."

"Oh, whatever. He probably sells drugs, too. I wouldn't put it past him. No judgment."

I shake my head. "Wow. I can't tell."

I love Jordan like a sister. I swear I do. But sometimes she can be so judgmental. And…well, disturbingly narrow-minded at times. Still, I wouldn't trade her for the world. She always has my back. And I'll always have hers.

Even though I know what her response is going to be, I decide to ask anyway. "Hey, you want to take a road trip over to Irvington to hang out with my cousins?"

I call it a *road trip*, because although Irvington is only like twenty-five minutes away from where we live, it's like worlds apart from the life she and I live. Where we have estates and circular driveways and tree-lined streets, they have dilapidated buildings, abandoned houses, and trash-littered streets. And they have more murders and robberies than any other town in the area. Still, I enjoy going there to visit my twin cousins Shaniqua and Kaniqua. They're my uncle Kent's—my father's brother's—daughters, and they're hilarious. They live with their mother, Tiny. Well, Tiny isn't really all that little. She's more like whopper size. My brothers used to call her Auntie Big Whopper. Not to her face, though.

Jordan's car almost swerves over into the other lane as she snaps her neck in my direction. "*Irvington? Thugville?* In my parents' Benz? Oh, I don't think so. So I can be robbed? Or worse...*raped?* Girl, you have really lost your mind."

I roll my eyes at her theatrics. "Ohmygod, stop! No one is going to rape you, girl. Besides, you know my cousins look out for us."

She sucks her teeth. "Girl, please. They look out for *you.* You know your cousins Boomquisha and Boomquita do not even like me. They'd save them roaches they keep for pets from getting stomped out before they'd ever look out for me."

I laugh. "Oooh, you're so wrong for that. And I'm dead wrong for laughing at it."

But she's right. They don't like her. They want to fight her. And she's never done anything to either of them. Well, maybe they might have caught her rolling her eyes up in her head when she thought one of them wasn't looking, or they caught her giving me one of her looks when they said or did something that was maybe a little bit on the ridiculous side. Like the time they both had on matching pink bodysuits, a pair of those glass-looking stripper heels, and bright fuchsia china doll wigs. I didn't want to admit it, but they did look like two circus acts. Most times they do.

Still...those are my first cousins and they like to party and have a good time. And they don't care who doesn't like it, or them. They do whatever they want. Whenever they want.

"Don't you sometimes just want to live on the edge a little?" I ask, shifting in my seat. "Don't you ever get bored following the rules, or coloring within the lines?"

Jordan gives me a blank look. Then bats her lashes. "I do live on the edge. I'm on the edge of my seat every time I'm out with you, wondering what craziness you're going to get into next, like kissing riffraff."

"What if I *did* want to kiss him? What's so wrong with that? He had nice lips. And he was cute."

"Do you even know him?" She lets out a disgusted sigh. "Never mind. Nice lips or not. That's nasty. I mean. Aside from probably sucking down pig's guts and chicken claws, do you even know where that boy's mouth's been?"

I swear. Jordan can be such a joy-kill sometimes. Okay, most of the time. She'll yammer on and on about this for most of the ride to her house if I don't quickly redirect the conversation.

"You're right. I don't know what I was thinking."

"That's just it. You weren't thinking."

"I'm sorry, mom," I say sarcastically. "I won't let it happen again."

She laughs. "Yeah, right."

"Soooo, did you end up buying that cute skirt you saw in Nordstrom?"

She shakes her head. "Oh, no. We're not even about to

change subjects. Not this time. I want to know where you know that boy from."

I tell her I don't know him. That I've only seen him a few times in the mall. That he's tried to talk to me several times, but he's always with his friends.

She shoots me a look, rolling her eyes. "So what's his name?"

"B-U," I tell her, shifting in my seat.

She brakes at the stop sign. *"B-U?* What kind of crazy name is that?" I tell her it's short for Born-Universe.

She frowns, pulling off. *"Born-Universe?* See. What I tell you? Strike one right there. Who in the world names their child *that?"*

I shrug. "I seriously doubt that's his real name. At least I hope it isn't."

She grunts. "Does this Born U . . . B-U, or whoever he is, even have a high school diploma?"

I shrug. "I didn't ask. It's not like I was conducting an interview."

"Well, you should have been."

"Jordan, ohmygod! You really need to learn how to relax a bit. I think you need to lay off the *CSI* episodes. They're causing you to overreact."

She reaches over and touches my forehead. "Kennedy, girl, either you must be coming down with something or you're an imposter. Because the Kennedy I *know* would never, ever, be caught dead trying to kiss some strange boy in the middle of a half-packed mall."

I swat her hand away. "No, I'm not coming down with anything. And no, I'm not an imposter. Tell the truth. You didn't think he was cute when you saw him?"

"Ummm, nooo. I thought he was *ratchet.*"

I crack up laughing. She sounded so funny saying that. "Jordan, girl. Stop. There was nothing *ratchet* about him. Do you even know what ratchet is?"

"Yeah, I know what it is. Him. Jeans sagging. Underwear showing. I bet you he doesn't even know the real meaning behind wearing his pants sagging like that. Advertising his butt like that. If he only knew all he was doing was giving booty bandits something to drool about. I bet if he were in prison walking around like that he'd break his neck trying to find a belt or rope to keep his pants up over his behind. Or he'd end up wearing Kool-Aid painted on his lips and being called Bubblicious, while Big Bubba and his sweet tooth crew humped up on him."

I playfully swat at her arm. "Ohmygod, that's so disgusting!"

"Mmmph. He's disgusting. His neck and arm inked up. And what were those teardrops on his face for. Ugh! Then top it off with a mouth full of gold. And there you have it. Ratchet. His teeth are probably all rotted out behind all that metal."

"Ohmygod, stop!" I bite the inside of my lip to keep from laughing.

"No. You need to stop being so naïve. Kennedy, those kinds of boys will do nothing but use you up, then break your heart. You remember Nyla's cousin Sheema, right?" I nod. "Well, she hooked up with some thug from Newark, and now she's a druggie and pregnant."

"A druggie?"

"Yes. All she does is smoke marijuana all day."

"That doesn't make her a druggie."

"Well, it makes her stupid; that's for sure. And three months pregnant."

"And you blame that on her boyfriend?"

"Correction. Her *thug*. And, yes, I do. He is and was her demise. Now back to you. Since when you start vying for the attention of thugs?"

I don't tell her that I've secretly lusted for bad boys since like forever. I'm not in the mood for a long, drawn-out lecture from her. Or being under her judgmental scrutiny for having a deep affinity for the street life.

I shrug. "I'm not vying for their attention. I'm simply trying to have a little fun. You know. Do something different."

She narrows her eyes. "So what is this, some sort of teen life crisis? You want to do something different, go snow-boarding. Go paragliding. Go shopping for a pair of red hooker heels. But you don't go rifling through the trash for a boyfriend."

I wave her on as she navigates traffic, my hand absently tracing the thick leather piping of my purse. "You're such a hater."

"I am most certainly not," she says, feigning insult. "I simply hate seeing my dearest bestie in the midst of making the most tragic mistake of her life. I thought I was going to collapse right there in the middle of the floor seeing the two of you all cozied up like that."

I laugh. "Then I guess he and those sexy lips of his would have been the ones to resuscitate you. It would serve you right for how rude you were to him."

"Ewww. Not! Leave me dead on the ground. Please and thank you! I wouldn't want that boy's hood cooties any-where near me, or my mouth."

I laugh and playfully suck my teeth. I decide to not mention that he thought she was stuck-up. It wouldn't matter to her, anyway, what he thought of her. She knows she's a snob. Well, as she says it, "I know I have snobbish ways."

She snorts. "I was not rude. I just wasn't interested in being nice."

"Same difference, girly. Same difference."

3

"I mean, like, seriously, Kennedy. What do you even see in them hoodlums? They are so..."

Fine.

"They're so...how can I delicately say this? They are so..."

Sexy.

"*Beneath* you," she says pointedly, shooting a glance over in my direction as she pulls around her circular driveway.

"Ohmygod, Jordan!" I exclaim, shaking my head. I can't believe she thinks that. That because a guy doesn't live in a gated community, or attend a private school, or drive a luxury car gifted to him by his parents (or grandparents) that he isn't worthy of dating, or falling in love with. "You are so out of control right now. What a classist thing to say."

She rolls her eyes, parking her car in front of the cobblestone walkway that leads to her front door. "No. You're the one out of control, Kennedy. Practically ready to kiss some derelict, and in public no less." She shakes her head, turning off the engine. "Is this some kind of crazy phase you're going through? I mean. We've been best friends for, like, forever, so you can tell me if it is. Because it seems to me like you might be struggling with some sort of teen life crisis or something."

I sigh, opening the car door. "*Noooo,* it's not a *phase.* And the *only* thing I'm struggling with at the moment is *you.*"

She opens her door, popping the trunk open. "Struggling with *me?* All I'm doing is stating the obvious."

I raise a brow at her. "Oh, really? What exactly is that?"

She grabs her bags, slamming the trunk shut. "That the only thing any boy from the *ghetto, hood, slums,* or whatever they're calling it these days can ever do is use and abuse you, Kennedy. They'll break your heart. Then toss you out like last night's trash while they lie in wait for their next unsuspecting suburban victim."

I frown. "Ohmygod! That is so not true. Having my heart broken has nothing to do with someone's socio-economic status, where they're brought up, or what race they are. Heartbreakers and users come from all walks of life."

"Well, that might be true. But they're being bred in the ghetto," she says dismissively. "Kennedy, I can't believe you're being so naïve right now."

"Well, that makes the two of us," I say defensively. "I can't believe you're being so dang biased."

"I'm not biased. Face it, Kennedy. Most of those so-called thug boys you're so fascinated with are high-school dropouts, use drugs, sell drugs, are in gangs, and in and out of juvy."

"That is so not true. There are plenty who graduate high school and even go off to college."

She laughs, shaking her head while sliding her key into

her door. *"Plenty?* Yeah, right. Wishful thinking. Try *plenty* of prison-bound losers. I don't know what TBS special you've been watching. But you need to either change stations, or remove those rose-colored lenses you're looking through. There are *plenty* of dropouts. There are *plenty* hanging on street corners."

I sigh. *It's time I face the blaring truth,* I think, following behind Jordan as she lets herself into her house replete with shopping bags galore. *There's nothing I can ever say that will make an ounce of sense to her about my affinity toward boys from the hood. So there's no sense in wasting my breath trying to explain it.*

She drops her bags onto the marble floor of her foyer. I walk behind her as she heads toward the kitchen. No one else's here. Her parents oftentimes work long hours. They are both corporate attorneys who work out of a Madison Avenue law firm in New York City. Like me, Jordan is the youngest. But instead of having three older, overprotective brothers, she has three older sisters who spoil her rotten. I so envy her for that. I wish I had sisters. I mean. Having older brothers is kind of cool. But they can be annoying. And bossy; especially when they're trying to be my fathers.

Anyway, like my siblings—who are all in the armed forces (my nineteen-year-old brother, Kent, is in his second year as a cadet at the Naval Academy; my twenty-one-year-old brother, Keith, just graduated from West Point; and my twenty-three-year-old brother, Kenneth, is a commissioned officer in the Air Force)—her sisters all live out on their own. So, for the most part, she has this big gigantic house all to herself, to do whatever she wants long before her parents' commute home comes to an end for the night.

"You want anything to eat?" she asks as she's grabbing two bottles of Fiji water and a large bowl of strawberries from the fridge. "I can heat up some chicken strips if you want."

I shake my head, reaching for the latest issue of *Seventeen* magazine lying on the aisle counter. "No. I'm fine." I flip through the pages. I roll my eyes when I stumble on an article on Miley Cyrus and her newest love interest. Jordan tells me to grab some napkins from the marble table. I shut the magazine, grab a handful of napkins, then follow her upstairs to her room.

I love Jordan's room. In addition to having a huge king-size bed and fifty-inch flat-screen TV, she has a massive walk-in closet, a huge bathroom with a Jacuzzi tub and separate shower stall, and a balcony.

My bedroom isn't anything to sneeze at, but it's definitely nothing like hers. I'd kill to have my own private bathroom in my room.

I open my water, take a few sips, then place the cap back on, and set it down on the floor beside her bed. I kick off my shoes and flop back against the big, fluffy pillows on her bed, flipping through the magazine I've been holding in my hand.

"So, what time is Hope getting here?"

She steps out of her bathroom, completely changed into a pair of red boy shorts and a black sports bra. "She should have been here by now. You know she's almost always never on time. That girl will probably be late to her own embalming."

I shake my head, laughing. "You're stupid."

The doorbell chimes three times as Jordan picks up her buzzing iPhone.

"Speaking of the Miss Late, that's her now."

She scurries out of the room and rushes down the stairs to get the ringing doorbell. A few seconds later, she returns with Hope following behind her.

"Ooh, you nasty heathen," she says pointedly as she drops her Burberry tote on Jordan's dresser. "I heard you were going to let some *thug* kiss you right out in the open at the mall. Please tell me it's all lies."

She looks cute. She's wearing all white, a pair of white capris with a white blouse that crisscrosses in the front. I glance down at her white Marc Jacobs leather wedged sneakers.

"Those are cute," I say, pointing at her feet. My feeble attempt to deflect the question. "Where'd you get those?"

"Nordstrom."

"Girl, later for them shoes," Jordan snorts, flicking her wrists. "They are cute, though. But that's irrelevant at this moment."

Hope's eyes widen. "Says who?"

"Says me," Jordan counters. "Now let's get back to Kennedy and Sir Kiss 'Em on the Lips."

I roll my eyes at her. "No. Let's not."

"Tell Hope what his name is. B-U, right?"

"B-U? What kind of name is that?"

I groan. "It's short for Born-Universe."

Hope blinks. "Dear God. How exotic."

Jordan snickers. "And original, right?"

Hope rolls her eyes. "Oh, definitely. Creativity and uniqueness at its best."

I suck my teeth. "Okay, okay; enough about my day at the mall." I shoot my gaze over at Jordan. "How about we talk about *you* and your break-up with Howie for the umpteenth time this month?"

Hope gasps. *"Again?* What the heck is wrong with y'all? What, this is like break-up number six in the last four weeks?" She shakes her head. "Y'all need therapy."

I laugh.

Jordan rolls her eyes. "We don't need therapy. What we need is a permanent break from each other."

I give her a "yeah right" look.

"No. I'm serious," Jordan insists. "I think we spend too much time together. And now we act more like brother and sister than we do boyfriend and girlfriend."

Hope shakes her head. "Uh, no. Y'all need relationship counseling, hun. I hate to be the bearer of bad news. But both of you seem to have problems with communicating. You do know communication is key to any successful relationship, right?"

I chuckle. "Ohmygod, you are starting to sound like your mom."

She giggles. "I know, right. It's getting scary. She keeps saying I'm going to end up becoming a therapist like her. But she's wrong. I'm going to practice law."

Jordan huffs. "I'm too young for relationship counseling. That counseling stuff's for old folks who are about to get divorced."

"Wrong," Hope corrects. "Counseling is for anyone with problems or issues they can't solve on their own. And you, girly, I don't mean to rain on your parade. Or pull the rug from under your feet. But *you* have some serious relationship issues. My mom says it's not healthy for couples to constantly keep breaking up. She says it's a sign that there are bigger problems in the relationship."

Oh, Lord! Here we go. Hope's about to get on her soap-

box again. Oh, goodie. I fake a yawn. Sitting here listening to this is enough to put me to sleep.

Jordan plops down on her bed. "Okay, Life Coach, I've heard enough. Next topic, *please.*"

Hope shrugs. "Well, don't say I didn't try to warn you, hun." She pulls out her iPhone and snaps a picture of the three of us, then posts it on her Instagram page. "Hey, y'all want to go shopping in the city tomorrow, then catch a movie?"

"Sounds like a plan to me," Jordan says enthusiastically. "Then we can go uptown to my favorite bakery so I can buy a dozen of my favorite red velvet cupcakes."

"Ohmygod!" Hope exclaims. "You and that bakery."

"Sorry. I can't go," I say, biting into a strawberry. Juice squirts from my mouth. I lick my lips. "I have to work to-morrow."

"Well, what time do you get off?" I tell her seven o'clock. "In the *evening*?"

"Uh, yeah. I go in at one."

Hope sighs. "And why are you working again? It's not like your parents have fallen on hard times. So it's not like you *need* the money. Right? Don't they still give you an al-lowance?"

"Yeah, I still get my allowance." I tell her I like working. That it makes me feel responsible and that I like earning my own money. But I leave out that the best part of going to work is that I get to see all the cute boys from the hood that I wouldn't be able to see otherwise if I weren't work-ing in the mall.

"Oh, okay. If you say so," she says, half interested in my reasoning. Aside from volunteering at the hospital as Candy

Stripers on the weekends during the school year, Jordan and Hope prefer to live off of their parents' money. And as long as they maintain straight A's they can do exactly that. I can as well. But choose not to.

"So what's going on with that trampy girl at the job who is always eyeballing you and rolling her eyes at you every time you walk by? She sounds scary."

I roll my eyes around in my head. "Oh, you're talking about Sasha. *Psst*. I don't know what her problem is. I've been nothing but nice to her. All she does is stare and talk about me behind my back, but she says it loud enough so I can hear her talking about me. I've never done anything to her." I shake my head. "It's like she wants to start something with me."

Jordan and Hope give me sympathetic looks.

"Poor thing," Hope says, shaking her head. "She sounds like she has issues. Didn't you say, like, she's real ghetto and trashy."

"Yeah. She is."

"Ugh. And she talks that stupid, annoying Ebonics, too," Jordan chimes in. "Now, that's who needs counseling."

Hope shudders. "Ugh. That's so not cute."

"Yeah. Tell me about it," I say, glancing at my watch.

Jordan reaches over and grabs my hand. "Maybe she's just jealous of you."

I groan. "I don't know what that girl's problem is. She has no reason to be jealous of *me*. She's really pretty. And has a really nice shape. And a lot of the guys who come in to order seem to always either know her or want to get to know her. So I don't think it's that. All I know is, I try to be nice to her, most times. But, she's always so nasty. So now

I try to avoid having any interaction with her as much as I can help it."

Hope gives me a pitiful look. "Well I don't know why you're working there anyway. Being around those bad elements isn't good for you. All those low-budget hood roaches." She shakes, feigning a chill. "What if you catch something from one of them, then what? You'll have to be quarantined for the whole summer."

I roll my eyes. "Ohmygod, Hope! Stop!"

She shrugs. "You never know."

Jordan says, "Anyway, you be careful. That ghetto girl sounds like major trouble." She reaches for her buzzing phone. She raises her brows and huffs when she sees who's calling her. "She sounds like she's cuckoo-crazy."

"O-M-G!" Hope exclaims, looking from Jordan to me. "You think she might be dangerous? You know them ghetto girls are always getting arrested for fighting and stabbing each other." Her brown eyes widen with alarm.

I smirk. Hope can be so over-the-top with her theatrics. She's more melodramatic than Jordan. "I seriously doubt she's dangerous," I protest. "Or *that* kind of crazy. I just think she's an angry girl."

Hope purses her lips. "Well, angry or not. I think you should report her to management the next time she says something to you. And get yourself a security team and a can of Mace in case she calls for backup from her ghetto friends."

I shake my head. "Let's hope it never has to come to that."

4

"So how was your day with the girls?" my mom wants to know, leaning up against the doorframe of my bedroom. She watches me as I remove my purchases from Forever 21 and Uniqlo from the shopping bags and hang them in my closet.

It's a little after seven o'clock in the evening.

"It was okay."

"I see you bought some really cute things," she says, eying my purchases. "How much did you spend?"

I shrug. Tell her not much, like three hundred dollars. She asks for her Amex card back. I walk over to my bag and pull it from my wallet, handing it to her.

"Now that summer is here, you should probably go through some of the clothes and shoes you haven't worn in a while and put them in a pile so that I can take them down to the Salvation Army, along with some of all your brothers' things."

"I will. I need to make room for all of the new stuff I'll

be getting over the next few weeks anyway. Daddy promised me a shopping spree if I got all A's on my finals."

She chuckles. "Your father knew that wouldn't be a challenge for you. He was going to buy you whatever you wanted, regardless."

I stick my head out from my closet and smile. "Yeah, I know. You, too."

"Shameful, I'll admit. We've spoiled you rotten," she says playfully. She steps into my room. "You're our only daughter. You've never given us any problems, so of course we'll give you whatever you want." I grin, stepping out of my closet. "Within reason," she quickly adds.

"Well, just be grateful I'm not like Jordan and Hope, who want S-series Benzes and expensive trinkets from Tiffany and Company."

She chuckles. "Yeah, I guess you've got a point. Those two are going to run their parents crazy."

I laugh.

"Your father wants you and me to fly over to Dubai to spend the month of August with him. Won't that be exciting?"

Daddy works in intelligence as a National Security officer and has been working over in Dubai for the last eight months. Before that, he worked in Afghanistan for eighteen months. Although over the last two years he's spent more time in the Middle East than home, he usually comes home for the holidays, and typically stays from anywhere from two weeks to a month, depending.

Last summer—before I was interested in having a life of my own—Daddy met mom and me in Morocco, where we spent three weeks vacationing in Casablanca. That was a lot of fun: learning about Moroccan culture, sailing the Mediterranean Sea, even hiking the Moroccan mountains was quite interesting. Still, during the day, it was viciously hot and I thought I would die in the sizzling heat.

But this summer I have plans that do not include travel abroad or being scorched under a blazing sun. I love Daddy, but I'd rather wait until he comes home to spend time with him than give up practically a whole chunk of what could potentially be one of the greatest summers of my life...ever!

I stare at her. *Is she kidding me? I can't spend a whole month away. Stuck up under her and Daddy. What kind of fun is that?*

"Mom," I whine. "I can't go to Dubai for a *whole* month. What about work? I can't leave them short-handed."

"I'm sure they'll manage," she says indifferently. "Besides, you'll be quitting a week or so before the school year starts anyway, right?"

I blink. Tell her that I hadn't planned on it. That I had hoped to stay on during the school year and work the weekends. She smiles at me. "Sweetheart, I think that's great you want to work and gain a sense of independence, but we already agreed that you'd only work for the summer. The only thing your father and I want you to concentrate on is your studies; that's it."

I poke my lip out. "I know. But I can do both. It's not going to interfere with my grades. I promise. I really like it there." Umm, no, what I really want to say is, "I really like seeing all the sexy boys who come through the mall with their pants sagging."

"We'll see," she says brusquely. Code for end of discussion. I take the hint, moving about my bedroom. "You know I ran into Craig and his mother at Short Hills mall this afternoon." She gauges my reaction. There is none. "He asked about you. And his mother told me to tell you hello."

"Oh. That's nice," I say nonchalantly. I'm still kind of put off that she expects me to stop working and wants to whisk me off to some desert country in the blazing heat. Anything to try and ruin my summer plans. So what if she doesn't know about them? That's the whole point. For her not to know.

I walk back into my closet. "Next time you see Mrs. Johnston, tell her I said hi."

"You should call her. I know she'd love to hear from you."

Craig Johnston is my mother's idea of the perfect guy for me. And yes, he was one of my parent-approved boyfriends last year. Thing is, he is a really, really nice guy. And he's cute, too. But I didn't like him like that. I mean. I tried to like him. But, after our first kiss and there weren't any fireworks going off in my head after he pulled back, I knew he wasn't the one for me. Still we talked/dated for almost three months after that, mostly because he was fun to be around and I really did like his company.

I just didn't like him for a boyfriend.

Still don't.

"He's such a fine young man," my mom continues. "I can't get over how tall he's gotten since the last time I saw him."

"I bet." I close my closet door, then walk over to my bed and plop down on it.

"I always wondered whatever happened to the two of you. I can tell he still likes you, Kennedy."

I roll my eyes up in my head. "There's not much to tell. It didn't work out, Mom. It's not the end of the world."

She sits on the edge of my bed. "I know, sweetheart. I'm not saying it is. It's just that . . . I can tell he really liked you. He still does."

"I liked him, too, Mom. Just not like *that*."

"Well, what was wrong with him?"

Umm, let's see.

Honor student, check.

Star athlete, check.

Respectful, check.

Boy Scout—no, Eagle Scout . . . excuse me, check. How could I have forgotten? It was one of the things he constantly talked about in between his incessant chatter about the debate team and his volunteer work with the SPCA.

Umm, what else?

Tall, check.

Good looking, check.

Parents loved him, check-check.

I shrug, sighing. "He just wasn't for me."

"He comes from such a nice family. And he seems like a really good kid."

I shrug dismissively, getting up from the bed. "I'm sure he is. Good, that is. But even good kids have problems, Mom."

She gives me a quizzical look. I can tell she wants me to elaborate, to gossip. Truth is, there's no chinwag to tell when it pertains to Craig.

Yawn. Boooooooring!

"I'm sure he's given his parents about as much trouble as you've given your father and me. All I'm saying is, maybe you should give him a call and invite him over."

I stop flitting about my room, turn to face her. "*Call* him? And *invite* him over? Are you serious? Why would I want to do that?"

I plop back on my bed, scooting back then sitting Indian-style. Aside from his dad and my dad being fraternity brothers and my mother and his mother being sorority sisters, Craig and I have nothing in common. We don't even have the same taste in music. He likes classical, pop, jazz, and rock. Whereas I love hip-hop and (believe it or not) some country music.

I decide to tell her, "I just wasn't that into him."

She pushes. "Why?"

"Mom . . ." I say wearily.

"What? I'm simply asking a question. I really want to know why the two of you didn't work out."

Well, for starters, because you and dad liked him.

I sigh. "Mom, I see what you're trying to do, but it isn't going to work."

"What am I *trying* to do?" she asks, feigning confusion. "All I'm suggesting is that you give Craig a call. That's all."

I guffaw. "Uh-huh. You're trying to play matchmaker again."

She reaches over and grabs one of my pillows and play-fully hits me with it. "I'm trying to do no such thing."

I give her a "yeah right" look.

She smiles. "Well, sweetheart, you can't knock me for trying. You've done everything your father and I have asked of you during the school year, so there's nothing wrong with me wanting to see you have some fun over the summer with someone from a good family background."

Oh no! I don't think so. I am not about to spend my summer looking into the silly face of some boring boy. I don't care how cute he is.

"I'm glad you want me to have fun," I say excitedly.

"That's exactly what I want. Lots and lots of summer excitement."

"Ooh, do tell," she says, smiling. "What kind of girlish mischief are you girls planning to get into this time?"

We have nothing planned. I, on the other hand, plan to explore the world on the other side of town.

But how?

Hope and Jordan are out.

"Well, um," I say, cautiously. "I was kind of hoping I could stay a week with the twins."

Mom blinks. "Your uncle *Kent's* twins?"

"Yeah, Mom. Who else's?"

She looks surprised. "Now, why in the world would you want to stay over there?"

I shrug. "I don't know. It'd be fun. Besides, I don't get to spend a lot of time with the twins."

"Sweetheart, I know Shaniqua and Kaniqua are your favorite cousins—only God knows why—but you know how your father and I feel about you spending too much time with them."

I sigh. "I know, I know. You and Daddy think they're bad influences. But that's so utterly ridiculous. I have a mind of my own."

"I know you do, sweetheart. It's just that—"

"What, they live in the hood? Is that it?"

She frowns. "I wasn't going to say that."

I make a face that says, "I don't believe you."

"There's no supervision. Or very little of it over there."

"I know they can be a little wild..."

She raises an arched brow. "*A little?* You think?"

"Okay, okay. They can't influence me to do anything I

don't want to do," I add. "I wish you and Daddy would trust me, just once."

"Your father and I do trust you. We just don't trust *them*."

"Same difference. You're still saying you don't trust *me*. Don't you think I know right from wrong?"

"Of course we do.

"That's so unfair. They're my cousins."

"Yes. They are. But they're also rude, disrespectful, and out of control, just like their mother. You can go visit for the day. But I don't want you over there unless there's supervision. That means your uncle Kent must be over there *and* your aunt Tiny must be sober."

"Ohmygod! You know Uncle Kent is not going to go over there just so that I can visit with the twins."

Uncle Kent moved out two years ago, and divorced the twins' mom like three months ago because all she wanted to do was hang out in the bars. From what I've overheard from my parents talking, Uncle Kent had had enough of Aunt Tiny's roguish ways.

"Then I guess you can't go," Mom says triumphantly. "Besides, I don't like the company Tiny keeps. Ever since your uncle moved out she keeps a lot of riff-raff coming in and out of there."

"How do you know that? You don't even talk to her."

"You're right, I don't. That still doesn't mean I don't know what's going on over there. Tiny wouldn't be half bad if she stayed out of the bars and stopped all that drinking."

"Dang, Mom. You make it sound like she's a drunk or something."

She shakes her head. "I'm not saying that. All I'm saying

is, your uncle's ex-wife is a bit too liberal when it comes to the twins. And she's a bit too loose for my liking."

Translation: She lets them do whatever they want. Well, almost whatever. They're not allowed to smoke in the house. And boys aren't allowed to stay over past one A.M.

"I tell you what. Why don't you call them and invite them here for a weekend. You could have a slumber party…"

With no boys allowed unless he's a nerd? With not being allowed to hang out anywhere, except at the mall? No, thank you!

"Why can't I stay over there?" I whine.

She gets up from the bed, her forehead creasing with frustration. "Kennedy, you're not staying a week in Irvington with your cousins. So you might as well let that crazy little dream go. If you really want to spend time with them, then you can invite them here for a week."

"Well, what about for a weekend? You or Daddy could drop me off on Friday, then pick me up Sunday morning, if you want."

"I have a better idea. How about they come *here* for the weekend?"

I blink. "And do what?"

"Oh I don't know. What did you plan on doing if I agreed to let you stay there?"

"Hang out and chill." I say this as if it's an obvious answer.

She smiles. "Then you can *hang out* and *chill* here."

"It's not the same," I argue. "It's boring here."

She tilts her head. "And *why* is that? Because there'll be supervision? Because you won't be able to crawl yourself up in here all hours of the day and night, like your cousins do?"

I huff. It's obvious this conversation is going nowhere.

She's not going to ever let me stay any more than an hour over there. So I might as well let it go.

You can always sneak over there while they're at work.

Yeah, that's true. They'd never know.

Yeah, right. Aunt Tiny would love nothing more than to have something to smear in Mom's face.

I sigh, deflated and defeated. Until I can devise a plan to get out of this castle of boredom, I'll simply have to grin and bear it. For now, anyway.

"Never mind," I say, folding my arms. "Forget I even asked."

5

"Next customer, please," I quickly say, scanning the crowded area the minute I am logged in to my register. It's Friday night. And the mall is always packed on Friday nights, especially since the food court is where most of the kids from the area hang out, along with the fact that it's right across from the entrance to the AMC movie theater. So it's extra busy up in here. And my feet are killing me.

I sigh, taking the next customer's order, then the next.

"Uh, *Special K*, you might wanna help get this line movin' a li'l faster," this girl Sasha Green says, popping her chewing gum as she breezes by me. She calls me Special K because "you're real special," she'd said to me, smirking as she looked me up and down my first day here, after I'd held out my hand and introduced myself to her. "Hi, I'm Kennedy."

She stared at my outstretched hand, turning her nose up as if I had dog poop caked up beneath my fingernails.

"And I'm not interested." She turned her head, shifting her body. Her rudeness was not expected, nor was it warranted. But after a month of working here I realize that's who and what she is. Rude.

She tosses her hips real hard and nasty-like to make her booty shake and bounce as she walks. Rumor around here is, she doesn't wear any underwear. Yuck. How nasty is that? Coming to work without underwear on. She's the shift tramp. The bossy, messy, always-trying-to-be-someone's-supervisor, who never has anything nice to say about anyone except herself.

Sasha's a little older than me, like eighteen. But she acts like she's a grown woman in her twenties. And she always has something snide to say to me. Still...I don't let anything she says or does bother me. Not really.

"Next in line, please," I say, trying not to roll my eyes at her. I hold my breath, looking over at an obnoxious group of guys standing one line over, all wearing white tees, True Religions, fitted hats, and the new Lebrons on their feet. They're loud, rude, and...disgustingly vulgar. Well...not all of them.

"Yo, suck on dis sac, mofo," the dark skinned guy with a thick neck says to one of the guys with him while grabbing the front of his baggy jeans.

His boys laugh at him. "Yo, this cat right here," the brown skinned guy with long, shoulder-length dreadlocks says, shaking his head. "You stay tryna get someone to suck up on sumthin'. Let me find out you a freak."

"Yeah, I'm freakin' ya moms, son." He starts rapidly thrusting his pelvis. "Bam, bam, bam. I stays knockin' dat down. I'm ya new daddy, muhfuckka." He laughs.

"Yeah, a'ight, yo," Locks says. "Don't get ya chin checked,

fam. I done tol' you 'bout dat dumb ish, yo." He mushes Thick Neck on the side of the head, causing him to go into a boxing stance, throwing playful jabs at Locks.

Please don't even bother coming over in my line.

"Next in line," I repeat, holding my breath. I'm not in the mood for any of these stupid boys clowning. No, not today. All I want to do is finish up the next twenty minutes of my shift stress free. Change out of this uniform, which smells like French fries and grease, and take a long, hot shower. No luck, though. I take a deep breath as the tallest of the three steps over to my register. He's muscular with bronze-colored skin. I try not to notice his fresh edge up, or the way his cornrows neatly zigzag around his perfectly round head, or the way his trimmed mustache and goatee frame his thick, full lips. Or how perfectly straight and white his teeth are.

I swallow. "Can I help you?"

He licks his lips, eyeing me. His hazel gaze slowly drops down to my name tag then onto my breasts before flickering up to the menu overhead, then back at me. The air around me heats up, causing me to feel flush. "Yeah, *Ken*nedy, let me get a triple Whopper, a Sprite. And a side order of *you*; you real sexy, *Ken*nedy."

The way he's said my name almost causes my knees to buckle.

He smirks.

I quickly recover without allowing myself to get caught up in his little flirt game. "Would you like to try one of our mocha or caramel frappés?"

He licks his lips again. "Nah. I'd like to try you, *Ken*nedy..."

I swallow. "Anything else?"

"Yeah, let me get ya number."

"I'm not on the menu. And you're holding up my line."

"I'm sayin', ma, I'd rather be holdin' you. But you frontin'."

Sasha pops her hips back over to me. All eyes are on her momentarily. And I'm glad. This guy standing in front of me is making me dizzy with all of his fineness. Sasha plants a hand up on her hip and wants to know why my line isn't moving. I give her a blank stare, tell her maybe she should help out, then go back to doing what I'm doing.

"Will that be all?"

Hazel Eyes glances at Sasha, then back at me. He grins, sliding his hand down into his pocket then pulling out a wad of money. "Yeah, I'm good, for now. But I'd be even better if you'd let me take you out to dinner 'n' a movie, then"—he licks his beautiful lips again—"if you act right, we can check into a telly 'n' I can give you da business."

Telly?

It takes me a minute to realize what he's referring to. A motel room. Ugh!

I frown. "Thanks, but no thanks," I say.

Thick Neck laughs. "Yo, you wildin', fam. You got that li'l girl scared."

I ring his order up. Tell him his total. Then wait for him to pay.

He hands me a fifty. Then tells me to keep the change when I try to hand it to him along with his receipt. When he refuses the money, I lay it on the counter.

"Next in line, please."

"She clownin' you, yo," Thick Neck instigates.

"No lie, son," Locks says, cutting in front of Thick Neck, glancing over at Hazel Eyes. "She bad, yo. I'd like to beat that thing-thing up, too. But, eff her, my nig. She prolly can't handle none'a da *D*. She ain't ready for it, fam. You can look at 'er 'n' tell. She a youngin', yo. You know dem li'l girls ain't ready for no real work, fam."

I blink.

Hazel eyes winks at me. "Nah, she a good girl I wanna turn bad. She ready. Ain't you, ma? I see it all in your eyes."

I suck my teeth.

"Yo, let me get two classic chicken sandwiches," Locks continues nonchalantly. "Cheese and ketchup only. And a thing of onion rings." He looks over at Thick Neck and asks him what he wants. "And let me get two double stacker combos for my manz."

"Anything else?" I ask, irritation rising in my tone.

He eyes me. "Hold da attitude, ma. You too pretty to be actin' all stank; feel me? All I'm tryna do is order my meal. And all my peeps was tryna do is holla at you, yo. But you wanna be all stuck up 'n' shit. You lucky I don't smack you in ya frontz."

I blink.

"Yo, dawg, chill da eff out, for real." Hazel Eyes elbows him in the side. "That ain't cool, yo."

"Nah, eff dis stupid *beyaatch*."

I frown. This is the first time a boy has ever called me the B word to my face. And I feel like I've just been sucker-punched in the gut.

Before I can say anything, Hazel Eyes checks him. Tells him he shouldn't disrespect females like that. Then pushes him out of the way. "Yo, my bad," Hazel Eyes says apologetically. "That mofo ain't always playin' wit' a full deck when he ain't on his meds."

I raise a brow. He's staring at me with puppy dog eyes

holding his heart, feigning hurt. "But I'm sayin', babe. You got me feelin' some kinda way. Let me get dem digits so you can make it up to me."

I roll my eyes. "Your orders will be up momentarily." I shoo him over, making room for the next customer. Hazel Eyes keeps his stare on me, while Thick Neck walks off to harass two females sitting at a nearby table with his flirty.ways. Hazel Eyes winks at me, again, then glides the tip of his reddish tongue over his bottom lip. And for some reason this whole encounter has my insides shaking. "Next in line," I call out. And all I can keep thinking as I take my next customer's order, trying to keep my attention on the task at hand while slyly cutting my eye over at Hazel Eyes as he and his two disrespectful friends finally walk out with their food is, *Dang, I should have given him my number. If I see him again, I will.*

6

So I got what I wanted. I *did* see him again. Hazel Eyes, that is. Two weeks later, but it happened. And I gave him my phone number. Right after my shift, he caught me walking through the food court toward the escalators heading down to the second level.

"Yo, ma? Wait up," he called out, jogging over toward me carrying three Macy's shopping bags. He looked so good. I tried to keep myself from smiling as he approached me. "So, what's good? Where you off to?"

"Home," I told him.

"Word? Home already? Yo, it's mad early, ma. And you too fine to be goin' home *alone*. You want some company?" He licked his succulent lips. And I suddenly felt my knees getting weak.

My mother would have fainted on the spot if I'd walked through the door with him in tow. "I can't have company like that."

"Oh, a'ight. It's all good. You feel like chillin', though? You can come through 'n' we can chill at my spot."

It was almost nine P.M. And as tempting as it sounded, I was hot and tired. And knew I wouldn't be able to go off to *chill* with him. Not unless I lied to my parents about where I was going. And that wasn't something I'd ever done. Telling them one thing just so I could go over to some guy's house, particularly one I'd only met standing in my line, ordering his food.

Besides, I wasn't allowed over to any boy's house without my parents having already spoken to his parents first. And definitely wouldn't be at this time of night. No. If I were going to be allowed over at a boy's house it had to be during the day, with a parent or another responsible adult—one my parents deemed suitable—home to supervise us. And we'd have to be sitting in an open area.

"I can't. I have to go home and take a shower."

He grinned. "Nah, you good, babe. You can shower at my crib. I got my own bathroom in my room."

I blinked, shaking my head.

"Yo, come on, Blaze!" Thick Neck yelled out, spreading his arms out holding up a bunch of shopping bags. "Leave dat li'l girl alone. We tryna roll out."

Hazel Eyes sucked his teeth, waving him on. "Yo, relax, fam. I'll be dere in a minute."

"You better go before they leave you," I said, pulling out my cell as it vibrated. It was a text from my mother telling me she was outside waiting for me.

"Nah, we good, yo. Them ninjas ain't goin' nowhere. I'm da one wit' da keys; feel me? And it's my whip so dey move when I move. I'm sayin' though. I been sittin' out here waitin' for you to clock out, ma. So what's good? You gonna let me get dem digits? Or are you gonna keep stylin' like you don't want me to have 'em when we both know you do?"

I felt myself heating from the inside out just listening to the way he spoke while watching him lick his lips in between each sentence. "I wasn't styling," I said defensively. "I was at work and you and your goons were being loud and embarrassing. Besides, I know you probably have a bunch of girls' numbers in your phone already so it's not like not having mine is going to be the end of the world for you."

"Nah, it's sumthin' light. I ain't even on it like dat, feel me? I'm checkin' for you; period, point blank. So what's it gonna be?" He pulled out his shiny new iPhone. "Bless a ninja wit' dem numbers, yo."

My mother sent another text. Without much thought, I sent her one back. Lied and told her I was finishing up my shift and was punching out in five more minutes. I felt bad for lying, but whatever guilty feelings I might have had were quickly dismissed as I watched Hazel Eyes type in my number, then call me.

"A'ght, bet. You can't get away now. You mine now. I got you on lock, *Ken*nedy." He smirked. "Yeah, you thought I forgot ya name, huh? And I ain't even have ta look down at ya nametag."

I laughed. "Yeah, right."

"Yo, check it. Since you ain't tryna chill tonight, I'ma get ready to bounce. I'll hit you up later tonight, a'ight?"

I nodded. "Okay. If you want."

"A'ight, bet." I eyed him as he turned to walk off.

"Wait. I don't even know your name."

"It's Blaze, babe."

I tilted my head. "Blaze? Why they call you that?"

He winked. "Why you think? 'Cause I'm hot like fire 'n' I gets it in like dat."

"So you gonna let me get up in dat, right?" Blaze asks in between large bites of his grilled turkey sub from Charley's. We're at Bridgewater Commons up on the third level sitting at one of the tables eating. We've been talking on the phone for the last three nights, and this is like...a date, I guess.

But I had to tell my mom a small fib last night just so I could be with him. I told her I was riding to Connecticut with Jordan and her father to pick up her sister, Amina, from Yale. Well, it wasn't a complete lie. Jordan and her father *are* picking up her sister from college today. I'm just not riding with them.

After three nights of texting, Skype, and talking on the phone, I was ready to get my summer rolling. So when he texted me last night and said he wanted to spend some time with me today, I had to see him. The tricky part was trying to figure out how I could get out of the house for the day. So I lied.

And now...here I sit on a Saturday at two in the afternoon staring at this boy with greasy, oil-slicked lips and a mouthful of food, chomping away.

I furrow my brows. Give him a confused look. "Huh?"

He tilts his head. "Yo, c'mon, ma. Don't front. You know what it is, yo." He reaches for a napkin and wipes his mouth. "I'm sayin'. We gonna hit up dis movie real quick, then..." He rubs his hands together. "We gonna go back to my spot 'n' make it do what it do."

It takes a few seconds for it to register. Get. Up. In that.

Ohhhh. Get up in that. He wants to crawl up on top of me and have sex.

I roll my eyes. Disgusted. Now, wait. I'll admit, I *am* boy crazy, like most girls my age. And, yes, you already know I am highly infatuated with guys from the hood. Okay, okay, thugs. But I'm not fast like *that*. I'm still a virgin. The most I've ever done is kiss a boy. Okay, okay, and let him feel up on my booty and play with my boobs a little. But that's it. And that was with only one guy. My ex-boyfriend Jake Lester who cheated on me, like five months ago, with this blonde-haired, blue-eyed Becky who didn't mind going all the way with him. Anyway, who cares? He was corny anyway.

Okay, wait. That's not completely true. Jake wasn't really corny. He was really a nice guy. And smart. And athletic. And he was really horny, like most boys. Still, he wasn't for me. But what he *was* is corny for cheating on me instead of just breaking up with me first. He didn't have to cheat.

I hate cheaters!

But, whatever. He's going off to Morehouse in a few weeks on a full academic scholarship to play tennis, major in journalism, and pledge Kappa like his grandfather, father, and his three older brothers. Good for him.

I'm over him.

But this boy right here. Mmmph. I don't know what kind of girl he *thinks* I am. But he has me confused. I am not easy. Therefore, I have no interest in letting him or anyone else getting up in anything over here.

I knew this was a terrible mistake! I should have never come out to meet this nasty dog!

"Apologies. But I'm not that kind of girl," I tell him,

shifting in my seat. "If sex is what you want, you've got the wrong one."

He raises his brow. "Nah, it's not all about da sex. But I'm sayin'... you lickin' da dome, though, right? 'Cause I ain't wit' wastin' my time on no broad who ain't tryna treat a muhfuckka right. I got needs, yo. And I need dis snake drained, nah mean?"

I blink. I hear the question, but I don't answer. Not right away, anyway. I am too stunned, like he'd just slung snot on me. I know lots of girls at my private school who sleep around with different boys, or who will sleep with a boy just so he can spend time with her, thinking that's going to get him to like her more. That's not me.

I know I'm from the suburbs and all, but that doesn't make me some dizzy, dumb girl either. My parents may have some silly rules that half the time make very little sense to me. But the one rule that I won't ever question is saving myself for that special someone. Although the waiting until I'm over twenty-one and finished with college part *is* debatable. But that's neither here nor there, because this boy is *real* special if he thinks I'm giving it up.

"No, I *don't* know what you mean." I set my fork down on my tray. And wait for his explanation. I glance at the big-faced designer watch on his wrist, then back up at him as he chews his food, swallowing.

"I'm sayin'... I'm tryna see what's really good wit' you."

I've suddenly lost my appetite.

"You already know what it is, so don't front. You stroke mine, I'ma stroke yours."

I lean in, mindful so that no one else around us can hear me. "So, let me understand this. Are you saying that the only reason we're out today is because you're looking for sex?"

"Nah, ma, dat's not what I'm sayin'." I eye him as he lifts his drink, places the straw between his lips, then takes three long sips.

I tilt my head, tucking my hair behind my ears. "Then what are you saying? Because that's what it sounded like to me."

He belches. Doesn't even excuse himself. I frown. "Oh, my bad. But, I'm sayin'. I ain't gonna front on da panties, ma. I wanna get up in 'em 'cause, yeah, you lookin' right. So yeah, I wanna stroke you up. But I ain't on it like dat. Its whateva, whateva. But, I'm sayin', you can still let me see what dem lips 'n' dat mouth is all about, nah mean."

Now I'm ready to go.

I push my chair back, pulling out my phone. But then I remember I can't call anyone. I'm supposed to be with Jordan and her dad and quickly toss it back into my bag. Now, I'm stuck with this boy. And I'm annoyed at myself for lying to my mother just so I could spend time with him.

I narrow my eyes. "Listen, *Blaze*. I don't know what impression I gave you, or what you think you know about me. And I definitely don't know how other girls are when they're with you. But I'm not a whore. And I'm definitely not playing head nurse to you or anyone else. So if that's what you're hoping for, then you're sadly mistaken and you have definitely wasted your time, and your money."

I dig down in my bag and pull out my wallet. I snatch out a twenty, tossing it at him, then stand up.

He starts grinning. "Yo, why you trippin'? What's dis for?"

"I'm not tripping. It's for your time and for my half of

lunch, plus the tip." I sling my bag up over my shoulder prepared to walk off.

"Yo, hol' up. Where you goin'?"

"To find me a way home."

He quickly stands and reaches for me. "Nah, nah. Chill, ma. You ain't gotta roll out like dat. I was only effen wit' you."

I fold my arms, giving him a "yeah right" look.

He puts his hands up in mock surrender. "You gon' break my heart, yo, if you bounce." He picks up the money, handing it to me. "Yo, take dis back. I don't need ya paper, yo."

I stare at his hand.

"C'mon, relax. Real spit, I'm not on it like dat. I was only testin' you. Here, take ya money, ma. I don't need ya paper. I got dis."

I raise my brow.

"I'm sayin'. I dig you."

I tsk him. "Boy, please. It seems like you're more focused on trying to *dig* something else instead. So if you are, then we need to leave now."

"Nah, we good, babe. I mean. Yeah, I wanna get up in dat. I ain't gonna front. I'm tryna cuddle up 'n' boo you up. But I'm not gonna press you for da panties. I respect how you get down."

I know just seconds ago I was ready to bolt for the door, but now I suddenly have a change of heart. I keep from smiling at the thought of cuddling up with him. Even though I know he's a horndog, there's still something about him I like. Still, I let him know, again, that I am not easy. And that I'm not going to allow him to treat me like I am.

He apologizes. Gives me a sad puppy-dog face. "I got you. My bad, a'ight. Let me make it up to you."

"How?"

He grins. "I'll figure sumthin' out, a'ight?"

I shrug, reluctantly pulling out my chair and taking a seat. "Well, let's see if we can get through the movie first.

He grins. "Oh, we will. Believe dat." He lifts his drink, taking long deep pulls as he glances at his watch. "C'mon, let's roll."

7

The movie was good. Hazel Eyes was a gentleman through most of the movie. I mean, yes. He did put his arm around me. And a few times his hand did *accidentally* wander a little too high up on my thigh. But other than that, I really enjoyed myself.

It's a little after six o'clock in the evening and now we are heading back to his place. I'm nervous. And, okay, I know I shouldn't be going over to his house. But I want to. Truth is, I'm not ready to go home. Well, I can't go home...not yet.

I sent Jordan a text to see if she and her dad were back from Connecticut. They're not. So that's that.

During the ride over to his place, August Alsina's CD is playing. August is so sexy to me. And I love his voice. I close my eyes, bobbing my head as "I Luv This Shit" starts playing. In my head, August is singing to me. I snap my fingers to the beat.

Blaze laughs. "Yo, what you know about dis?"

I open my eyes and look over at him. "What, you think I don't listen to this kind of music? I love August. And his music is dope. I'm not gonna lie. At first, when I first heard this song on the radio, I thought he was Chris Brown singing."

"Yeah, he do sound kinda like Chris Breezy. Dude is def doin' his thing. But I ain't tryna talk about him." He turns the volume down. "What's good wit' you? You sure you wanna chill?"

I nod. "Yeah. I'm sure."

"So you gonna let me push dem panties to da side?" He grins, moving his eyebrows up and down. I give him the evil eye and he laughs. "Chill, chill. I'm only effen wit' you."

I roll my eyes, sucking my teeth. "Yeah, right. Please don't have me Mace you." I shift my body in my seat, folding my arms across my chest.

"Yo, real spit, ma. I got you. Trust. You in good hands."

I give him a "yeah right" look.

"Word is bond. I got you."

"Yeah, we'll see," I mumble, reaching over and turning up the volume to the radio. Future's song "Honest" is playing. I lean back in my seat, bouncing my head to the beat, pretending like I know what the heck he's sing-rapping. Truth is, I don't understand his country grammar, but I like the beat. I'm just being honest.

When we finally pull up in front of a yellow house with green shutters and a big bay window on a quiet street, I look over at Hazel Eyes, confused. "I thought we were going to your place."

He looks over at me, shutting off the engine. "This *is* my spot." He frowns. "What, you think e'eryone who lives in da hood is livin' in da projects or sumthin'?"

Busted.

I won't lie.

I did kind of think, expect, that maybe he did. Suddenly I feel guilty for thinking like that. But then I know it's part out of ignorance and part out of fascination that I hoped he did live in the projects.

I look over at him sheepishly. "I wasn't sure; that's all."

"Yeah, a'ight. And just so you know. My moms isn't on drugs. My crib isn't dirty. And I don't have roaches. And we ain't on section eight." He opens his door. "C'mon. Let's go in."

I immediately feel asinine for thinking—okay, *hoping*— he did. I unfasten my seat belt, then open the door and slowly ease myself out, shutting it behind me.

He walks over and takes my hand. Surprisingly, I don't pull away. It feels good, my hand in his.

"You smoke?" he asks, grabbing a shoebox from out of his closet, then pulling out a plastic baggie stuffed with what looks like oregano. But I know better. It's marijuana. We're up in his room. His room is small but nice. He has a full-size bed that's actually made up. The walls are painted light blue. And he has large framed posters of basketball players on them. A gigantic picture of a half-naked girl with an enormous butt is hanging over his bed. She looks Spanish. There's a stereo system up on a dresser and a huge flat-screen TV up on his wall. His closet is packed with clothes. And along the right wall there are boxes of sneakers neatly stacked up.

He shuts his closet door, then comes and sits on the side of the bed, next to his nightstand. I stare at his profile and it's really hard to think straight, let alone talk. His skin is smooth and clear, the kind of skin girls at my school pay hundreds, maybe even thousands, of dollars in skincare products and spas for.

I shake my head. I've never smoked anything in my life. And, although I've had fleeting thoughts of curiosity as to what it'd be like, I'm not sure if I'm ready to find out. I tell him no as he pulls out a cigar. He glances over at me, his lips curl into a crooked grin. "Yeah, you one of dem good girls. I like dat."

Fascination dances in my eyes as I watch him slice open a cigar, remove the tobacco, then pack it with marijuana. I eye him with excitement as he places it between his lips and slides his tongue over it, just so. Then he takes it between his thumbs, index fingers and middle fingers and slowly rolls it to perfection.

"So why do you like the fact that I'm a good girl?" I finally ask, pulling my gaze away from the thick blunt Blaze places on the nightstand before he starts slicing open another cigar, then packing it with marijuana.

"Because you ain't all hard 'n' gutter like a lotta these birds cluckin' 'round here. You got ya head on straight. And you ain't got no rep in da streets. You def wifey material."

"I am? Why you say that?"

"Why I say what?"

"That I'm wifey material. What does that mean?"

His lighter flicks, and the air around me immediately fills with the strong scent of weed. I blink and swallow as he takes deep, long pulls. Aside from seeing it in movies and videos, this is the first time I've actually seen anyone actually roll a blunt, let alone smoke it, live and direct. I can't lie. I find myself becoming enchanted with how the thick smoke rolls around his tongue then floats out of his mouth and up through his nose.

The more he smokes, the more odorous his room becomes. Scary thing is, I'm not even bothered by the pungent smell.

"It means what it means." He exhales a mouthful of smoke, getting up, holding his sagging pants up with one hand as he walks over to the window and opens it. His blunt dangles from his lips. "You a good girl."

"But what if I *don't* want to be that, a good girl?"

He comes back over and sits beside me, then leans back on his forearm. He takes another pull from the blunt. "You ain't ready for dat life, ma." He blows smoke in my face. I cough a little. And he laughs. "You drink?"

I shake my head.

"You puttin' in dat neck work?" I blink. He looks down at his lap. "Don't act like you don't know what I'm talkin' 'bout. Givin' up dat dome. Head."

I frown. I thought we already went through this. Thought I already put him in his place. Boys. They only hear what they want to hear. I shake my head.

"I know what you meant. No, I'm not doing that."

I refrain from telling him how gross I think oral sex is. Still, I sometimes find myself wondering why girls enjoy doing it and why every boy I know goes crazy over it. The first time I heard the term oral sex used I was like eleven. I was on the school bus en route home when this white girl in back of me, Katie Livingston, started talking about how she performed it on her brother's friend in their garage. He was in high school. Ninth grade. We were in sixth grade. I remember how Katie described the white stuff that filled her mouth and how he had wanted her to swallow it.

I couldn't wait to get home to ask my mother all about what I'd heard. When I asked her what oral sex was, she explained what it was, then added, "It isn't ladylike. Fast, nasty girls are the only ones out there putting their mouths on a boy's penis."

When I asked her what the white stuff was Katie was talking about, she said, "Make sure you don't ever drink or eat anything from that little nasty girl. It's semen. And swallowing it will give you throat cancer and make your tonsils fall out."

I believed her. The idea of getting cancer or having my tonsils fall out scared me to death. And even though I know better now, I still think putting my mouth on a boy's thing is gross. And it's definitely something I'm not interested in ever doing.

"And you ain't lettin' anyone smash so dat makes you nun-like. You pure."

"Ohmygod! Is that your nice way of calling me corny?"

He laughs again. "Nah, nah. You a good girl, that's all. Don't let anyone change dat. On some real ish, ya innocence is mad sexy, yo."

I smile. He reaches down into his nightstand drawer and pulls out a bottle of Hennessey and two plastic cups. "You want some?"

I shake my head. He laughs again, opening the bottle, then filling his cup halfway.

"What's so funny?" I ask, feeling myself becoming slightly annoyed. I'm not sure if he's laughing at me or not. All I know is I don't like it.

He smirks. "Like I said, you a good girl."

Feeling curious about the drink, almost dared if you will—even if it's only my imagination—I reach for Blaze's cup and take one small sip. As soon as it hits my tongue, my face twists into a grimace and my eyes water. Just the small drop of brown liquid sends a trail of fire down my throat and into my belly. For a moment, I think I'm going to die.

Blaze laughs. "See. You ain't ready."

I roll my watering eyes, determined not to be deterred from taking another sip. I place the cup up to my lips again, and this time I take a bigger sip. I swallow. And the wet heat instantly sweeps through my body, causing me to feel an unexpected tingle all over that rushes to my head.

I hand Blaze back his cup. He grins, then takes a large gulp of his drink. He takes the bottle and pours himself some more.

"Are you sure you should be drinking?" I ask him, trying to maintain my composure. Trying not to let the simmering heat and pleasure coursing through my veins overcome me. "I mean, you still need to take me home."

"Oh, I'm good. I got you. I'm not tryna get twisted, babe. I drink and drive responsibly."

He drinks and drives responsibly? I frown. How in the heck is that being responsible? He isn't twenty-one, so I guess he failed to get the memo on underage drinking. I decide against reminding him of that important detail.

"I'm sure you do. I just would like you to be even more responsible before you get behind the wheel. I want to get home in one piece." I glance at my watch. It's seven fifteen. I reach for my buzzing phone. It's a text from my mother wanting to know how things are going and around what time I think we'll be home.

I text her back. Tell her what Jordan told me. WE SHLD B HOME BY 10. WE'RE STOPPING TO GET SOMETHING TO EAT ☺

Ok, sweetheart. See you then. Be safe & enjoy

I swallow, slipping my phone down into my front pocket.

"Yo, you pretty," Blaze says, reaching over and stroking my cheek. "You mad sexy, you know that?"

I blush, shrugging. "Not really. I mean. I know I'm not butt-ugly."

He chuckles. "Nah, you def not dat. You pretty in da face, small in da waist 'n' dem hips mad thick, yo. I'm feelin' you, real spit, ma."

My nerves start to get the best of me. I start to second-guess myself for coming over here, thinking maybe I've made a mistake. But then a little voice in my head tells me to relax. Reminds me that it's the summer. School is out. To have a little fun. And that's what I want to do.

I take a deep breath. "Umm, I like you, too." *I think.*

"That's wassup." He stands up and removes his shirt. Then his wife-beater comes off. I look away. "You good?" he wants to know, trying to hold his sagging pants up with one hand while holding his blunt up to his lips with the other.

I nod my head. "Yeah, I'm good." The words come out sounding meek. Unbelieving. But I am. Strangely, I am enjoying myself. There's something about him I really like. And I want to know more about him.

But I am scared.

He pulls the blinds down, dimming the light in the room. Then turns on his stereo. Trey Songz starts pouring out of his speakers real low and sexy. Next thing I know we are kissing. Hazel Eyes has a long tongue. I can smell and taste the mix of alcohol and weed on his breath and tongue. My head starts to spin. And I don't know if it's from his kiss, or from the sip of his drink. Or if it's from the faint scent of his cologne tickling my senses, or from his wandering hands that seem to be slowly melting everything inside of me. He's a good—no, great—kisser.

His body is hot against mine, causing a deep burning wave of heat to course through me. All I know is, all of this deep kissing is going to lead somewhere way beyond our parted lips and dancing tongues if I don't get a hold of my senses and move his hands from up under my shirt, from off my breasts.

This isn't the first time I'm kissing a guy. And it isn't the first time anyone's touched my breasts, but it is the first time I feel like I'm riding a waterslide.

I'm wet, like a waterfall.

8

"Ohmygod, Kennedy!" Hope exclaims, covering her mouth in shock. Her eyebrows shoot up. "You little tramp! I can't believe you lied to your mother, then went to that boy's house and made out with him."

"I went to the movies first, before making out with him," I say jokingly.

"Well, how was it?"

"What, the movie?"

"No, silly." She playfully swats a hand at me. "Making out with him?"

"See, if I tell you, I might have to kill you," I say, laughing.

She rolls her eyes. "Okay, then. Be like that. Selfish."

I laugh.

I close my eyes, reliving the whole night. How he kissed me on my neck. Dipped his tongue into my mouth. And how I had to try to keep up with him, losing my breath in his warm kisses.

"Dag, it was like that?" she asks, laughing.

I nod. "It was heaven."

She shakes her head. "I can't believe you."

I feign ignorance. "What? What can't you believe?"

"This new you; sneaking over to some boy's house and lying to your mother. I never knew you had it in you."

"It's not that serious. It's not like I went out and committed a crime or something. All I did is make out with a boy."

"Yeah. A boy who you know your parents would disapprove of if they ever found out."

I grin. "And that's what makes it so much more exciting. Knowing my parents would have a fit."

She shakes her head. "I don't know, Kennedy. Seems so not worth all the trouble you could get in if you ever got caught. I mean, lying to your mom. That's so not cool. What if she found out you were lying to her?"

I shrug. "She won't." She wants to know if I've lied before to my mom in order to sneak off with a boy. I tell her no. Tell her that I've never had any reason to because I'd always done what is expeted of me by my parents.

"So why the change now?"

"I don't know. It's not like I intentionally set out to lie to her. I was on the phone talking to him and he was talking all low and sexy, telling me how much he wanted to hang out with me. I got caught up in the moment. Anyway, I wanted to see him, too."

"You know, Kennedy. Nothing good is going to come out of you being deceitful. One day it's all going to come out, then what?"

I look at her, confused. "What do you mean?"

She gives me a funny look. "Why do you like boys like that?"

"Like what?"

She huffs. "You know, ruffians. Thugs."

"I don't know. They're interesting and exciting."

"They're nothing but trouble."

I furrow my brows. "That's so not true, Hope. All that is is a negative stereotype. All guys who wear sagging pants and from urban areas aren't bad news. A lot of them are simply misunderstood."

She rolls her eyes, waving me on. "Oh, please, Kennedy. All they do is run around drinking and smoking and having wild, nasty sex and getting a bunch of girls pregnant and spreading around diseases."

I blink. "Ohmygod, Hope! You have got to be kidding me. I can't believe what's just come out of your mouth. You can not possibly believe what you've said."

She makes a face. "Well, it's true. So before you get on your soapbox, spare me the song and dance about the plight and misfortunes of the boys in the hood. Their apathy and disregard for the world around them is nothing but an excuse for them to go out and sell drugs and tear down their communities, killing and robbing each other, instead of staying in school, getting an education, and doing something positive and constructive with their lives."

"It's not always that cut and dried," I say, feeling a headache pushing its way to the center of my forehead.

She snorts. "I don't see why it's not. You either want to do right, or you don't. No one forces them to do what they do. It's a choice. So whatever negative light is being shone on them is by their own doing."

"That's so not fair. How can you say that? You don't know what it's like to walk in their shoes. Many who live in the hood want out. They want to do what's right, but when they aren't given the tools or allowed access to resources that can help them, then they start to feel hopeless and helpless."

She sucks her teeth. "So that makes it right?"

I shake my head. "No. That makes it real. You know like I do that the system is designed to see people fail, especially young black men. So you shouldn't be so quick to judge."

"Okay, so maybe I shouldn't judge. And maybe you're right. But I'll say this, then I'm going to let it go. They're all damaged if you ask me. And before long, if you choose to keep chasing behind boys like that, you'll end up damaged, too."

I am stunned, speechless.

9

"So why do they call you Blaze?" I ask Hazel Eyes two days later. We've been on Skype for the last twenty minutes. There's something about him I like. I know, I know. At first I thought it wasn't going to work out. But after our movie date and spending time with him alone at his house, he's really not all that bad. And, besides, he's really, really nice to look at.

Eye candy. Yeah, that's what they call guys who look like him.

He lights his second blunt, taking two deep pulls then holding it in his lungs.

"Don't you think that maybe you smoke too much?"

He coughs. "Nah, not like I used to. I cut back."

"You *cut back*?" I ask, surprised. "Really?"

"Yeah. I used to burn like nine, ten blunts a day."

I stare at him through the screen incredulously. "Are you for real? Even during the school year?"

"No doubt. Weed helped me concentrate better. I got

most of my A's when I was high, yo. Word is bond. I'd smoke a blunt before school, then another one for lunch. Then soon as two forty-five hit and dat bell rang, I'd be out da door sparking up wit' my boyz until it was time to take it down."

"So, is that why they call you *Blaze*? Because of all the marijuana you smoke?"

He shifts his eyes from my inquiring gaze. "Yeah, sumthin' like dat. So you wanna catch another movie tomorrow night?"

I chuckle. "Hey-hey, not so fast. Don't even try to change the subject. Not until you tell me what 'something like that' means. "

He brings his face close to his computer screen, and blows smoke at me. "See. If I tell you, I'ma have ta kidnap you." He laughs and coughs at the same time.

I tsk him. "Just tell me, please."

He sighs. "Yo, you really wanna know?"

I nod. "I wouldn't have asked if I didn't."

He sighs again. "When I was like eight I found my older brother's stash..."

"Oh, you have an older brother? How old is he? What kind of stash?"

He shakes his head. "Chill, chill. You want me to tell you da story or not?"

I nod.

"A'ight then. My brother, Brent, is twenty-three. Anyway, I found his stash of weed in a Timberland box under his bed. I remember watching him roll up and seein' him smoke and I thought it was cool. So dis one night when he was out doin' him, I snuck in his room wit' two of my friendz at da time. He had like six blunts already rolled 'n' ready to burn so I took one 'n' lit it. Me 'n' my boyz started smokin' it like we knew what we was doin' but we ain't know jack; feel me?"

I nod. "So what happened?"

Blaze looks off for a split second, then lands his gaze back on me. "We heard someone comin' 'n' got spooked. I tossed all da blunts 'n' da lighter back into the box 'n' pushed it back under his bed, then me 'n' my friendz dipped outta his room before we got caught. My moms woulda beat me if she caught me smokin'." He shakes his head. "Later dat night, I went to bed, then the next thing I know my moms is bargin' in my room shakin' me 'n' screamin' for me to get up 'cause there's a fire."

I gasp. "Ohmygod! Did your house burn down?"

He shakes his head. "Nah. It was just a lotta smoke. I mean, it did burn through the box 'n' my brother's mattress got scorched, but we ain't lose e'erything. My moms was just happy no one got hurt 'n' dat our crib didn't burn down to da ground."

"Y'all were real lucky," I say sincerely.

"True."

"So did they know how his bed caught fire?"

"Not at first. But then dem fire marshall cats came 'n' tol' my moms what caused it. She blacked on my brother for havin' dat stuff in her house."

"Did she put him out?"

"Nah. She just made him give her money for da damages. And started chargin' him rent to live wit' us. Soon as she spun off, he started spazzin' on me 'n' yoked me up for goin' into his ish. He knew da only way da fire coulda popped off da way it did is if someone was in his room messin' wit' his stash. Man, dude tried to beat da crap outta me. After dat he got a lock on his door, then started callin' me Blaze."

"Wow."

He licks his lips. "Now, what about dat movie?"

I grin. "Tell me your real name, and it's a yes."

He shakes his head. "See, why you gotta know all dat? It's Blaze."

"Yeah, okay. And my name's Tinkerbell from *Once Upon a Time*."

"Hahahaha. Well, once upon a time, there was dis dude named Blaze who had another name. Nice to meet you, Tinker. Now come ring my bell."

I join in his laughter. "You're so silly."

Although he doesn't tell me his real name, he does share with me that his mother's a single mom. That his dad was killed in car crash when he was six. And his brother's in prison for three years for selling drugs.

I also learn that he's going into his senior year. And that he plays basketball for his high school. That he's their star point guard. And he plans to go away to college.

I'm impressed.

"Where do plan on attending?" I ask, genuinely interested.

"I don't know. NYU, Georgetown, and Duke universities want me real bad."

Oh, wow," I say, excitedly. "That's great! Which one will you choose?"

He shrugs. "I don't know. My mom wants me to go get out of Jersey. But I ain't really tryna leave her, feel me?"

"Yeah. But where would you like to go if you had a choice?"

He thinks for a moment then says, "On some real, I'd like to go to either Howard, Hampton, Fisk, or North Carolina A & T University."

I give him a quizzical look. "Really? Wow. Why those schools? I mean, I know they're historically black universities and all, but why them when Georgetown, NYU, and Duke already have their eyes on you—why wouldn't you go to one of them? They're really good schools."

He gives me a funny look. "Why not those schools? They're just as good as Georgetown, Duke, NYU, Princeton, Harvard, Yale, or any other prestigious Ivy League school, feel me? Besides, they're listed among Forbes's top colleges and universities to attend."

"Forbes?" I say. "What you know about Forbes?"

"See," he says, smirking. "I know more than you think, yo. Don't sleep on ya future man, yo."

I laugh. "Oh, is that what you're going to be, my man?"

"Yeah. One day."

I raise a brow. "Oh, really?"

"Yeah. When you ready for me."

"Ohmygod! You are so full of yourself. What makes you *think* I'm not ready for you?"

"Don't worry about all dat. I can tell."

I tsk. "*Annnny*way, moving on. Sounds like you have a promising future ahead of you."

"True indeed. Every black boy from da hood ain't a dropout, or out slingin' packs, yo. Yeah, I dress hood 'n' I talk dat talk, but I ain't a derelict or destined for a prison cell."

I smile at him. "I know not to judge a book by its cover."

"Exactly. Most of us got dreams, feel me?"

I nod.

"I bet you thought I was just some hood nucca wit' nothin' goin' for himself, didn't you?"

"No. I didn't think that."

He laughs. "C'mon. Don't front. Yes, you did."

"Honestly. I didn't."

He gives me a "yeah right" look.

"Ohmygod! I'm serious. I really didn't know what to think when I first saw you."

"Yeah, right. You know you thought I looked good, yo. I saw you eyein' my swag."

I feign insult. "O-M-G! I was not eyeing your swag." I bust out laughing. "Okay, okay. Maybe I was; just a little."

"Hahaha. Yeah, that's what I thought." He pauses, moving his face up into his computer screen. "I'm sayin', though. I wanna see you, yo."

I smile. "I want to see you, too."

He pulls in his bottom lip. "A'ight then. So what's good?"

I glance at the time in the upper right corner of my MacBook. It's almost one in the morning. Already *waaaay* past my curfew. "I can't," I say. "My mom will kill me."

"Oh, a'ight, it's cool," he says without even trying to convince me to come out.

I won't pretend that I'm not a little taken aback for some reason that he isn't pressing me to sneak out to see him. I guess I kind of wanted him to. So, okay, okay, I'm disappointed.

"Well, alright then. I guess I'll go to sleep."

He laughs. "What, you want me to tell you to sneak outta ya crib to come chill wit' me?"

"No," I lie.

He keeps laughing. "Yeah, a'ight. Whatever you say, ma. But don't get it twisted, yo. I wanna def chill wit' you again. But I ain't tryna have you do nothin' you don't already do. Good girls don't sneak outta dey parents' crib. Bad girls do."

10

"Hey, y'all want to go check out that new movie with Jennifer Hudson?" Jordan asks, tossing her *Teen People* magazine over on her bed.

No, I'd rather go riding around, I think. My mind drifts back to the other night with Hazel Eyes. I snuck out of my house to hang out with him. And guess what? I don't even feel bad about doing it. A part of me knows I should feel horrible for doing what I did, climbing out of my bedroom window like that. But I don't. In fact, it was daring and exciting.

Yes, I was really nervous about getting caught, but the risk was worth it. Not that Blaze asked me to do it. Or expected me to. But his *good girl* comment made me want to not only prove to him that I could be a bad girl, too, but to see what it was like to break a rule. To sneak out.

And I got caught up in the thrill of it all.

It was fun. It was out of character. It was spontaneous. It was sooo not me. I climbed out of my bedroom window, grabbed onto the ledge, then shimmied my way down. Then I walked-ran outside the gates of my development and met Blaze at the WaWa's three blocks down from my street. We didn't really do much except ride around, then park in some secluded area and kiss and make out. I almost smoked some marijuana with him, too. Well, I wanted to. But he wouldn't let me.

He laughed and coughed as he smoked. "Yo, why you call it marijuana? That sounds mad white, yo."

"Well, that's what it is," I said, playfully swatting his arm. "Well, actually it's called cannabis because it comes from the cannabis plant."

He smirked, blowing smoke out of the side of his mouth. "Yeah, a'ight. Call it what you want, good girl. And I'ma call it what it is: Weed. Bud. Chronic. Loud. I don't know nuthin' 'bout no cannabis. All I know is, dis some good ish, yo."

"Can I try some?" I asked, surprising myself.

He looked at me, gave me a funny stare. "Nah. You ain't ready for dis, yo. I ain't tryna corrupt you."

I smirk. "Whatever."

He took a few more deep pulls, then put it out. But he didn't dare indulge my curiosity. And I'm kind of glad he didn't. Still, I don't like when he says I'm a good girl. For some reason, it sounds like being good is really a bad thing.

Anyway, next thing I knew, Blaze's hands were all over me. And mine were all over him. And before I knew it, we were in the backseat of his car getting all hot and bothered. But when he went for my panties, surprisingly, he didn't make a big deal out of it when I stopped him from pulling them down, or sticking his hand in them. We just grinded and kissed, then he finally said, "I better get you home, good girl. Before ya parents find out you missing."

"I'm not missing. I'm out with you."

"Yeah, true-true. You know what I mean." We both fixed ourselves, then got back in the front seats. He started his engine then drove me right back where he dropped me off at.

"You think I'm corny, don't you?"

He turned to look at me, then knitted his brows together. "Nah, not at all."

I shifted my body toward him. "Yeah, right," I said sarcastically, sucking my teeth. "Then why you keep calling me a good girl?"

"Because that's what you are. It's a compliment. Don't ever change."

I frowned. "Then why doesn't it feel like one when you say it?"

He shrugged. "You tell me, ma. I mean it no other way; real spit."

I eyed him unconvinced. "So you really don't think I'm a cornball?"

He grinned. "Nah." He leaned over and kissed me on the lips then. "I think you're mad sexy. Real sweet."

I'm not going to lie. He made me blush. And there was something about the way he stared into my eyes that made me excited. I mean, really, really excited. Like I wanted to make out with him right there in the parking lot of WaWa's.

"I really like you, yo," he said, kissing me one last time before I climbed out of his car and made my way back home—at almost two thirty in the morning. Even though he wanted to drive me all the way to my house, I wouldn't let him. I didn't—and don't—want him or anyone else to know where I live. Even if he does know that the area is really nice. He still doesn't know exactly how nice. It's not something he needs to know.

I climbed back up the side of the house and slipped back into my bedroom, breaking a nail in the process. But it was well worth it.

Will I do it again?

Ummm. Maybe not. We'll see. Okay, okay…probably. But only if there's something going on that I really want to be a part of. Then, yes. I think I will. Okay, okay…I know I will.

Fingers crossed, I don't ever get caught.

"Ummm, no thanks," Hope says, pulling me from my thoughts. I look over at her as she's shaking her head. "She won't be getting my money."

"Who won't be getting your money?" I ask.

Hope sighs. "Jennifer Hudson. Weren't you listening? I was telling Jordan that I'll sit this one out. I'm not interested in seeing her C-list acting in any movie."

"Ohmygod, Hope, that's so not nice," I say, grabbing one of the pillows off the bed and playfully hitting her with it.

She shrugs. "Don't get me wrong. I like Jennifer and all, but she really needs to stick to singing. I'd rather put that thirteen dollars, plus another fifteen dollars for snacks and drinks, toward a cute pair of sandals."

Jordan gives a dismissive wave.

"Well, what about you, Kennedy? You want to go?"

"Huh? What about me?"

Jordan repeats the question. I shake my head. "No. I'll pass."

She huffs. "Well, dang. Both of you sure know how to

be party duds. I thought it would be kind of fun to see a movie."

"Please. I'd rather watch Netflix," Hope says dismissively, "before going to see a Jennifer Hudson movie. She has an Oscar for Christ's sake. And this is the best she can do?" She shakes her head. "Tragic. Just real tragic." She scrolls through her phone. "But what about seeing that movie with Idris Alba? He's so...mmph."

"Ewwww. *Old*," Jordan retorts, twisting her face up. "And that's so nasty!"

I laugh. "Well, he's distinguished."

"And dirt old," Jordan says again.

"But he's still cute for an old guy," Hope says defensively. "Old guys can be cute, too."

Jordan rolls her eyes. "Yuck. Not when they're old enough to be your father."

Hope waves Jordan on, dismissing her comment. "So do y'all want to see the movie or not?"

I shrug. "I guess."

Jordan says, "Okay, I guess. I'm game. Let me text my mother to let her know we're going to the movies."

Not that this is my ideal way of spending a Friday night. I mean, really? It's real nice out. Now that the sun is down, it's not as hot and humid out like it was earlier. It's like eighty degrees out now. And I know the streets in the hood are jumping with excitement. Maybe I'll be able to convince Jordan to at least roll up all the windows real tight, lock all the doors, and speed through the hood to see who's out. Yeah, right. Not!

"Yo, what's good wit' ya peeps?" this brown-skinned guy with box-braids asks. He'd reached out and touched my hand, stopping me when Hope and Jordan and I walked by him at the concession stand. He spoke to Jordan and Hope, but they both looked him up and down, like he was a commoner, then told me they'd wait for me by the theater doors. He's wearing a pair of baggy cargo shorts that hang off his waist, showing the waistband of his American Eagle underwear with a black wife beater. He has a thick chain hanging from his neck with a bulldog pendant dangling from it. He's not as tall as I like, but he's still a cutie-pie. He kind of reminds me of a younger and very much shorter, stockier version of that basketball player Dwyane Wade.

"Why they actin' all stank?" he wants to know, eyeing Hope and Jordan as they walk off. Well, correction...practically stomp off.

Because they're snobs. I shrug. "Don't mind them. They're in love with their boyfriends and don't believe in speaking to other guys." Of course, it's a lie. But I can't flat-out tell him that they just turned their noses up at him because of the way he's dressed. That he *looks* like a thug.

"Oh, word? Well, I wasn't checkin' for either of 'em, anyway. But, I'm sayin', yo. What's good wit' you, ma? You gotta man?"

I shake my head. "No."

"Why not?"

I shrug. "I don't know."

"You want one?"

I smile. "I don't know. Depends."

He licks his lips. "Well, how 'bout you let me know ya name, love? You got Facebook?"

"It's—"

"C'mon, Kennedy," Jordan calls out, stomping her foot. "Dang. The movie's about to start."

He smirks. "Kennedy, huh? I like that."

"What's your name?"

"Oh, my bad, love. It's Rocky."

"Why they call you that?"

He grins. "'Cause I go hard, like Sylvester Stallone in them old Rocky Balboa flicks." He starts shadow boxing. "My knuckle game real right."

I laugh.

"Nah. I'm dead serious. So anybody eff wit' you, you come holla at me, a'ight?"

I nod, smiling. "Okay. If you say so."

We chat a few seconds more before he wants me to text him my number. I don't have the heart to tell him I'm not that interested in him. Still... I take his phone and type in my number.

Hopefully, he won't call.

"A'ight, bet." He wraps his arm loosely around my shoulder and whispers in my ear as he walks me over toward Hope and Jordan. "You real pretty, love. I wanna chill wit' you. I might even wanna wife you up."

I giggle. "If I let you."

Hope and Jordan are both gaping at me with their jaws dropped open. Jordan looks mortified. Hope looks confused.

And I want to laugh at the two of them.

"I'ma call you, a'ight?"

"Okay," I say softly, eyeing him as he walks off.

"Dear Jesus!" Jordan huffs the minute he's out of earshot. "You're like a magnet for the riffraff."

I roll my eyes. "Oh, shush. Let's go in."

She doesn't let it go. Not that I expected her to. "I mean, like really, Kennedy. Can't we take you anywhere without you picking up strays?"

"*Ohmygod!*" I shriek, playfully pushing her. "That is so messed up. You're such a hater."

"Yeah, you're right," she says over her shoulder as she walks into the darkened theater, "I *hate* to see you making a fool out of yourself."

Hope pushes Jordan farther into the theater. "Jordan, chill out. Kennedy wasn't making a fool of herself. She was just being nice. That's part of her community service. Being nice. You know that boy isn't even her type."

I laugh, following behind the two of them. "You got that right." *He's too short.* "Thanks, Hope. At least somebody knows me."

Jordan sucks her teeth. "Whatever. I *know* you, too. And I *know* I missed all the movie previews because of *you*. You know I like to catch all the upcoming movie attractions."

Oh joy!

11

"Hey Special K," the Sasha girl says in a tone friendlier than usual, walking over to me as I'm closing out my register. I silently roll my eyes up in my head, wondering what she could possibly want now. All this week, she's been working my nerves to the point that I am starting to not like coming in for work if I know she's working. It's as if she wants me to quit. And, honestly, I don't know how much more of her rudeness I can take. Yesterday, I heard her mumble, "This Oreo," when she walked by and saw my line was backed up. Then today when I almost ran smack into her as she was coming out of the bathroom and I was going in, she acted like she was ready to fight me.

I apologized for almost hitting her with the door. She rolled eyes. "Why don't you watch da *fuqq* where you goin'!" she snapped, brushing by me. "Stupid *bish*!"

And now here she is standing beside me with this phony-like grin plastered on her face like she's up to something.

"Yeah?" I say cautiously, refusing to give her eye contact.

"Crissy wants to know if you want OT tonight?"

"Not interested," I say nastily.

"Oh, okay." She doesn't move. I feel her eyes on me. Can practically feel her breath on my neck. That's how close she's up on me.

I frown. "Anything else?"

"*Meeeeeeeeeooooooow,*" she caterwauls. "Put da claws in. No need to wanna scratch my eyes out. I come in peace."

I finally look at her, giving her a blank stare. "Oh, really?" I snap, finally deciding it's time to say what's been on my mind. Inside, I'm a nervous wreck, hoping like heck that she doesn't try to slap me or punch me out. But I don't let my fear stop me from saying what I have to say. "That's a switch. Seems like all you've been to me since I've started working here is nasty and disrespectful. And I've done nothing but try to be nice to you."

"That's because you came up in here with dis uppity attitude 'n' I wasn't checkin' for dat."

I give her an incredulous look. "You know what you are? A bully."

"Pop, pop. Shots fired," she says, stepping back. "Put da gun down, boo. No need for all da 'tude."

I slam my register shut. "No. I have every right to have an attitude. There's been no need for you being rude and nasty to me, but you have. If you don't like me, fine. But that doesn't mean you have the right to say nasty things to me or about me under your breath when you don't even know me. And quite frankly, I've had about enough of your insolence."

She blinks. "My what?"

I huff. "Your rudeness."

She rolls her eyes and twists up her lips. "Ooh, look at Special K tryna—"

"And stop calling me *that*; my name is *Kennedy*."

She smirks. "Oh, okay, *Kennedy*. I guess *youuuu* told me, huh? Looks like li'l Miss Uppity got a li'l heart after all."

I frown, storming off. I can hear her laughing in back of me, but I don't care. *Screw that girl,* I think, heading toward the time clock to punch out. I've had enough of her for one day.

My parents have raised me to treat people the way I want to be treated. And if I don't have anything nice to say about someone, then to keep my mouth shut. Obviously, she hasn't been afforded the same mindset.

I don't need this crap! Jordan is right. It's not like I need the money. So why should I put up with that girl's stankness. *Maybe I should just quit!*

"Next customer, please." My breath immediately catches in the back of my throat as I look up from my register and this dream boy steps up to the counter to place his order. He's like six-three, at least, with delicious dark chocolate skin and muscles bulging everywhere. He has on a crisp white wife-beater tank top that fits him oh so perfect, showing the ripples in his abs. An eight-pack, I muse, trying like heck not to stare. But I can't help it. I just want to reach out and touch him.

He looks to be like eighteen, or nineteen. He's definitely grown.

All I keep thinking is, swaggerlicious.

"Hi, would you like to try one of our mocha or caramel frappés?"

"Nah, I'm good," he says, grinning. "Let me get a number three. Hold the lettuce and pickle."

"Okay. Anything else?"

"Nah," he says, looking over my shoulder. He does a head nod to whoever is in back of me.

For some reason I am not surprised when Sasha comes out from the back and starts prancing back and forth. He ogles her every move, his eyes locking on her booty.

I roll my eyes up in my head.

It's been two days since that incident with her and so far she hasn't been as brusque toward me. In fact she spoke to me today when I first started my shift and walked by, averting my eyes from hers.

She smirked. "Well, hello to you, too."

"Oh, hi," I said, surprised.

"What time you get off?" she asked, sliding a hand over her bangs.

"Six."

"Oh, okay. Make sure you see me before you leave."

She walked off, saying nothing more. And that's the last thing she's said to me all day. Now she's conveniently standing here at my register while I'm finishing up Sexy Chocolate's order, instead of working her station in the back.

"That'll be eight-dollars and thirty-seven cents," I tell him, eyeing him gawking at Sasha. There's no way I can compete with a girl whose boobs are practically bursting out of her uniform top.

He digs into his front pocket, pulling out a wad of money and handing me a twenty.

"Ooh, you fine," she says to him, fully aware that she's caught his attention.

"What's gucci, yo?" he says to her, grinning.

What's gucci?

"Chillin', boo. Tryna make these coins. What's good wit' you?"

Oh, that's what that means.

He licks his lips. "Right, right."

I hand him his receipt. Tell him his order will be up soon, then call for the next customer. He steps to the side and waits.

"Hey, girl," Sasha says. "You wanna roll wit' me to a party dis weekend?"

I can't believe what I am hearing. I give her a confused look, not sure if I've heard her right. "Huh?"

She snaps her fingers in my face. "Umm, hello? Party. Finger pop. Fine boys. Wit' *me*. You do know how to pop dem hips 'n' drop it like it's hot, don't you?"

Heck no. Well, only in the mirror, in private. Alone.

I don't feel comfortable telling her that.

Ohmygod! I can't believe she's standing here asking me *if I want to go to a party with her. Me!*

"Um, I don't know. When is it?"

"This Saturday."

I eye her curiously, wondering why she's inviting me to hang out with her, when she hasn't had one kind thing to say to me since I started here. Now all of a sudden she wants to party with me.

I can hear Jordan's voice in my head saying, "Unh-uh. Don't do it. That girl's ratchet and crazy! It's probably a setup, girl. Don't. Do. It."

Girl, get over it. This could be the start of the exciting summer you've been looking for.

I decide it really doesn't matter why she's asked me. Point is, I'm ready to have some fun. And it's not like anyone else is banging down my door to let me in on the happenings. So I need to take whomever I can get.

"Okay, sure. I guess," I say tentatively.

"Good. I'll give you my address so you can come through early."

I raise a brow. "Why?"

"Girl, have you looked in the mirror lately? For a makeover, boo."

I swallow. "A makeover? There's nothing wrong with the way I dress," I say, offended.

"Yeah, okay. That preppy look might work where you from. But you can't even be tryna roll out wit' me lookin' all church-girl. No, we gonna have ta put a li'l beat on ya face 'n' step ya fashion game up."

Put a li'l beat on my face?

"You mean makeup?"

"Yeah. Just a li'l to make ya eyes pop 'n' ya mouth real juicy."

"Oh."

"So you down?"

"I guess."

"Good." She smirks. "And you better not flake out on me, either. Or I'ma come to work on Monday 'n' bust you in ya head."

I frown.

She laughs. "Girl, relax. I'm only playing wit' you. I'm not workin' tomorrow so make sure you come see me before you get off so we can exchange info. I'ma 'bout to break you in real right, Miss Goodie-Goodie. So be ready."

I nod, bringing my attention to the next customer as she walks off. "Hi, would you like to try one of our mocha or caramel frappés?"

12

Saturday afternoon, at a little after two P.M., I arrive at Sasha's apartment building after having my mom drop me off at the mall as if I had to go to work, then calling a cab to bring me over here.

"So, you ready for your makeover?" Sasha says excitedly. "Out with that ole preppy white girl look 'n' in wit' the boss lady swag."

I shrug. "I guess."

She plants a hand up on her hip. "You *guess*? Girl, bye! Miss me wit' that. Already tol' you, if you gonna roll wit' me, then you gonna need to step ya dress game up, boo. 'Cause what you stay rockin' ain't it."

I frown, glancing down at my Century 21 pink cami, Adiktd Mystery jeans, and expensive sandals. "What's wrong with what I have on?"

Sasha gives me a blank look. Then rapidly bats her lashes. "Well, nothing, I suppose. If you tryna go for suburban white girl, then you're a smash hit. But if you wanna rise to the top 'n' be a fly girl then I'ma need for you to sit back 'n' let me work my magic. I can't have you rollin' in the hood wit' me lookin' all wack 'n' whatnot. Not gonna happen, honey boo-boo. If we gonna roll then you gonna have to represent for the boss chicks. I promise you. When I'm finished you'll have all the cutie-boos checkin' for you. I'ma 'bout to turn you from a plain chick into bein' a real problem. Watch 'n' see."

"And what's *a problem*?" I ask with raised eyebrows.

She runs her hands up and down her body. "All'a this, boo. I'm problem number one. And now I'ma 'bout to make you problem number two. Thought you knew."

I blink. No offense, but Sasha dresses kind of...um, well, let's see. What's the right word I'm looking for? Skanky. Yeah, that's it. Everything she wears is always so tight. Even her uniforms fit snugly, causing the seams to stretch over her curvy body. It's like she feels the need to put on display everything she's blessed with.

It's like she thinks less is sexiness.

"Well, okay. I guess I can go along with the makeover. But I don't want to wear anything that screams boy-hungry hooker."

She waves me on. "Ain't nothing wrong wit' showin' off a whole lotta thigh. Just be classy wit' it."

I take in her teensy-weeny black boy shorts and skimpy white off-the-shoulder see-through blouse. She's sitting up on her dresser with her legs gaping wide open, showing all of her goodies. I'm almost certain she doesn't have on any panties. The thought makes me gag.

"I guess," I say, shifting on her bed. "It all depends on how you define classy."

"Okay, Miss Lady. How do you define it?"

I shrug. "I don't know. For me, it's about the way you carry yourself. Being a lady. Polite. Knowing how to sit and walk and talk. Not being all loud and crude. Knowing how to act in public. Someone with impressive character. Elegantly stylish. High quality."

"Wow."

"Wow, what?" I ask innocently. She's looking at me as if I've said something crazy. "Why are you looking at me like that?"

"Like what?" She tilts her head. "Like you're *crazy*?"

"Yeah."

"Because you are," she snaps, jumping off her dresser.

I blink, taken aback at how quickly she's flipped on me.

"How the eff you gonna sit up here in my face 'n' try'n call me ghetto, huh? Where they teaching that at? The 'burbs? Because, honey, you got the right one."

She starts removing her earrings.

I blink again. Shift in my seat. "That's not what I meant," I quickly say, trying to defuse the situation. The last thing I want is a fight with her. "I apologize if I said something that offended you. That wasn't my intention. I thought we were speaking freely. You asked me to define a word. And I gave you my best definition."

"*Tsk*. Definition my ass. Sounded like you were tryna throw shade to me." She tsks me again. "You uppity hoes kill me, turnin' ya noses up at us hood chicks. *Bish*, be clear. Ain't nothin' ghetto 'bout me. I'ma hood classy chick. Believe that."

Hood classy? Wow, okay. That's a new one.

"Sasha, I really apologize if I gave you the impression I was implying that you weren't classy. I definitely wasn't trying to disrespect you."

"Oh, I'ma let it slide this time, boo-boo. But the next time I'ma take it straight to ya face."

I blink.

She stares me down, then cracks up laughing. "Psych! Gotcha!"

I don't see anything funny.

"Girl, you shoulda seen your face. It was priceless! I had you going. Hahahaha."

I let out a slight sigh of relief. Although I finally relax a little, in the back of my mind, I'm thinking, *This girl is a loose cannon.*

"Yeah, you definitely got me." I let out a nervous chuckle. "I thought you were getting ready to attack me."

She waves me on dismissively. "Girl, please. Unless you cross me, you'll never have to worry about me doin' you dirty."

"Oh, you won't have to worry about that," I say truthfully. "I'd never do anything to cross you."

"Then I'll always have your back."

She walks over to her closet and flings open the mirrored door. My mouth drops open. Her closet is packed tight to the seams with designer clothes, shoes, and handbags, many of them still with tags on them.

I have a lot of clothes, but nothing compared to this. Then again, I have a walk-in closet and all of my things aren't all cramped up into one space. "Wow. Your mom must really work around the clock to make sure you have all this nice stuff."

"*Pfft.* My moms? Girl, stop. I wish. That stingy *bish* ain't hardly comin' up off'a no paper for me. If I wanna keep nice clothes on my back, then I gotta get out there 'n' get it the best way I know how. I been doin' me ever since."

I cringe at her calling her own mother the B-word. I would never. My mom would have my head if I even thought it. "Oh, wow." I don't know what else to say. My parents buy me anything I want within reason. Not that I ever ask for much.

Now, I'm looking at her and kind of feeling sorry for her, understanding a little bit better why she's the way she is. Mean-spirited.

Sasha keeps talking as she pulls clothes from off the rack. "Soon as I turned sixteen that trick told me I was grown 'n' needed to finance my own needs. If I wanna eat, I gotta buy my own groceries."

I blink.

"And that ole greedy heifer was still gettin' EBT benefits for me up until last year."

She sees the confusion on my face.

She lets out an annoyed sigh. "Food stamps. Girl, keep up."

"Oh. Okay. What about your dad?"

She screws her face up at me. "My *dad?* Why you askin' 'bout him? What, you a social worker now?"

I apologize for asking. But then I turn around and I ask her how she affords all of this stuff on her paycheck if her parents don't buy them for her.

She bucks her eyes, then scrunches up her face. "See. Now you still doin' too much. But since you asked, I'm on the ballers 'n' boosters program."

I give her a confused look.

She sucks her teeth. "You don't know much of anything, do you?" She shakes her head. "You suburban hoes got a lot to learn. I forget y'all kinda slow."

"Not knowing what something is doesn't make me slow," I say, feeling insulted by her.

"Yeah, okay. Whatever. I only rock wit' ballers who can finance my wears. And if they not tryna come up off them dollars, then I roll up on the boosters 'n' put my order in. They can get whatever you want. From the knock-offs to the official ish." She pulls what I'm sure she believes is an *official* Louis Vuitton bag from off a hook, holding it up. "I'm serious 'bout mine. This bag costs almost fifteen hunnid in the store, but, thanks to my connect over in the Bricks, I got it for only three hunnid."

Although I don't personally carry the coveted luxury bags, my mom does. And I've been inside enough Louis Vuitton stores in my lifetime to know what's real and what's not. This poor bag she's holding up, bragging about, isn't legit.

"That's nice," I lie. I don't have the heart to tell her that she's been scammed. Bamboozled. Then again, it's not my business and I don't want to be "doin' too much," as she said.

She tries to give it to me. "Here, you can rock it today, if you want. I'm goin' to serve 'em my Gucci satchel."

I shake my head. Decline the offer. Although it's a really good replica of the real thing, I wouldn't be caught dead carrying it. "Oh, no thanks. I appreciate the offer, though." I point over to my lipstick (that's the name of color) Tumi crossbody bag. "But my little ole bag will do just fine."

She makes a face, tossing the bag back into her crammed closet. "Suit yaself." She shuts the door, then walks over to her bed and tosses an armful of clothes onto the center of it. "Pick through these outfits 'n' see which one you wanna rock. I'll be right back."

She heads for the door, leaving me wondering what I'm getting myself into by befriending her. Reluctantly, I sift through the pile of designer clothes on her bed. Everything she's pulled out is skimpy. But I won't lie. A lot of it is very nice. Still. The idea of having all of my business out doesn't sit right with me.

But I did say I wanted to be adventurous this summer, didn't I?

Five minutes later, Sasha comes back into the room carrying a bottle of Hennessey and two shot glasses. "I brought us some Hen dog to get the party juices flowin'." I eye her as she pours herself the first shot. I quickly say no thanks when she's about to pour me a glass.

She looks at me and shrugs. "Whatever. More for me." She snaps her head back and swallows the dark elixir in one gulp. She refills her shot glass and tosses it back. "Aaah." She shakes her shoulders and shakes out her hands as if she's having a seizure. "Whew! The devil is a lie. Henny does the body right. We need some music up in here."

I watch her as she scuttles over toward her Sony Bluetooth speaker, holding up her phone. A few seconds later, Trinidad James's "All Gold Everything" starts playing.

"Woo-oooh!" She snaps her fingers. "This ish right here goes hard."

I shrug.

She dances over to where she's left the drinks and pours another shot, then tosses it back. "And please don't tell me you wearin' some big ole nasty granny panties underneath them jeans. Please, don't. I'm goin' to hop in the shower. Don't be goin' thru my ish, either, *bish*." She laughs. "Let me stop effen wit' you. I'll be back in a sec."

She shakes her butt out of the room.

Several minutes go by and her Samsung rings over on the dresser. She quickly stalks back into the bedroom with only her purple thong on. "Ooh, I thought I heard my phone. It's about time this ninja hit me back."

Her naked breasts sway. I quickly avert my eyes, reaching over and picking up the latest issue of *Ebony*. I flip through the pages, pretending to be interested. But, honestly, my mind is starting to race about this party we're going to. Like who's going to be there? What types of guys are going to be there? Stuff like that.

"Hello? Yeah...uh-uh...where you...? Oh, okay...We gettin' dressed now...Yeah, yeah, blah, blah, blah...I know..."

I feign interest in some article about the woes of the music industry until I stumble on an article about how most New Yorkers don't use condoms during sex. I cringe. "Ohmygod, that's so nasty," I mumble, reading on. It states that only one out of three adults in New York used a condom the last time they had sex. I read on, wondering why anyone would jeopardize their health like that, knowing the risks involved. I shake my head as I finish reading.

"Yeah, she's here..." I look up from the magazine, glancing over at Sasha as she prances around the room half-naked. "Yeah...the chick I was tellin' you 'bout...hol' on..."

"Here," she says, shoving her cell into my face. "My boy wants to holla at you."

I frown, staring at her hand. "Who is he?"

"Someone who's gonna change your life; that's who."

I shake my head, pushing her hand away from me.

"Girl, don't play. I been talkin' you up to him 'n' he's tryna get at you. So you better act like you know 'n' get wit' the program. I'm tryna upgrade you, boo."

Upgrade me?

"You can thank me later. Now here." She shoves the phone back in my face. "Hello," I say in a low whisper.

"Yo, wat's good, ma?" I hear the smooth voice on the other end of the line say. I'm not going to lie. He has a really nice voice. "I've heard a lot 'bout you from my peoples."

I shoot a look over at Sasha as she heads out of the door, telling me over her shoulder that she's going to take her shower.

"Oh," I say, fidgeting with the diamond Tiffany cross around my neck. A gift from my grandparents given to me on my thirteenth birthday. "Who is this?"

"Malik. But cats in the streets call me Money."

"Oh," I say again. Not sure what I'm supposed to say after that.

"So what's good? You got a man?"

I shake my head. *No, but I want one.* Hazel Eyes comes to mind. But I immediately shake any thoughts of him being my boo from my head. "No."

"That's what it is. You gonna be at my people's party, right?"

"Yeah."

"True. I'ma holla at you then, a'ight?"

"Okay."

"True. Tell Sash I'ma get up wit' her a li'l later."

We disconnect. I walk over and set Sasha's phone down on her dresser, then go back through the pile of clothes she has on her bed. This time I go through each outfit with a renewed purpose—to look fly.

13

"Maybe I shouldn't have worn this," I say, feeling uncomfortable as I step out of her car and my heeled foot hits the curb. "I feel naked."

"Girl, stop. You got that fire, boo. And you thick 'n' curvy in all the right places. You better stop playin' 'n' work what ya momma gave you." She slaps my butt. I jump. "Ooh, you have a nice bouncy booty, too. I don't even know why you be hidin' it in all them corny clothes. Show some boob crack! Show some booty crack! Ninjas are visual. They need to *see* what they *think* they *might* be gettin' even if you ain't really tryna give 'em nothin'. They're like dogs. You gotta know how to dangle a bone in front of 'em long enough to get whatever it is you want outa 'em. Then all you gotta do is give him a li'l treat for his generosity."

I shake my head. "Oh, I don't need a guy to buy me things. All I have to do is ask my parents or one of my brothers and they'll just get it for me."

She rolls her eyes. "Well, ex*cuuuuse* me, Miss Uppity. We all don't have Mommy and Daddy's wit' endless bank."

"I'm not uppity," I say defensively, shutting her car door. "And my parents work hard. We're not rich."

"Mmph. Whatever. Everyone doesn't have it like you, Miss I Get Whatever I Want. Some of us started from the bottom 'n' had to scheme our way up on top."

She stops, digs in her purse and pulls out a compact mirror. She checks herself in it. Glides a coat of lipgloss over her lips then blows herself a kiss before finally snapping her compact shut and tossing it back down into her bag.

"C'mon, let's go."

We walk up to the house. There's like six guys on the side of the two-story house that looks like it's seen better days, shooting dice and smoking. And I want nothing more than to go over and watch and listen and learn. But Sasha isn't trying to hear it.

"Girl, please. Leave them dust busters alone. They ain't pushing no real paper. You need a baller in ya life. Not some lightweight."

Begrudgingly, I follow behind her trying to mask my disappointment. There's a group of ten guys either standing or sitting on the porch in wife-beaters and sagging jeans with sparkling chains dangling from their necks, blinged-out watches on their wrists—a few have huge diamonds in their earlobes—drinking and smoking weed. One by one, Sasha introduces me to all of the thugged-out guys.

I smile, feeling like I've just died and gone to thug heaven.

They all say, "What's good…"

I eye them, taking in their bulging muscles. Most of

them look as if they've spent most of their time in the gym lifting weights, sculpting their bodies. A few look like they will shoot first and ask questions later. I feel a tingly sensation creep down my spine at their hoodness as they all drink me in with their wandering eyes.

"Ma, you fine," a tall, dark-skinned guy with half-sleeve tattoos on both of his arms says, licking his lips. "Where you been hidin' all my life?"

"Away from you," Sasha jumps in, playfully pushing him out of the way. "Now back up off my girl."

I glance at her; surprised she's called me her *girl*. I mean, just a few weeks ago I was *corny* and I *thought* I was cute. Today, I'm upgraded to *girl* status. I'm not complaining, though. Still, I wonder for a brief moment if she means it or if it's simply a figure of speech.

Tall, Dark, and Tatted mushes her in the head. "Sash, go 'head wit' that slickness, yo. 'Fore I take it to ya skull. Ain't nobody talkin' to you." He brings his attention to me. "What's good wit' you, ma? Who ya man?"

I open my mouth to speak, but Sasha cuts in before I can get a word out.

"Don't worry about all dat," Sasha snaps.

"She gotta phatty," I hear someone say in back of me. I glance over my shoulder straight into the face of a reddish-brown skinned guy with cornrows and juicy red lips that he licks as he gazes at my butt. "Yo, I need dat in my life; word to mother. I need dat."

"Slick, fall back, boo. Malik's already got dibs on dat."

Malik? Got dibs on that? I haven't even met him yet. What if I don't like him? I mean, yeah. We spoke on the phone. And he sounded okay. But that didn't mean I'd *want* him to have dibs on me. I keep from frowning. The

way she said *on that* makes me feel like I'm a piece of fur-
niture or something.

Truth is, I kinda like Hazel Eyes. And I know he likes
me. I've only gone out with him once. And I haven't been
back over to his house since that one time. But we Skype
almost every night and we text each other every day. And,
okay...I snuck out to see him once.

"Oh a'ight, a'ight. That's what it is." He winks at me.
"Yo, you mad sexy, though. That ninja don't treat you
right, come holla at ya boy. I got a pet snake that would
love to crawl up in da sheets wit' you; ya heard?"

Everyone in earshot laughs.

"Someone else says, "Word is bond. I'd tap that up.
She's fresh meat, son; real fresh, just like how I like it."

I blink, hoping like heck my nervousness and shyness
isn't too obvious.

"Girl, c'mon in the house," Sasha says, pulling me by
the arm and guiding me through the cloud of smoke.
"Don't pay them fools no mind. They all a bunch of horny
hounds."

"So where's this Malik guy you've been bragging about?"
I ask once we've made it into the house and through the
throng of bodies and thick fog of weed smoke. A few girls
either shoot me the evil eye or kind of roll their eyes at me
as I pass by, but I don't really mind. I know I'm looking
cute in my short white tennis skirt and halter top. And my
red-painted toes look real cute in the strappy sandals
Sasha let me borrow.

"*Braggin'* about?" she says with attitude. "Oh, no, boo.
Never that. I don't need to brag, hun. It is what it is. That
mofo's fine. But don't worry, girl. He'll be here. Trust.

Then you can see for yaself. In the meantime, let's get you loose. You're a li'l too tight for me."

"I am not. I'm loose."

She laughs. "Yeah, okay. Not. You're 'bout as loose as a virgin in a chastity belt, but I'ma break you in real right."

I shrug, not really sure exactly what it is she means. I let it go over my head, following behind her into the kitchen. As I walk past a group of girls, I hear some girl say as Sasha walks by, "Yeah, there goes that grimy *bish*. She gave my brother chlamydia."

"Well, Loquita, that's what he gets for goin' in raw. He shoulda strapped it up before he tapped it up."

"*Biatch*, please. What you tryna say? That it's his fault that that *bish* is nasty? Girl, bye! She shouldn't be servin' up effen cooties. I should run up on her 'n' punch her in da back of the head."

I blink, quickly glancing over at them. They are both cute girls. One is brown-skinned. She has shoulder-length hair dyed pink and green-colored eyes. Contacts, I muse. Her lip is pierced, as is her nose and eyebrow. I don't get a real good look at the dark-skinned girl with the bright red hair standing next to her because Pink Hair blasts me.

"Trick, why you all over here? Snap ya neck back around 'n' keep it movin' before you find ya face on the floor."

Her friend laughs, shaking her head. "Nosy hoes, I tell you."

I look away real quick. Don't say a word. Just walk. Fast.

When I walk up to where Sasha is, she introduces me to this string-bean-thin girl with humongous boobs. She's kind of okay looking, I guess. She has a little too much purple eye shadow going on, but then again…what do I know? I'm not a makeup kind of girl.

"Kennedy, this is my girl Shayneetha. Shay, this is Kennedy."

"Hi," I say, extending my hand out to her.

She dismisses my outstretched hand. "That's nice."

Taken aback by her rudeness, I quickly drop my hand down to my side.

"Ooh, Shay-Shay, play nice." Sasha looks over at me. "Girl, don't pay her no mind. She's shady like that wit' everyone. I'ma go grab us a couple of drinks."

I nod my head. "Okay."

Now I'm standing here next to this girl, feeling insecure. I can feel her sizing me up and I don't even know why. It's not like I've done or said anything to offend her. I think I might have heard her mumble *This corny bish*, under her breath, but then some brown-skinned guy with dreads walks over and whispers something in her ear, but he's looking over at me.

She shrugs. Says something back to him in his ear. He grins. Then licks his lips and winks at me before walking off. I cringe inside, thinking that maybe this was a bad idea for me to come here. I feel so out of place. Like I'm the weakest link or something. I know it's all in my head, but I feel like everyone in the room is pointing fingers over at me, laughing.

I'm feeling alone in a room full of strangers.

I am tempted to run out the door. But then Sasha is back from wherever she disappeared to, carrying two plastic cups in her hands; one red and one blue.

Jay-Z's "Holy Grail" starts playing.

"Girl," the girl Shayneetha says, cutting her eyes at me,

"I'ma go find that fine Snoopy 'n' get my pop on. I saw him earlier pinned up on some bubble head."

"Do you, boo," Sasha says, handing me the red cup in her hand.

"What's this?"

She smirks. "Something to help get your mind right. Thug Passion, boo."

"Oh, okay. Thanks." I reluctantly take it, looking inside the cup. I smell it. I'd never had it before, but I knew what it was: A mixture of Alizé and champagne. I also knew it was the title of one Tupac's songs where he'd referenced the drink in his song. I only knew this because I'd read it in a *Vibe* magazine article they'd written about the late, great rapper. "Isn't this drink kind of old school? I mean. I didn't think kids my age drank this."

"Oh, it's all 'bout the Ciroc, boo. But I figured you needed you some Thug Passion in ya life since you tryna be down. But this one has a whole lot of thug and a little less passion in it."

I give her a confused look, not knowing what she meant by that. She notices the look on my face. "Girl, stop tryna analyze everything I say. Stay in the moment and drink up." She taps her cup to mine. "Here's to that thug life."

"Mmmm. I like the sound of that." I take a slow sip of my drink. Make a face as it slides down the back of my throat. I feel a slow heat course through my chest. And by the time I'm on my third, or maybe it's my fifth sip, I'm melting all over myself from the flames. By the time the cup is empty, I am practically floating.

By my second cup, I'm soaring. And everything around me is moving in slo-mo. My skin is tingling. My sense of smell and sound seems magnified. Next thing I know, an August Alsina song is playing, "Nobody Knows," and I'm in the middle of the floor dancing. Alone. Swirling and twirling.

One arm is up over my head. I rock my hips in big circles. I hike up my tiny skirt and start doing nasty things I'd never done before. It's like I've become possessed. The beat hypnotizes me. I slowly twirl around. My eyes close. I sway left to right. Then throw my head back. Run my hands through my hair. I lose myself to the music. Become everything I've ever watched in Beyoncé and Ciara videos.

It feels like I'm slipping in and out of consciousness.

Dang, that drink really has my head spinning.

I feel my body overheating.

Oooh, it's so hot in here.

I try to stop myself from untying my halter, but it's like my hands, my fingers, my arms, have a mind of their own.

What's happening to me?

I'm in the spotlight. And somehow I am feeling like I've just become the life of the party.

And everyone's entertainment...

14

I will a bleary eye open. Then wince. My head is spinning. "Oooh, you kept it real *classy,* li'l Miss Party Girl," Sasha says, smirking. "Mmph. You turned the party out. I didn't think you had it in you, Miss Suburbs. But you turnt it up—all the way up—last night."

I groan, trying to lift my head up from the pillow. My head is pounding. Regretting ever trying to move, I plop my head back onto the pillow, pulling the covers over my head then lower them enough to peer over the edge. My stomach sloshes. And I feel like I'm ready to vomit at any moment.

Please God. Let me get through this and I promise to never, ever drink another Thug Passion drink or anything with the word thug *attached to it, for as long as I live. Please and thank you…*

I don't remember much of anything after Sasha handed me my second drink. I remember taking slow sips. Then I started swaying. Everything else is one big blur. And I'm afraid to even ask what happened. I'm not sure if I want her to fill in the blanks, either.

"Girl, I couldn't get you off the dance floor. You gave Beyoncé a run for her money last night, boo." She laughs, falling back on her bed. "Ohmygod! You should have seen you. A hot slutty mess!"

She tells me how I was booty popping and hip thrusting it, dropping down on my knees and crawling on the floor, swinging my hair around. *"Yasss,* Miss Peaches! You showed out."

"Miss Peaches?"

She cracks up laughing.

"Yesss! That's what you had dem ninjas callin' you last night after you took off ya top 'n' started flashin' e'eryone. You shoulda seen dey faces, starin' at dem big juicy boobs of yours."

I am mortified. All I can see in my mind's eye is my slumped, drunk body being tossed around like a dirty rag doll. "Oh, God!" I grumble. "Please don't tell me." My face heats with embarrassment.

This is tragic! How could I be so stupid?!

I try to replay the events that took place before the booze and my lapse in judgment kicked in. But keep coming up blank.

Ohmgod! What was in that drink?

I'm never drinking that mess again! Ever!

"Girl, relax. You were just doin' you. Lettin' ya hair down 'n' havin' a good time. Shiiiiit, I was twisted. But not like you." She laughs, reaching for a can of Red Bull on her nightstand. "I thought I was gonna have ta beat the brakes off some'a them ninjas. They kept tryna take you upstairs to get that train ride."

My eyes pop open.

She senses my fear. Assures me that nothing happened. This *time*. "But, girl, you owe me. I coulda made a killin' off you last night. Had I let them horny ninjas get at you I woulda had me enough for a down payment on a cute li'l BMW, or somethin'. And you fresh meat, too. Mmph."

I blink. I can't believe she's talking as if she was considering pimping me out for the night. Although she's laughing, the look in her eyes tells me if there were a way she could have gotten away with it, that's exactly what she would have done. Rented me out to the whole party.

"You lucky Malik got there when he did and was able to keep them fools in check 'cause dey wasn't even tryna hear me after a while. You had them horny ninjas goin' through it."

I swallow, wincing. My throat is dry. Sore. "Ohmygod! He was there, too?" My voice is hoarse, feels raw. Like I'd been screaming at the top of my lungs all night. Or as if someone scrubbed the back of my throat with sandpaper then rubbed salt over it.

"Girrrl, was he! Looking so fine. And trust. Drunk or not, I could tell he liked *e'very*thing about you." She made a popping sound with her mouth.

My eyes become unnaturally wide as she recounts the events from the night before. Tells me I danced eight songs straight. That I hiked my skirt up over my hips and showed the whole party my bare essentials.

Dear God!

She chuckles. "Next time, though, I'ma need you to handle ya liquor a li'l better."

I cover my face. Shame courses through every inch of my body. Panic rises inside of me, making me feel sweaty and cold all at the same time. *This can't be happening! It has to be a terrible mistake!*

"What time is it?" I finally croak out, feeling sick to my stomach.

"It's almost ten o'clock."

I jolt up in the bed, causing my mushy brain to swish around in my head. *"Ten o'clock?* In the morning? Ohgodohgod! I am sooo dead!" My feet hit the dirty beige carpet and scatter over to my bag, frantically searching from my phone. "Ohgod! My parents are going to kill me."

"Girl, relax. It's not like they're gonna kill you over being late once in your li'l perfect life. It's not like you break your curfew all the time and stay out all night."

"No, I don't. But still…ohgod! I'm so done. I'll probably get grounded for the next two weeks."

I close my eyes. My eyeballs throb behind my lids. I let out a loud groan.

"You're overreactin' if you ask me. I bet all your parents are gonna do is put you in timeout, then take away your allowance for the next week or so."

I keep my eyes shut, slowly shaking my head. "No. They are going to be livid. Trust me; especially my mother."

"Not if you come up with a good lie," she offers matter-of-factly.

I frown. "Are you kidding me? I've been out *all* night. And I didn't even call home to let anyone know I was okay. What kind of lie could I possibly say that would keep my mother from wringing my neck? She's going to kill me."

"Poor thing," she says nonchalantly, taking a swig of her Red Bull. She offers me some. "Here. This'll help give you a boost of energy."

I shake my head. Tell her thanks, but no thanks. I've

had enough of her handing me drinks for one lifetime. She shrugs. "More for me." She pulls out a little baggie from out of her nightstand top drawer. It's packed with marijuana. I watch with wide-eyed amazement as she empties the tobacco of a blunt out on her nightstand and fills it with the weed, sealing it by licking and pushing the seams together. Next she lights it and takes a long pull from it. She starts coughing instantly as if she were coughing up a lung.

She clutches her chest. "Ooh, yesss! This that good ish right here." She laughs in between coughs, a puff of thick smoke curling out of her mouth.

I frown.

She holds her blunt out to me. "You sure you don't want some of this? I'm tellin' you, it'll help you wit' that hangover. "

I shake my head. "No. I don't do drugs."

She bucks her eyes. "*Bish*, what you tryna say? I know you not even tryna call me out. I don't do drugs either. I mean, yeah. E'ery now and then I might do a li'l molly wit' my girl Shay-Shay. But that's it. I don't eff wit' none'a that hard ish. So don't even get it twisted. I'm no druggie, trick."

I cringe. "I'm not a trick," I say evenly. "So please don't call me one."

She grunts. "Mmmph. I can't tell. From what I saw last night looked to me like you was trickin' for somethin' 'n' it sure wasn't for dollars, boo."

"I got drunk," I retort defensively.

She takes another pull from her blunt, then blows smoke in my direction. "Yeah, whatever. Blame it on da a-a-a-alcohol. Chile, please. I may not be da sharpest knife in the drawer, but I'm no idiot, boo. You a real live freak and a half. I bet if I hadn't been there to save you, you woulda let 'em all get a taste of ya goodies. So you can front if you want. But I know ya kind."

I blink. "My *kind*? What kind is that?"

She takes another long pull from her blunt, eyeing me. "Pssst. Like you don't know. An undercover freak; dat's what kind."

Seeing the smug look on her face makes me angry. I squirm. Not wanting a confrontation, I decide to take the high road and tread lightly. "Well, I'm not a freak. And I wasn't trying to call you a druggie or anything. I was just saying I don't do any drugs; that's all."

She frowns. "Girl, you silly. Weed ain't no drug. It's from da earth. There's nothing wrong wit' smokin' weed. It does da body good. Trust." She takes two pulls, holds the smoke in her lungs and coughs.

"Well, it's against the law," I counter. "And I'd rather not indulge in anything illegal."

She rolls her eyes, blowing circles up at the water-stained ceiling. "Girl, miss me wit' dat moral code ish. So is underage drinkin', but you didn't have a problem doin' dat, did you?" She gives me a hard stare, then rolls her eyes. "Like I said, weed comes from the Mother Earth. It's one of God's greatest wonders. So if he didn't want us to smoke it, he wouldn't have created it. Now would he?"

I have no comeback for her. It's clear she has all the answers.

I give her a blank stare, deciding it's time to slip back into the clothes I'd come here wearing before my world got turned upside down, and head home to face my fate.

15

"**K**ennedy, *where* have you been?!" my mother snaps the minute I step through the double doors. Hand on hip, nose flaring, eyes drawn to narrow slits. She's fuming.

"I-I-I," I stammer nervously. I've never seen her so mad. "I was..."

"Before you open your mouth with a lie, think about what you are going to say to me. Because I know, and you know, that you weren't with Hope or Jordan because I've spoken to both of them. Now where were you?"

"Ohmygod. I can't believe you'd call me a liar. Have I ever lied to you?"

"I'm not calling *you* a liar. I'm warning you to not let any lies fall from your lips in case you wanted to."

I stand here silently, racking my brain as to what I'll tell her. She has me cornered. I've never been in this situation so I don't know what to do to get out of it. Finally, I hang my head. My lashes wet with tears.

"I-I-I'm sorry. It won't happen again."

"Oh, no, young lady. You're not getting off the hook that easy. I want to know where you were and why your phone is off? I've been calling it all night. And all morning."

That's strange. I don't remember turning my phone off. I reach in my bag, pulling it out. Yup . . . it's off. "My battery died," I lie. "And I didn't have a way of charging it."

"And no one else had a phone you could use."

"No. There wasn't any service."

"Excuse you? What do you mean, there wasn't any service? Well, where were you that you couldn't make calls or get your butt home before your curfew?"

"At a friend's house."

She tilts her head. "Don't try my patience, Kennedy. What *friend's* house? And who are this *friend's* parents?"

"It's just her and her mom. Her dad died." That's a lie. But I don't think she'd like hearing that Sasha's father is in prison for armed robbery. And I think she told me drug charges, too. Or maybe it was a gun charge. I can't remember. All I know is, this information is on a need-to-know basis.

She eyes me. "That's not telling me what I want to know, Kennedy."

I'm starting to feel light-headed.

"Mom, please. Not right now. I don't feel well."

She huffs. "Who do you think you're telling *not right now*, huh? Like I'm bothering you. You don't get to strut up in here twelve hours after your curfew without one phone call and tell me *not right now*. I will smack the piss, the snot, and everything else out of you. Do you understand me?"

I clutch my churning stomach. *Ohgodohgod! I'm going to throw up!*

I don't answer. I take off running toward the powder room across from the sunken great room. She's hot on my heels.

"Don't you dare run off from me while I'm talking to you. Kennedy! I want to know where you've been! I've been up all night, worried sick about you! I've called all over town looking for you! And you have the gall to stroll up in here like everything is fine! This is not acceptable, Kennedy!"

"Not now, mom, please!" I slam the bathroom door in her face. Flip up the toilet seat and grip the cool porcelain, throwing my guts up. I cling to the coolness with all my might. Tears spurting from my eyes as I empty the remaining contents of my cramped stomach out.

I stay in this position—face inside the bowl, hands squeezing the sides, until I am coughing and dry heaving. And then I do the unthinkable.

I poop on myself.

Four P.M., my mom is at the foot of my bed, shaking me. "Wake up! Rise and shine!"

I groan as she walks over and flips on my nightstand lamp. I don't remember how I got into bed. Or when I took off my clothes and slipped into my pajamas. But somehow I did.

My mind is blank.

Completely gone.

Mom starts shaking my bed again. "Let's go, Kennedy! It's time to get up. You should have gotten your sleep wherever you were last night. Sleep time is over."

Ohmygod, nooo! I can't believe this!

I groan again. Everything around me is still spinning from the night before. I've spent most of the morning throwing up. I'm exhausted. And now all I want to do is sleep. Sleep. Sleep!

But it doesn't look like that's going to happen with my mom breathing down my neck doing everything she can to kill my sleep mode.

I close my eyes. Snatches of last night flitter through my head. I'm in the middle of the floor dancing. Alone. Swirling and twirling. Guys are pressed up against me, grinding and groping me. My boobs are exposed. The teenie-tiny skirt I was wearing is hiked up over my hips. Someone tries to slide his hands in my panties. I remember, now, telling him no. I pushed his hand away.

Ohgod!

I think I see Sasha over in the corner with her friends, laughing at me. But why would she do that when she cursed those boys out for trying to hump me all up on the dance floor?

"Mom, *please*. I don't feel well," I grumble, pulling the covers up over my head.

"That's not my problem. That's yours." She snatches the covers off me. "Now get up out of this bed."

"Why can't I sleep?" I whine. "We can talk later tonight, or tomorrow."

"Oh, no, little Miss Party Girl. You don't get to choose when we talk. We talk when I say we talk. So get up. You are sadly mistaken if you think you're going to lie in this bed and sleep the rest of the day away. I was nice enough to let you sleep off whatever it is you *drank* or *smoked* last night. Now it's time for you and me to have a little chat."

She shakes the bed again. My stomach churns and I feel like screaming at the top of my lungs. I take two deep breaths, then roll and stretch. I rub my burning eyes. They can barely open.

It takes a few minutes for my eyes to finally adjust to the brightness in the room. There she is. My mom. Standing at the foot of my bed with her arms folded, scowling. She's pissed. Very pissed. And I know I'm in big trouble.

And I know I have no one to blame except myself. I should have never had all those drinks. But I only had three, I think. Or was it four? I remember the first drink. And the second one after that.

Ohgod! All I know is, my head feels like someone is stomping around on my brain with cement boots. It even hurts behind my eyeballs.

If this is what drinking does to you, then I want no further part of it. None. Never. Ever.

"I'm waiting, Kennedy," Mom says through clenched teeth. "You and I are going to have a serious conversation, starting with where you were *all* night. And who dropped you off this morning with all that loud music playing, like this is some ghetto yard drop-stop."

I cringe as my ears pop. Although she isn't really yelling, it feels as if she has a bullhorn up to her lips and she's screaming into my ear.

"Okay, okay. I'm up. Can I at least take a shower and put some clothes on before I have to face my inquisition, *please*?"

She narrows her eyes at me. I can tell she's ready to go off. She takes a deep breath. Then finally says, "You have ten minutes. And not a second over." She glances at her watch. "Starting now."

16

"I'm very disappointed in you, Kennedy," Mom says, eyeing me. We are siting at the kitchen table. A cup of green tea with honey is in front of me. Mom shakes her head. "I raised you better than this. No young respectable girl comes dragging herself into the house way past the crack of dawn, reeking of alcohol and marijuana smoke."

"I wasn't smoking marijuana, Mom." I say this as if it's going to make that big of a difference. As if it will lessen the consequences.

She eyes me incredulously. "So you think underage drinking makes it better?" She tilts her head. "Is that supposed to make me feel better knowing that *my* sixteen-year-old daughter was only out God knows where *drinking* instead of *using* illicit drugs? Is that what you're telling me, Kennedy?"

"No ma'am."

"So how was it?"

I blink. Give her a confused look. "How was what?"

"The party you were at? You know, the one you thought it was okay not to come home from."

I lower my eyes from her burning stare. I fidget with the spoon in my hand, then dip it back into my steaming mug, stirring thoughtlessly.

Mom's fingers tap against the tabletop impatiently. "I'm waiting for an answer, Kennedy."

"I'm sorry," I say softly.

"No. Don't be sorry. I didn't ask for an apology. I want answers."

I think to tell her some elaborate tale, but I can't remember exactly what I told her when I walked through the door this morning. I don't want to tell a lie that doesn't match whatever I've already told her. I am relieved when my mom unknowingly lets me off the hook from having to remember exactly what I told her when she asks me who this *friend* is I was out with last night.

"Her name is Sasha."

She tilts her head. "And *how* do you know this *Sasha* girl?"

"From work." I blow into my cup, then take a slow sip of my tea.

She purses her lips. "Mmm. Where does she live?"

"Across town," I offer, hoping that'll be enough to satisfy her inquiry. It isn't. She wants to know exactly where *across* town she lives. I tell her not too far from the Flatlands, a subsidized housing development.

She purses her lips and keeps silent. I can tell she's thinking. "I see," she finally says calmly. I can tell by the look in her eyes she isn't too happy about me being in the hood, but she doesn't say so. "And how old is she?" I tell her eighteen. "And you thought it was okay to stay out over this Sasha's house without me knowing anything about her or her family, is that right?"

I shake my head. "No. I know it wasn't okay. I was wrong for not coming home, or calling you to let you know where I was or that I was okay. I know I know better. I thought I'd be home before curfew, I really did."

"So, let me get this straight. My sixteen-year-old daughter stayed the night over at some eighteen-year-old girl's house where her parent allowed underage drinking?"

"Her mom didn't know we were drinking."

"So the two of you snuck alcohol into her parents' house, is that what you're telling me?"

"No. She kind of already had the alcohol in the house." Okay, I know it's a lie.

"I see. And were there boys at this little party?"

"It wasn't a party." Okay, it's another lie. And I feel horrible for looking my mom in the eye telling her this. I shift in my seat. "There weren't any boys there, just Sasha and a few of her girlfriends."

"Kennedy, you know the rules. No sleepovers over anyone's house unless we've met the parents. No drinking. No smoking. No drugs. And definitely no sex."

"I only drank."

"But there was marijuana there...at this party, right?"

"It wasn't a party. And there wasn't any marijuana there."

She gives me a blank stare. "Look, Kennedy. Do I look like I need to be in a clown suit or something to you?"

I shake my head. "No, ma'am."

"Then why are you sitting here trying to insult my intelligence? I was your age once. You stumbled up in here reeking of alcohol, which you admit to drinking, and smelling like you were rolling around in a cloud of marijuana smoke."

"But I didn't smoke any. I swear."

She lets out a frustrated sigh. "But you were around it. Kennedy, I raised you better than that. Why would you be around someone smoking marijuana, huh?"

I shrug. "I didn't know there was going to be marijuana there."

"And what if someone had called the cops and ended up raiding the place, then what? You would have been arrested, too."

I lower my head. "I wasn't thinking. All I wanted was to have some fun, that's all. I didn't plan on getting drunk or staying out past curfew, or coming home hung over. I feel horrible for what I did."

"And so you should." She eyes me, then reaches over and places her hand over mine. "I'm angry and extremely upset with you. But I'm relieved that you're okay. That still doesn't mean you aren't punished."

"I know I am. It won't happen again. I promise."

"Let's hope, for your sake, it doesn't."

Mom slides her chair back from the table, then stands. "Look, sweetheart. I know what it's like to be sixteen and wanting to be adventurous. You've always been inquisitive. And a good kid. And I don't want anything to change that. There can be a lot of peer pressure to sometimes do what's not right. I just don't want to see you getting caught up in peer pressure. Your father and I have taught you to make your own decisions, haven't we?"

I nod. "Yes. But I wasn't being pressured to do anything."

She eyes me. "You should not be drinking. First of all,

you're not old enough to drink. And secondly, anything could have happened to you out there being intoxicated. Young women get taken advantage of all the time."

"I know, Mom," I say sheepishly. "And I'm sorry. It won't happen again." *Not getting drunk, that is.*

She stares at me, then squeezes my hand. "Listen, sweetheart. I know my little baby girl is growing up. And I know your father and I have to trust you to do the right things. But all I'm asking is that you not grow up too fast. You have a bright future ahead of you."

"I know, Mom," I say.

She stares at me. Then narrows her eyes. "Are you sure you're not using drugs?" I tell her I'm sure. She wants to know if I've ever tried them. Again, I answer no. She eyes me as if she's trying to decide whether or not she should believe me. Technically, she shouldn't. I know it. Thankfully, she doesn't.

I run my hands across my eyes and over the crown of my head. I'm feeling queasy.

"I'm not naïve, Kennedy. I know what goes on at teen parties. The last thing I want is for you to get yourself caught up in something you can't get out of."

"Mom, I won't."

"You have one more year left, sweetheart, then you are off to Harvard or Yale."

I swallow. "Can we please not talk about that right now?"

She sighs. "How long has this drinking been going on?"

"Last night was the first—and my *last*—time." I groan. "I feel awful. I don't like it."

She smiles. "Then I guess what you're going through should be punishment enough."

"Are you going to tell Daddy?"

"No. You're going to get a pass, this time. But don't let it happen again."

"I promise. I won't."

The next day I'm on my thirty-minute lunch break sitting at a table in the food court filling Sasha in on all the drama with my mom.

"That lady better get her life," she says, tilting her head, causing her bright fuchsia bangs to swing over her left eye. I've finished telling her that my mom wants to meet her. And she's not the least bit pleased about it. "I know dat's your momz 'n' all, but where dey do dat at? I ain't even 'bout to come to ya house 'n' let ya momz scrutinize me like I'm some backyard trash. I be done cussed her out, okay? She bet' not even try it. I'm too grown for da mom games, boo."

I blink. "She's not trying it. Or playing games. She's only interested in seeing who I'm hanging out with."

She snorts. "She better go have several seats at da Garden."

I give her a blank stare.

"I know how dem uppity broadz like your momz move. They think their precious daughters are too good for chicks like me."

"That's so not true," I say defensively.

"Yeah, right. Lies. Rich broadz like your momz stay lookin' down at girls from da hood like we lepers or like we have a bad case of herpes. No ma'am. Dat ain't gonna happen. Not today. Not any other day. "

"That's not her intention—to scrutinize you," I say softly. "She just wants see who I'm hanging out with; that's all."

She huffs. "Yeah, right. More lies you tell. What, she wanna make sure I'm good enough for her precious little princess to hang out wit'?" She rolls her eyes. "Girl, bye. Miss me wit' dat. Ain't no momz I know checkin' for dey kidz' friends. Ya momz is buggin' for real, girl. She doin' way too much."

I shrug. "Yeah, I guess."

"Mmmph. Well, guess dat ish somewhere else 'cause ain't nobody got time to be meetin' her." She waves me on dismissively. "Movin' on. So you tryna hit dis party up wit' me dis weekend or what?"

"I don't know," I say. "I kind of promised my mom I wouldn't get into anymore trouble."

She frowns. "Girl, bye! You betta get ya life! All dat good girl ish gonna get you is a buncha borin' nights at home. I know you ain't even 'bout to let her ruin ya summer fun, boo."

She's right! I said I wanted to party and have fun. So why should I stop now when the fun is just getting started?

"What time are we going?"

She grins. "*Bish*, dat's what I'm talkin' 'bout. It's gonna be live. Trust."

17

"So what's good, yo?" The voice blares into my ear over Busta's "Thank You" playing loudly out of the three large speakers situated around the basement. I'm at a house party in East Orange with Sasha. Somewhere I shouldn't be, of course. But the energy is live. The music is all that. And there's a pack of thug cuties here. Once again, I lied. Told my mom that I was staying the night at Hope's. That I'd be home tomorrow around one or two. Luckily for me, she believed me.

I keep my gaze low and avoid making eye contact with most of the kids here, mostly because the boys who are ogling me are making me uncomfortable. And the first time I do look up and scan the room, I'm being greeted with girls eyeballing me nastily.

"I see you all over here by yaself," he says, looking me up and down, slowly dragging the pink-colored tip of his tongue over his dark brown lips. I remember him from the last party Sasha brought me to. He was one of the guys standing out on the porch smoking a blunt. He's a brown-skinned guy with slanted, bloodshot eyes. Probably from drinking and smoking. He's about six feet with a muscular build. He's wearing a white T-shirt and a pair of baggy jeans. True Religions, I think.

I sweep my eyes around the party and notice guys grinding up on girls. And girls doing strip club moves on the dance floor. A few are pressed up in corners making out. Or smoking weed.

Without thought, I bob my head from side to side.

"You wanna dance?" he asks, taking me in with his gaze. I look up at him, then glance around the space. The floor is packed with hoochie-type girls grinding their booties up on crotches, twerking and bouncing real hard to a Jay-Z song now playing.

I shake my head. "No, thanks."

It's so packed that bodies are practically pressing into each other just to walk by. And there's a thick fog of smoke hovering in the air. I feel myself getting light-headed from all of the marijuana smoke.

He leans into my ear. "Oh, a'ight." He grins, then licks his lips.

"Why are you looking at me like that?"

"Like what?"

I shrug. "I don't know. Like you're trying to figure me out or something."

He laughs. "Oh, nah-nah. You lookin' mad sexy, though."

"Thank you," I say over the music, trying to avoid the narrowed eyes glaring at me from across the room. There are like four girls standing over on the other side of the dance floor giving me nasty looks. I don't even know any of them. But because they don't like Sasha—for whatever reasons—they don't like me. So whatever problems she has with girls I've inherited. Guilty by association.

Speaking of Sasha, she disappeared up the stairs with some boy with dreads, leaving me holding up the wall, like the lone wallflower that I am.

I glance at my watch.

Ohmygod, I can't believe she's been missing in action for almost half an hour.

"Yo, you too pretty to be standing here looking like a bored statue," he says, reaching for my hand. "Let me holla at you for a minute."

I pull my hand back.

He laughs. "Oh, word? It's like dat? I ain't gonna bite, ma; not unless you want me to. I just wanna get away from all'a dis loud music; feel me?"

I nod. "Yeah, it is kind of loud."

He gestures his head toward the stairs. "Let's go upstairs for a sec."

I glance over at the group of girls across the room. One of them grabs her crotch, then flips me off with her middle finger. I cringe. Another girl takes her finger and slides it across her throat. The threat clear: "I'm going to slice your throat."

I swallow.

He looks over at the group of girls. "Yo, don't pay them birds no mind. They hatin', that's all."

"But why?" I ask innocently.

He scrunches his face. "*Why?* You fresh meat, babe. E'ery dude in here wanna get at you. And them haters know it."

I blink. Then glance over toward the staircase when I see a guy and a girl coming down the stairs. I hope to see Sasha. But I'm disappointed when it's not her.

"Yo, you can stand here if you want, but Sasha's upstairs doin' her, so you might as well do you."

I guess he's right. Anything is better than standing here feeling stupid. Maybe I'll find Sasha upstairs, and she'll be ready to go.

"I was told to never walk off with strangers," I joke.

"I'm not a stranger, baby."

"Uh, um, if I don't know your name you are."

He smirks. "Yo, I dig you. It's Shaheed. But my peoples call me Sha."

"Nice to meet you, Shaheed," I say, trying to flirt without seeming flirty. I mean, I don't want to give off any mixed messages. I only want to have some fun.

It's a party for Christ's sake.

And Sasha is nowhere to be seen.

What else am I supposed to do? Stand here and look lost and silly?

I don't think so.

Shaheed lightly grabs me by the elbow and leads the way. I follow him through the throng of partygoers, then up the dark stairs. There's a slit of light coming from under a door. The bathroom, I think.

We walk past another door which is slightly open, a slice of light creeping out from beneath it. Save from the slivers of light and the glow of a nightlight stuck in a wall outlet, the whole upstairs is dimly lit.

We walk a short ways down the hall. I count six doors, including the two I assume are the bathroom and a bedroom, in my head. Music is playing up here as well, so it's hard to hear anything being said behind any of the doors.

Shaheed turns the knob to the third door on the left, pushing it open. It's a bedroom. There's a twin bed, a dresser, a nightstand, and a big flat-screen television mounted up on the wall across from the bed. A nightlight is plugged into an outlet near the door.

I step inside and Shaheed shuts the door behind us. My eyes have to adjust to the darkness. I blink several times.

"So, I'm sayin'...what's good? When you gonna let me show you my long stroke?"

I raise a brow. "Your *long stroke?* What, you swim? I used to belong to the swim team at my school."

He laughs. "Yeah. I swim a'ight. Up in dem guts."

I blink, caught off guard. "What did you say?"

"Nah, I'm sayin'. I gotta long stroke, but it ain't for da pool, feel me."

"Wait. You want to have *sex* with me?"

He grins. "You already know what it is, ma. Yeah I wanna hit dat." He steps in, pulling me into him. He reeks of weed and alcohol. He licks his lips. "I ain't even gonna front, yo. I've been eyein' you all night, ma. From da moment you stepped through da door I started schemin' on dat phatty, yo. I'm tryna see what's really good wit' all'a dat."

He grabs at the front of his jeans. "You got my ish on rock, yo."

He is groping me in the dark, pressing himself into me.

I wrestle my way out of his grasp. Tell him to please keep his hands to himself. That I'm not easy like that.

He laughs. "C'mon, yo. Don't front. You ripe 'n' ready for da D, yo. I can smell it. You stay comin' around lookin'

all good, like you want mofos tryna get at you. Don't think
I haven't peeped you eyein' me."

I shake my head. "That's not true. I mean. Yeah, I've
glanced at you the few times I've seen you. But that doesn't
mean I like you."

He frowns. "Oh, so you sayin' you ain't feelin' me? Is
that it?"

"Yes. I mean. No."

"Which is it? You feelin' me or you not?"

"I-I-I don't even know you," I say wearily.

"So you a tease then, huh? You one'a dem hoes who
likes to go 'round teasin' mofos, huh? Get all up in a
mofo's head 'n' play mind games. Is that it?"

"N-n-no," I stammer, trying to back away from him.
"That's not what I was doing. I swear to you. I thought you
were just being nice when you asked me to come up here.
I really thought you wanted to talk."

"Yeah, I wanted to talk you outta dem panties. That's it."

"But I don't like you like that."

"Yeah, but I'm tryna change all'a dat. But you wanna
front."

He leans in and tries to kiss me on the lips. I jerk my
head back just as his lips hit the side of my neck. I can see
the drool sliding out of the corners of his mouth as his
lusty gaze drinks my body in.

"Ma, you mad sexy. You got my head goin' 'n' I ain't
even hit dat yet. I bet you mad juicy, too."

I shake my head. "No. I'm not juicy. I mean, I'm not trying to let you hit that, I mean, this."

"Yo, let me be da judge of dat. Let me feel it." I blink as
he grabs me and pulls me into him, sliding his big hand
over the curve of my hip, then onto my butt.

I push his hand off of me. Tell him no thanks. But he's not trying to hear it.

"Nah, baby. You in my space. I'm tryna get it in. So don't front. You know what time it is."

"This is all wrong," I say, stepping back.

"Nah, shorty, this is all right." He licks his already wet lips with the tip of his tongue. "And I'ma 'bout to make you feel right in a minute if you stop frontin' 'n' get wit' da program."

"I don't want to have sex with you," I stutter, hoping he'll see the pleading in my eyes.

Ohmygod! What have I gotten myself into? Please don't let this boy rape me.

Sasha, where the heck are you?!

"Please," I stammer. "I just want to go find my friend, then leave."

He grunts. "Who, Sasha? Yo, dat broad's somewhere gettin' twisted 'n' her back blown out."

I don't really know what he means by 'she's getting twisted.' But I knew what he meant about her back.

"Yo, ya girl ain't 'bout to bounce no time soon, real spit. She's 'bout to take dat ride on da express train. So you might as well relax, ma. I ain't gonna hurt you."

Express train?

What in the heck is he talking about?

"Yo, don't act like you don't know what time it is." He starts making train sounds. "*Choo-choo.* All aboard," he says, deepening his voice. "Come get up on dis hard stick."

I gasp. *Ohmygod! Sasha is somewhere letting a bunch of guys take turns on her.* I feel queasy now. I tell him I can't do this. That I didn't know this is what he wanted.

"Then what you come up here for if you ain't know what time it was, huh, trick?"

"I-I-I thought you wanted to talk," I say, fighting back an avalanche of tears.

He snorts. *"Talk?* Is you effen retarded, yo. I brought you up here to beat that box up. I ain't tryna talk. I'm tryna stroke."

He grabs me again.

"Please, stop!" I plead, trying to break free from his grip. However, to no avail. He's much stronger than me. He keeps pawing at me. "Get off me! I don't want to have sex with you."

My pleas fall on deaf ears as he tries to force himself on me. I start screaming at the top of my lungs, hoping somewhere will hear me over the loud music.

They don't.

Shaheed's hand is up my skirt now and he's trying to pull at my underwear. I press my thighs together. My heart is jumping in my chest a mile a minute. I'm kicking myself for wearing this short skirt.

I knew I should have worn jeans like I wanted to in the first place.

Ohmygod! This isn't how I want to lose my virginity! By some drunk boy I don't even know or like!

Shaheed's all over me. And I can't take it anymore. I scream as loud as I can.

"Yo, shut da eff up, you effen trick-tease!"

He slams me down on the bed. I am screaming and kicking. Scared to death. As he tries to climb on top of me, I knee him in the groin, hard, then hit him in his face, causing him to double over in pain.

I run for the door, swinging it open, banging on all the doors, screaming out for Sasha until one finally opens. It's the second one to the left.

A tall, thin guy with long box braids and a bunch of tattoos covering his chest and arms opens the door—*butt-naked*. He doesn't even have the decency to cover himself.

Oh my God...

"Is Sasha in here? Sasha?!"

I glance around the large bedroom and notice there are four other guys in the room. Naked.

"Yo, Slim," a voice calls out, "you tryna get next?"

"Yeah, man, hol'up. We got company."

I croak out a scream as I look over and see Sasha on her knees in the middle of the bed with some guy humping her like a mad man. I back out of the room and flee toward the stairs like there's a fire. I have to get out of here, now. I run smack into Sasha's friend, Malik, as he's coming up the stairs.

"Yo, wat's gud, ma?"

My lips quiver.

He frowns. "Yo, ma, you a'ight?"

I collapse in his arms and burst into tears.

18

"Yo, run dat ish by me again," Malik says, staring deep into my eyes. His intense gaze makes me uncomfortable. But not in a frightening, creepy kind of way. When I fell into his arms as he was coming up the stairs, he saw how distraught I was and wrapped an arm around me, and walked me outside for some air. We're standing next to his parked truck and he's intently listening as I repeat what almost happened to me upstairs. He narrows his eyes. "Dat muhfuggah did *what?*"

The edge in his tone is so sharp it slices into the air around me. His voice is deep and hypnotizing. I fight to keep from closing my eyes and falling under his spell. Slowly, I am melting under his heated gaze. I am so nervous. But, for some strange reason, I feel safe with him.

Crazy, right?

"H-h-he tried to *rape* me," I repeat, wiping my tears with the handful of napkins he'd grabbed from inside the party before walking me out to his Range Rover.

"What dis niqqa look like, yo?"

I tell him. He frowns. "Hol'up. What you say his name was?"

"S-s-shaheed."

He scowls as he repeats his name. "*Shaheed?* Oh word? Dat's how he doin' it. A'ight. He must really wanna start his summer off wit' a black eye 'n' broken nose." I watch him slide his hand into his front pocket and pull out his cell. "Yo, where you at, son? You here? Oh, a'ight. Cool-cool. Word. Yeah, I'm out front hollerin' at my peoples..."

His peoples? He's talking like he's known me for a long time.

I stare at him through tear-filled eyes, swiping tears as they fall. I feel so humiliated. Maybe if I had had a few drinks, like before, and was too inebriated to know what was going on around me, it wouldn't feel so bad.

Malik opens the driver's side door, then reaches inside and pulls out some more napkins, handing them to me. He takes the balled up ones I've used to blow my nose and wipe my eyes from me. I thank him with a faint smile.

"...Nah, nah...I just got here. Man, eff dem dumb hoes, yo. I ain't checkin' for none'a dat right now. I need you to get at dat cat Shaheed for me. He somewhere up in there. He tried to do some foul ish to my peoples 'n' I ain't feelin' dat, feel me? Yeah, yeah. Get at him. Say wat? Break his shit, yo. That's wat."

I blink.

Ohmygod! He's going to have his boys do something to him.

Maybe I shouldn't have told him.

Nooo, maybe he shouldn't have tried to force himself on me.

He gets what he gets.

I swallow, glance over at a black Acura that is parallel parking across the street. The girl behind the wheel is struggling to get the car into the tight space. Someone hops out of the front passenger side and starts trying to direct her.

"Ohmygod, Meeka, whoever gave you ya license needs to be drop-kicked in the throat."

"Eat me," the driver snaps back. "All I asked is for you to make sure I don't hit that stupid car in back of me. Ain't nobody ask you for no extras."

"Well, if you knew how to park I wouldn't haveta be out here tryna play traffic cop. I'd already be inside the party gettin' my drop 'n' pop on."

I eye her as she does a booty shake right in the middle of the street. Her hips shake wildly as the rear passenger window rolls down and another girl sticks her head out the window cheering her on. "Don't stop! Get it! Get it! Do dat ole nasty ish, Kee-Kee. Air dat ole stank coochie out."

The girl and the driver burst into laughter, causing her to back into the parked car behind her. The future stripper gives her friends the finger. Tells them to kiss her butt. Well, her a-double-s.

I blow my nose, feeling less shaken. I pull out my cell and check my messages. I have two missed calls from Hope. And a text message from Blaze saying: WATZ GUD? HAD U ON DA BRAIN JUS WANTED TO C HOW U DOIN. HIT ME BACK

"Party or no party," I hear Malik say into his phone, bringing my attention back to him. "He tried to violate my peoples, yo. Handle him. And if da mofo leaps, you already know wat it is." The call ends and he slides his phone back down into his pocket.

"It's handled, yo."

I blink, once, twice. "It's *handled*...how?"

He furrows his brow. "Don't worry 'bout dat. All you need'a know is, dat clown ain't gonna ever step outa pocket wit' you again. Word is bond, yo."

"What are you going to do to him?"

His jaw clenches. "I already tol' you don't worry 'bout dat, yo. You let me deal wit' dat, a'ight?" I nod. "Cool. Now who you out here wit', anyway? I know you ain't out here solo."

I shake my head. Tell him I came with Sasha. "But somehow she went missing with some guy," I add, purposefully leaving out the fact that I'd seen her upstairs having an orgy.

"Sasha?" He frowns, shaking his head. "See. Dat's dat bullshit, for real for real. How y'all get here?"

"She drove," I say, glancing over at the girls getting out of the Acura. They're all wearing short hairdos and extra-short skirts with extra-high heels that they can barely walk in.

All that just to get noticed. Mmmph. I shake my head, glancing down at my own attire. *Like I have room to talk.*

"She ain't even hit me up to let me know you was gonna be here." I knit my brows together. "Oh, you ain't know I was checkin' for you? Sasha ain't tell you?"

I shake my head. "No. Why would she need to do that? I don't even know you."

"Not yet you don't. But you 'bout to real soon." I give him a confused look. "Yo, c'mon, ma. Don't front. You really ain't know?"

I shake my head. "No, not really."

"Well, I am." He tells me how he's had his eye on me since he first spotted me at work. That he asked Sasha who

I was, but she acted like she didn't want him to know at first. But he kept pressing her.

"Oh," I say.

"Yeah. But it's all good. I got at you now. So relax, baby. In a minute, I'ma 'bout to be da best thing that's ever happened to you."

I frown.

He starts laughing. "Relax, yo. I'm only effen wit' you. But I'm 'bout you gettin' to know me. How you feel 'bout dat?"

I shrug. Honestly, I don't know what to feel. My brain is still fogged from what almost happened earlier, and from what I witnessed upstairs. But I'll admit I'm relieved that I ran into him when I did. I don't know what I would have done, being way out here.

"Well, check it. We ain't gonna talk 'bout none'a dat right now. I gotta make sure you get home be—"

"Yo, wat's poppin', Money?" a light-skinned guy with slanted eyes and cornrows says, walking over and giving Malik a pound. He glances over at me and nods. "What's good, ma?"

"Nothing," I say, trying not to stare at him. He's really, really tall. Like at least six four, six five. And he's really, really cute.

"Ain't nuthin', yo," Malik says to him. "Just out here kickin' it wit' my peoples."

"Oh, a'ight, a'ight." He glances back over at me. "I see you, son. She mad sexy, fam."

I catch Malik, grinning. "True indeed, yo. But, dig. I'ma holla at you in a bit, a'ight?"

"Yo, true, true. Fo' sho'. I'ma 'bout to go inside 'n' see wat it lookin' like." They give each other one of those brotherly hugs with the handshake thingy they all do. I think they call it *dap*, or something like that.

Malik stands in front of me, leaning up against the door of his truck. He keeps staring at me; his eyes roaming all over me. And I am feeling hot under his gaze. I shift my weight from one heeled foot to the other.

Nervously, I tuck a strand of hair behind my ear. Then fidget with the hem of my skirt. All I can think about is getting home and taking a hot shower to scrub Shaheed's grimy hands off of me.

"Yo, you got some pretty legs," Malik says, finally slicing through the awkward silence between us. "I see why you got these fools out here buggin'."

"It's not intentional," I say defensively. The way he says that makes me feel like I need to defend the way I'm dressed. And I shouldn't have to.

"Nah, I ain't sayin' it is. You old enough to dress however you wanna. All I'm sayin' is, li'l boys can't always handle a sexy woman showin' 'em a lotta skin; especially some dumb mofo wit' a few drinks or dat other ish in his system."

Wow, he thinks I'm sexy!

"I'm not grown," I say. "I'm only sixteen."

"Is dat right?" he smirks, amusement dancing in his eyes. "Sixteen, huh? Well, check it. You might be *only* sixteen. But you got a body like a grown woman. See. If you had a man in ya life you wouldn't have to worry about no punk busta tryna violate you."

I tilt my head. "And who says I don't have a boyfriend?"

"See. Who said anything 'bout a *boy*friend. I said a *man*. Big difference. Li'l girls have *boy*friends. Baby, you need a real man to keep you safe, ya heard? Like I said, these li'l boyz ain't ready for you, ma."

"*Heyyy,* Maaaaalik," a voice coos in back of me. I glance over my shoulder and see a mocha-brown girl wearing a platinum blonde weave—or maybe it's a wig, I don't know—and a white fishnet bodysuit with a white thong.

Ohmygod! She has on pasties over her nipples. How gross!

"Yo, what's good, Melody?" Malik says, looking over my head to speak to her.

"Nothin' much, boo. Please tell me it's not busted up in there." Fishnet is now standing a few inches away from us. I quickly take in her outfit, glancing down at her feet. She has on a pair of seven-inch platform heels. I say hello and she doesn't bother to speak back or even look my way.

How rude?

"I don't know. I've been out here chillin'."

"Oh, all right. Well, let me get up in here to see what— or who—I can turn out tonight."

Malik laughs. "Go do you, baby. I already know how you do it."

As soon as Fishnet walks off, here come two more girls, walking over to Malik. They are both dark chocolate with extremely long, glittery lash extensions. One is wearing a short white dress with a scoop neck and cut-out-back with black heels. The other is wearing the same exact outfit; except her dress is black and she's wearing white heels. Both of their dresses barely cover their butts.

"Heyyy, Malik," they both say in unison.

He grins. "Yo, wat it do?"

"You wat it do, boo," White Dress says, flashing her bright white smile.

"Oh, word? Dat's wasssup."

"Boy, when you gonna call me?" Black Dress asks, batting her eyes at him.

They both glance over at me, looking me up and down. Then bring their attention back to Malik like I'm invisible.

"Oh, my bad. Kia 'n' Mia, dis my peoples, Kennedy. Kennedy dis Kia 'n' Mia."

I open my mouth to ask them if they are twins, even though they don't look alike, but I am immediately stunned into silence when people from the party come running out of the front door. Girls are screaming and scattering around frantically as someone gets thrown out the door and onto the sidewalk. Then pounced on by five guys, punching and stomping him.

I blink.

It takes a few seconds for it to register in my brain, for me to realize who it is being beaten almost to death.

My eyes pop open in horror.

It's that boy Shaheed.

19

A few days later, I'm at Sasha's house. We're locked up in her bedroom with the window wide open. It's sweltering in her room, like a sauna. It's bad enough that it's humid outside. But it's torturous to be inside sweating. I try not to think about it. But I can't help wondering how anyone can live like this, without central air. But Sasha doesn't seem fazed by the heat steaming up her room. There are two oscillating fans over in either corner of the room.

"Ooh, I'm so mad I missed dat party last weekend," Sasha's friend Shay-Shay says as she splits open a cigar with her long fingernails. I eye her as she lets the tobacco fall out into the trash can. "Dat ish wit' Sha wouldn't even had gone down like dat, either." She shoots me a dirty look. I look away from her. "Mmph. Silly tricks stay frontin' on da *D*. Then wanna cry *rape.*"

I blink.

"Girl, stop," Sasha says, shaking her head. "You wasn't even there so don't go poppin' off 'cause you don't know what happened up in dat room. Ain't dat right, girl?" She looks over at me. "Tell her to eat da inside of ya crack."

"I'd really rather not talk about it," I say, shifting in my seat. "I mean. I have no reason to lie on anyone."

Shay-Shay grunts, pulling out a plastic bag stuffed with dark green leaves and evenly sprinkling some out onto the gutted cigar skin.

"Girl, no judgment over here," Sasha says. "I know how nuccas do when they get all liquored up. Trust. Nuccas don't know howta take no for an answer."

"Whatever, Sasha. You know Sha ain't hardly try'n rape her. She prolly wanted it, then got mad when he turned her down."

I frown. "I'm not a tease."

She glares at me. "Oh, don't get it effed up. You better have a seat 'fore I take it to ya face." She licks and rolls the cigar, then pulls out a lighter and runs the flame along the sides of the cigar. "You had no bidness goin' up to dat room if you ain't wanna get that thang stretched out."

"*Bish*," Sasha snaps. "She should be able to go wherever she wants. He ain't have no business tryna force her. You know dat nucca is a panty-hound so stop. You just mad 'cause da mofo ain't tryna break you off none'a dat lollipop." She cracks up laughing. "Oh, Miss Goody Two-shoes had all dem ninjas tryna get up in dem drawz. Seems like I can't take *Peaches* nowhere."

She cracks up laughing.

"That's so not true," I say.

Shay-Shay frowns as she lights her blunt, then inhales

deeply. *"Peaches?"* She blows a big curl of white smoke from her lips. She takes three more pulls then passes it to Sasha.

"Inside joke, girl," Sasha says, taking the blunt from her. She takes a pull then starts telling her how I carried on the first time she took me to a party. "Girl, you shoulda seen Miss Strip Tease, flashin' her boobs 'n' gettin' all freaky wit' it."

I cringe at the memory of being intoxicated and not remembering half of what I supposedly did. The Shay-Shay girl glares at me as Sasha reaches over and tries to pass me the blunt.

I shake my head. "No. That's okay. I'm good."

Shay-Shay rolls her eyes. "Mmph. And da *bish* thinks she's too good to smoke wit' us. Why she even here?"

" 'Cause I invited her," Sasha snaps. "So you need'a chill da *fuqq* out."

Shay waves her off. "Trick, pass me da blunt 'n' stop hoggin' it like you tryna eat it."

"Whatever." She takes another pull, then hands it back over to Shay-Shay. She blows smoke up at the ceiling. "But she right, though, girly. You need'a come up off'a all dat goody two-shoes ish 'n' kick back wit' us. It ain't like we askin' you to do coke or pop an E-pill. All it is is weed. Dat ain't gonna kill you."

"Yeah, I know. I never said it would."

"Then, girl, wat you scared of?"

I start coughing from the thick cloud of smoke that's blowing my way. The room is getting thick with it, making it feel ten times hotter than it already is in here.

Shay-Shay sucks her teeth. "Girl, bye. Don't beg her to smoke wit' us. I ain't really checkin' for her liked dat anyway."

Sasha rolls her eyes. "Here, girl." She takes two long pulls from the blunt, then hands it to me. "I know you a newbie so I'ma break you in real easy breezy. Here."

Reluctantly, I take the blunt from her, looking at it with both excitement and nervousness. I'd wanted to smoke with Hazel Eyes but he wouldn't. And now here is my opportunity to see what it's like.

I put it to my lips.

"All you gotta do is pull on it until you feel a light burn, then hold da smoke in ya chest for like a few seconds, then blow it out."

I do as she instructs and immediately my throat tightens and I start coughing and choking as if I'm about to have an asthma attack. My eyes start watering and my chest feels like it's on fire. Shay-Shay and Sasha look at each other and burst out laughing. And now I am laughing with them, coughing and wiping tears from my eyes.

I'm floating.

I roll my head back and look up at the ceiling as we pass the blunt back and forth. I see a bunch of cracks in the paint and start to wonder if those cracks have always been there or if I was just seeing things from smoking the blunt.

We smoke the blunt down until I can barely grip it with my fingers. Shay-Shay calls it a roach, then pulls out some kind of clipper thing and keeps on smoking it down to almost nothing.

Wow, she's real greedy.

I peel my eyes from the cracks in the ceiling and glance over at Shay-Shay, who's rolling another blunt.

She puts it up to her lips and lights it up.

Dang, she has some big, fluffy lips.

I start giggling.

By the time we finish the second blunt. I can't stop looking at Shay-Shay's lips. They look like they've gotten bigger than they already were.

She sucks her teeth. "What you doin' all dat stupid laughin' for? What's so effen funny?"

"Bwaaahahahaaahaha. I can't stop laughing at your lips," I say without any thought.

Sasha starts laughing. "Ooh, she callin' you Horselips, boo. Girl, you dead wrong for dat."

"Hahahaha. I know, right. Her lips so big they look like they'll suck a boy's whole face off if he tries to kiss her."

I'm laughing so hard that I don't notice that Shay-Shay isn't laughing. I don't notice the evil look she gives me, either. In fact, I don't even realize that Sasha is no longer laughing with me because I am so caught up in laughter.

Out of nowhere, Shay-Shay lunges at me, pulling out a knife and flipping it open. She grabs me by my shirt collar, slamming me back onto the bed and catching me completely off guard. "Bish, I will slice ya effen throat! No. Then again, I'll slash up ya face 'n' cut off ya gawtdamn lips, don't come for me unless I call you!"

My heart drops.

"I-I-I was only playing."

"We ain't cool like dat! I will bust you in yo' face!" She starts digging her nails into my neck, trying to choke me with one hand. "Laugh now!"

I start scratching and clawing at her hand trying to get her off of me.

Sasha hops up from the floor. "*Sheeeit*! See you heifers effen wit' my high. C'mon Shay, you know dis girl can't even handle you. So let her go."

"No! She wanna laugh. But I don't see her laughin' now. Is you? Huh, *bish!*" She swings a fist upside my head. And I hear myself scream in my head. "I should stab ya!" She mushes me, then lets go and starts pacing the floor like a wild woman.

I gasp and gulp in air, trying to catch my breath.

"Ohmygod!" I rub my neck and shake my head. "I can't believe you tried to kill me!"

"Believe it! You don't know me! I will bring it ya head! You lucky I don't bust ya mouff open right now. I know I got big lips, I don't need you tryna make fun of 'em."

I try to apologize but she isn't interested.

She clenches her teeth, pounding her fist into the palm of her hand. "You ain't 'bout dis life, so you need to stop tryna be 'n' get back to da 'burbs where you belong."

The wild look in her eyes tells me she's two steps from crazy. She charges at me and punches me in my jaw, causing my head to snap back. Blood gushes from my mouth.

I scream, glancing over at Sasha.

She shrugs. "Next time watch what you say."

20

Three days later, I am out spending the day with Malik. I was surprised when he called and said he wanted to take me shopping. No guy has ever offered to take me out to buy me whatever I want. But Malik did. Now, after four hours of mall and outlet hopping, Malik suggests we go grab a quick bite to eat. He asks what I have a taste for. I tell him whatever he wants is fine with me. Truth is, I don't really have much of an appetite. For some reason, I'm starting to feel...I don't know. Like, um, maybe I really shouldn't have let him spend so much money on me.

A part of me is also feeling bad about lying to my mom again. But what other choice did I have? I wanted to see him. And I know if I'd told her the truth she would have forbidden it.

I shrug off the guilt that is slowly stirring in the pit of my stomach as I settle into the plush leather seat. I lean my head back on the headrest and stare out the window, wondering how in the heck I am going to sneak all of these shopping bags into my house without my mother asking me a million questions.

"Yo, you a'ight over there?" Malik asks, looking over at me.

I nod, soaking in all of his fineness. My milk-chocolate dreamboat. Malik. Six feet tall, rippled abs, chiseled biceps, and sweet, juicy lips. He is so *fine*. He melts me into a puddle of sweet nothings every time he looks into my soul with his beautiful, deep, piercing, dark brown eyes with the thick lashes.

He's perfect.

The way Malik gazes into my eyes is intoxicating. Intense. It's as if he wants to see everything there is to see in me. It makes me feel special. I've never had any boy look at me the way he does. And I think that's one of the reasons why I wanted to see him today. *Had* to see him.

I can almost see myself becoming addicted to Malik in the way that I am to Reese's Peanut Butter Cups. I know that I'm allergic to chocolate, yet still indulge myself. It's starting to feel the same way with Malik. I know too much of him might not be good for me, but for some reason I can't seem to get enough of him. And that kinda frightens and excites me at the same time.

"Yo, real spit, babe. You 'bout to have me catch a charge; for real for real. I'ma kidnap ya for the weekend, then have my way wit' you; you know that right?" A slow grin creeps over his lips.

I shift in my seat, feeling heat spread through my body. I don't know what to say to that. I push out a chuckle. "I wish. My parents would ground me indefinitely if they ever found out I was off somewhere spending the weekend with some guy, if they didn't kill me first."

"Nah, you sixteen. You grown, baby." He reaches over

and lightly squeezes my knee, then glides his hand up my leg. "You can do whatever you want, babe. And, legally, there's nothing they can do to stop you. Besides, who said they'd have to know; nah'mean?"

I smile at him, not knowing what else to say. I mean, I know what the age of consent is: sixteen. But does that mean that legally there isn't anything my parents could do if I went and spent the weekend with him?

Ohmygod, why am I even thinking about any of this? He's only kidding. Relax.

Fifteen minutes later, Malik parks his SUV, then gets out and walks around to my side and opens the door, helping me out. "You sexy, babe."

I smile, feeling like the luckiest girl alive. Malik is everything I have ever wished for in a guy. He's so sweet. No, he's a whole lot more than just sweet. He's . . . perfect!

I've had to pinch myself at least four times to make sure it's real. Because to be honest, it all feels too good to be true.

I know nineteen isn't really that old. But for me it is. He's the oldest guy I've ever spent any time with. Compared to the other guys I've dated or liked, Malik isn't a boy. He's a grown man.

And he seems *waaaay* too old for me. But I know age is nothing but a number. It's how someone treats you and makes you feel that really matters, right?

I breathe in his cologne as he takes me by the hand and leads me toward the entrance of Applebee's, where we are seated within minutes. I'm glad there wasn't a long wait, like usual on a Saturday night.

We sit at a table near the bar. "You know what you wanna get?" he asks, picking up his menu and flipping through it.

I want to tell him that I've never eaten here before. But decide it isn't important. Being with him is.

I flip through my menu as well, trying to decide. "No, not yet," I say, glancing up at him as he pulls out his Samsung and starts texting.

A few minutes later our waiter comes to the table to take our orders. I order the three-cheese chicken penne. He gets an appetizer sampler, and the honey pepper chicken and shrimp. We both order pomegranate lemonades.

Malik waits for the waiter to walk off, then rests his arms on the table, leaning in. Just as he opens his mouth to speak, he's interrupted by this brown-skinned girl wearing a short blonde pixie hairstyle with streaks of orange in her bangs and bright yellow, purple, and gold highlights in each spike of her hair.

She looks like she stuck her head into a bowl of melted Skittles.

"Oh, no, this mofo ain't sittin' up here with some other chick. *Malik?!*"

He looks up and over in the direction of the ruckus. Skittles stomps over toward our table with three other girls in tow, all looking like they'd slice, shoot, and stomp, then ask questions later. Her multicolored fingernails are at least four inches long. Both of her wrists are wrapped in gold bangles. And she has a bunch of rings on almost every finger.

"So dis why you ain't been pickin' up ya phone all day. You was s'posed to come through dis mornin' 'n' instead you out trickin' up my baby's milk 'n' Pampers on dis li'l uppity, yellow thot."

I blink.

I don't know why, but suddenly this trashy girl makes me think of old rerun shows of *Martin*. Now I know who she reminds me of. The character Sheneneh. And the three girls with her all look just as colorful and crazy as she does. If I wasn't so scared of what's about to unfold in here, I'd laugh.

She snarls at me. "Trick, what you doin' out wit' *my* man, coo-cooin' all up in his face like you in love, huh?"

I blink.

Skittles looks mean and good dang crazy.

"Yo, go 'head with that dumb shit, Henney."

Henney? Ohmygod, what kind of name is that?

She slams a hand on her narrow hip. She has a real small waist, itty-bitty breasts that look like they could easily be mistaken for plums, and a gigantic booty that looks like it's been attached to the wrong body. I try not to gawk at her.

"Don't 'Henney' me, you sneaky black sonofabitch! I been callin' ya all day, nucca. Why ain't you been through to see about ya son, huh?"

"Yo go 'head wit' dat. You already know what it is. How many times we gonna keep goin' through dis?"

I swallow. *Ohmygod! I can't believe Malik has a baby with this crazy girl.*

"What you lookin' at, trick?"

"N-n-othing," I stutter, shifting my eyes around the restaurant. Several tables around us have already started taking in the spectacle unfolding. And all I keep thinking is, *please don't let these ghetto girls jump me in here*.

Truth is, aside from the fights I've had with my three older brothers, I'd never had a *real* fight in my entire life with a girl, or with anyone, for that matter until that girl Shay-Shay attacked me. Not even an argument. Well, not one where there are curse words and yelling and threatening going back and forth.

I know I said that I'm fascinated with the fast, gritty streets of the hood. But that doesn't mean I want to experience a firsthand fight with any of these girls, eying me real nasty-like. They all look like they know how to spit razors out and slice a face without blinking an eye.

I shift in my seat.

"Yo, what you want, Hennessey? Don't you see I'm tryna eat? Why you gotta be on effen ten all da effen time, huh?"

"I ain't on ten, yet, ninja. But I'ma 'bout to be real quick if you don't tell me what you doin' out here wit' her."

My eyes pop open. I swallow. "My name's Kennedy," I say meekly.

She glances over at her three friends, who are all smirking. "Oh, y'all hear dat. Her name's *Kennnnedy*," she says, mockingly. Her friends laugh. "Soundin' all tighty-whitey. Trick, please. Take dat Cracker Jack ish back to da 'burbs where you belong. I'll call you what I wanna call you. And *what?*"

I shift back in my seat, cutting my eye over at Malik.

"I don't know what you lookin' over dere at him for, like he gonna save you or sumthin'. What, you need daddy to save you? I ain't over here for you anyway, li'l girl. So don't go pissin' ya panties up. But trust. If I wanted to bring it to ya face, there wouldn't be all dis talkin' goin' on."

Her friends laugh.

Malik's jaw tightens. "Yo, Hennessey, for real. You 'bout to have me take it there. Word is bond, yo. You better step, a'ight?"

"Nucca, I ain't better do ish. I know you don't even wanna see me turn up up in here so don't even try'n play me."

Malik grits his teeth. "Before I split ya shit, yo, I'm warnin' you."

She ignores him, shooting a dirty look over at me. Her glare is hot enough to melt steel. "How long you been neck-bobbin' him, huh, li'l girl? What, you deaf? You hear me talkin' to you."

"Yo, what da—" Malik hops up from the table and snaps on her, goes from nice to nasty in a flash. And it startles me for a second. I'm not accustomed to this kind of stuff; especially not out in public. I see a thick vein pump in his forehead as snatches her by the arm and starts roughing her up. "Didn't I tell you to take ya to stop, huh? But you wanna keep poppin' ya jaws, right?"

She pushes him off of her. "I'm not tryna hear you. You think you can come through 'n' hit dis good stuff whenever you effen want, then turn around 'n' play me. I don't think so. I'm not da one." She lunges toward the table, causing me to jump. "*Beeyotch,* he ain't eva gonna be yours so you might as well cash out now before you find yaself stomped out. That ninja ain' eva lettin' go of dis wet-wet ova here, boo. Trust. You just a sidepiece."

Malik yanks her by the arm again. Tells her to shut her mouth. The whole scene starts to turn ugly as she fights him off of her, calling him all types of dirty, cruel names. She's a real gutter mouth.

Next thing I know, her three friends all jump on Malik, snatching plates off nearby tables and smashing them upside his head. He lets Skittles go and tries to manhandle her friends. I watch in horror as Malik tosses them around the restaurant and they jump on his back until they've finally gotten him down on the floor, stomping and kicking and punching him.

I am so scared I've peed on myself.

"And since you wanna choose dat stuck-up slut over all'a dis hood goodness, I got sumthin' for you if I ever catch her alone! You watch, punk!"

21

"Where have you been, young lady?" my mom wants to know, swinging open my bedroom door and stepping into my room. I can tell she's pissed by the sternness in her voice.

"I was out with...out with Sasha," I blurt out.

"Sasha?" She raises her brow. "Oh really? And where were you with this *Sasha*?"

"Hanging out at her house."

She blinks. "And where does this Sasha live, again?"

I never told you! Besides, it's none of your business!

"Across town," I offer, moving around my room, trying to avoid her roving eyes. She's studying my every move. And it's making me uncomfortable. Lying isn't my greatest asset. But it's something I'm slowly becoming better at. Concealing the truth from her is a whole lot easier than telling her that I was with Malik; that he had to manhandle an ex-girlfriend and I witnessed him getting jumped in a restaurant by her and her ghetto squad. Telling her this will only send her through the roof. Mom leans up against my dresser, her arms folded and head tilted.

"Across town *where*? And were her parents home?"

I suck my teeth. "Mom, she's eighteen. She doesn't need supervision. And, yes, her mother was there." I purposefully don't mention where she lives, or that her mom was passed out on the sofa drunk with a half bottle of Jack Daniels between her legs.

She grunts. "Don't you suck your teeth at me. It's past your curfew. You do know that, right?"

"I'm only a few minutes late. What's the big deal? You've never had any problem before."

"Well, before you would call to let me know where you were and what time to expect you. Anything can happen out there."

I huff. "Dang, mom. I'm not a little girl. Fall back. I'm only thirty minutes late. Okay, I get it. I didn't call. It won't happen again, okay? Geesh. Relax. It's not..."

"*Relax? Fall back?*" she shrieks, glaring at me as if I've gone completely insane. Maybe I have. I have never spoken to her in this manner before. Never.

"Have you lost your mind, Kennedy, huh? Have you? You don't tell *me* to relax. Since when do you think it's okay to speak to me like that, huh? Since when did you start talking like that? I tell you when. When you started associating with that Sasha girl. I don't like her. She's a little too fast to my liking. And she's obviously becoming a bad influence on you if you think you can disrespect me in my own home and tell me to *fall back* and *relax*."

"I wasn't saying it to be disrespectful. It's a figure of speech."

She plants a hand up on her hip. "Figure of speech or

not, it's disrespectful. I am your mother, not one of your new little homegirls you've taken up with. I don't want you hanging with that Sasha girl anymore. You understand me?"

"Ohmygod! That's so unfair! Why? What has she done to you?"

"She's a bad influence."

"You don't even know her. She's *not* a bad influence on me," I protest, sounding like a whiny brat.

"I don't need to know her to know that she's trouble."

"It's all my fault. I should have called you, but I got caught up and lost track of time. I apologize. You don't have to act like it's the end of the world."

"It's not the end of the world, Kennedy. But it will be the end of your outings if you can't get in this house on time. Do I make myself clear?"

I silently roll my eyes up in my head. "Yeah."

"*Yeah?* Girl, you had better regroup and remember whom you are speaking to. Am I clear?"

"Yes."

"Yes? Girl, I'm warning you. You had better put a handle on it before you find yourself grounded for the next two weeks."

I bite into my lip to keep from screaming.

I pull in a deep breath. Blow it out slowly. "Yes, Mom."

"Good. You're grounded for the rest of the weekend."

"But—"

"'But' nothing. I don't want to hear another word about it. Grounded."

I open my mouth to speak, but she puts a hand up and shuts me down. "I said, not another word."

I quickly shut my mouth.

"Now go shower and get yourself ready for bed. You

smell like marijuana smoke. And you better not even think about smoking that mess."

"I'm not."

She eyes me real hard, then spins on her heel and walks out, leaving me standing here in the middle of my room, feeling like my whole world is about to end being on punishment for the next two days.

"She spazzed out on you like dat?" Sasha says, shaking her head. We're sitting in the food court on our thirty-minute break and I just finished filling her in on the drama that happened last night.

"Yeah, she was pretty pissed."

"Girl, couldn't be me. My momz tried dat punishment ish on me 'n' I tol' her to kiss my juicy..." She leans over on one butt cheek then reaches in back of her and smacks it. "And I tol' her to kiss it real good. Ain't nobody got time for dat."

"Ohmygod! What'd she do after that?"

"Girl, please. What you think she did? Not a thang. The only thing she could do was sit there 'n' deal wit' it. I was sixteen 'n' grown. She couldn't do a thang but get wit' da program 'n' let me do me."

"Well, my parents, especially my mom, would never just let me *do* me."

She grunts. "Mmmph. I don't know why not. Aren't you almost seventeen?"

"Yeah."

"Well, then you grown, girl. You better get ya life, boo. Its summertime 'n' ain't nobody tryna be cooped up in some box all weekend."

I nod, taking in what she says. "True. But—"

"'But' nothin', girl. You need to be ready to hit dis party wit' me tomorrow night 'n' stop frontin'. It's gonna be fire. Trust."

My heart skips at the thought of going out, being swept up in the music and all the cuties that I know are going to be there. Then reality sets in. And my excitement deflates. "Ooh, I wish I could go. There's no way I'll be able to get out without my mom catching me, then grounding me for the rest of the summer."

"Umm, *hellllloooo*." She snaps her fingers in my face. "Earth to Kennedy. Who says she has to know? Sneak out."

Sneak out? Ohmygod! She can't be serious. My mom would kill me. Then again, it's not like I haven't done it before.

I shake my head. "Well…maybe. I just don't want to get caught."

She gives me a pitiful look. "Poor thing." She plucks a French fry from her plate, dips it into her little cup of ketchup then takes a bite. "Well, good luck with that. *Annny*way, movin' on. What's up wit' you 'n' my boy Malik? You feelin' him or what?"

I shrug. "He's nice. I guess."

She gives me an incredulous look. "He's *nice?* You *guess*? Girl, bye. Miss me wit' dat. Didn't y'all go out?"

I nod. "Yeah. We did. And then his baby mother showed up and started making a scene?"

She makes a face. "Which baby muhver?" I tell her. She rolls her eyes. "Henney ain't nothin' but a buncha mouth. It prolly ain't his baby anyway."

"Really?"

"Girl, please. She gave it up to da whole block one time. She nasty like dat."

I blink. *She has a whole lot of nerve calling someone nasty when I caught her naked with a room full of half-naked guys, letting them have their way with her.*

I keep my thought to myself.

"But back to Malik," she says, plucking another fry from her plate, then stuffing it into her mouth. "What you mean you guess?" She chews, then swallows. "Girl, bye. There's nothin' to guess. Dat nucca's mad fly. His swag's sick 'n' he stays on one. Girl, please. He's *e'ery*thing."

I've heard the phrase "on one" used before many times in rap lyrics and from Sasha, but I still don't quite understand what it means. Embarrassed, I ask Sasha to explain it to me.

She gives me a strange look, shaking her head. "Girl, you really don't know much of nothin', do you?" she laughs. "See. Dat's wat happens when you ain't from da hood. You stay lost. Anyway, let me bring you into da light. It means dat you either high or drunk. But in Malik's case it means he does him 'n' he don't give a eff what mofos out in da streets gotta say or think about it."

"Oh," I say, nodding.

She takes a sip of her Mountain Dew. "Now out in Cali if you hear 'em say dat den it means they high off dat crystal meth. Well, dat's wat my girl Lisa says since all'a her fam from out dat way. Meth head junkies."

She shakes her head.

"Isn't that what you use sometimes?" I ask, immediately regretting it ever falling from my lips.

She shoots me a nasty look. *Oh God!* "What, *meth?*" I slowly nod, bracing myself for what's to come. "*Bish*, don't you *ever* dis me. I ain't never used no effen meth.

Maybe a li'l molly here 'n' dere, but dat's it. And I only use dat when I really wanna let my hair down 'n' just do me."

"Oh," I say, apologetically. "I didn't know. I thought they were the same thing."

"Trick, do your homework, first, before you go tryna label someone. No, dey ain't da same thang. You uppity hoes stay tryna look down at chicks from the hood when you bishes do more whorin' 'n' druggin' than any of us."

"Sasha," I say calmly. "Please don't call me names. It's disrespectful."

She slams a hand up on her hip, zigzagging her neck from one side to the other. "Tramp, bye. Miss me wit' dat. I'll call you what I want, especially when you come out ya face tryna dis me. You try'n call me out, then I'ma call you out, too. Trust. I don't know what kinda games you tryna play. But I ain't da one, boo-boo. So don't do me."

I blink.

"Look, Sasha. I'm not exactly sure what I said to set you off. But I wasn't trying to *do* you. Or label you. I only asked a simple question."

"Girl, bye. It was disrespectful."

Honestly, I am not seeing what was so disrespectful about what I asked her. But for some reason, the fact that I've asked seems to be a problem for her. So in hopes to restore peace between us I say, "I apologize. Really. I didn't think asking a question would upset you."

"Well, it sounded like judgment to me."

"Ohmygod! *Judgment?* Sasha, that's the last thing I do to anyone. I swear. I accept people for who they are and for what they do, even if it's not what I'm into. I really didn't know it wasn't the same thing."

"Well now you do."

"I apologize. I didn't mean to offend you."

She clucks her tongue. "Well, it sounded dat way to me, like you better than me. Dat's da problem wit' you uppity suburban *bishes,* you all think you better than us hood *bishes*, but you stay tryna come to da hood to eff our men."

I give her an incredulous look. "That's so not true."

"Girl, bye. Miss me wit' dat."

She gets up and snatches her tray from off the table, storming off.

I am left sitting at the table, looking around like, "What just happened here?" while feeling completely flabbergasted.

22

Three days later, I'm at Jordan's house with Hope. We've just gotten back from the salon getting manicures and pedicures, along with cucumber and mint facials. And now we're up in her bedroom listening to Sevyn Streeter's album *Call Me Crazy, But...*

Yo I wanna c u

It's a text from Malik. We've spoken a few times since that incident at the restaurant. And although seeing those crazy girls jump him made me real nervous, I still like him. Maybe I'm crazy. I don't know. All I know is, there's something about Malik I really, really like.

I smile. It's been a few days since I've seen him. But now that I am off punishment, I am so looking forward to spending time with him.

I wanna c u 2

"Hey, you want to go to the mall today?" Jordan asked.

"Which one?" Hope wants to know, looking up from her iPhone over at Jordan.

"Garden State."

Hope shakes her head. "Oh, no thank you. I'm not up for that drive to Paramus today."

"What? Are you serious? It's less than thirty minutes. So what do you mean you're not up for driving to Paramus? You're acting like it's an hour drive or something."

Hope sighs. "I have to go to some Jack and Jill thing with my mother at three. Then I have ballet at five. Raincheck?"

"Oh," Jordan says, sounding disappointed. "What about you, Kennedy? You game?"

"I can't," I say, looking up from my phone. "I have to work."

Jordan huffs. "Ohmygod! This is ridiculous. All you do is work."

U gotta work?

No, I text back.

"Huh?" I look up from my phone. "Are you talking to me?"

She sucks her teeth. "Yessss. I'm talking to you. Who are you texting and grinning over, anyway?"

"A friend," I say casually.

"Uh-huh. And does this friend have a name?" Hope inquires.

I'm not ready to share with them his name just yet. "Yup. None-ya."

"Let me guess," Jordan retorts, twisting her lips up. "He's one of them thug boys you're so fascinated with."

I roll my eyes. "Whatever."

Ima kidnap u, yo.

I grin.

Jordan sighs. "That's so rude."

I roll my eyes. "Girl, bye. Don't hate. Like you don't do

it too. Let it be Howard. Mmph. You stay with your face stuck to your screen." Malik sends another text, saying he'll be free around eight.

"I *saaaaid,* all you do is work. It's like you'd rather spend time at that ratchet job than spend time with your best friends."

I text him back, OK 😊

I set my phone beside me on the bed. "That is so not true, Jordan." I look over at Hope. "Hope, do you feel that way, too?"

She puts her hands up. "Don't put me in this. My name is Switzerland. And I'm staying neutral."

My cell chimes, alerting me I have a new text message. I reach for it, glancing at the screen. It's another text from Malik. IMA SCOOP U UP @ 9. U GONNA B READY 4 ME?

Yes.

"Really, Kennedy?" Jordan says, frowning. "You're going to keep texting like that and not tell us who you're texting? Since when you start keeping secrets?"

"I'm not keeping any secrets," I lie. "I was texting my manager to let her know I was sick. So we can hang out at the mall."

"Goody," she says, clapping. Hope gets up from the bed, shouldering her oversized D&G bag. "Well, kiddies. I gotta go. My mom's outside already."

She air-kisses me, then Jordan, then is out the door.

"Well," Jordan says, looking over at me. "It's just you and me." She glances at my phone in my hand. "Oh, and your cell."

"Girl, stop. Let's go to Newport Mall."

Her eyes pop out of her head. "*Whaaat?* Why are you

trying to drag me to that hood mall? You know I'm allergic to those type of malls. There's no Gucci! No Prada! No Bloomingdale's! No Neiman Marcus!"

"Okay, okay...I get it. You're a label junkie."

She sucks her teeth. "And you're a hood junkie."

"C'mon. It'll be fun."

"Yeah, okay," she says relunctantly, getting up from her chaise. "We'll see. Let me go put on my Kevlar."

I crack up laughing.

23

"Awww, shiiiiiiiiit. Looka here, looka here. Dere goes dat dirty trick right dere," I hear someone say, pointing over in my direction.

Oh, god noo!

I stop dead in my tracks. My knees buckle. It's that Hennessey girl wobbling in our direction with two other girls on either side of her.

Jordan whispers out of the side of her mouth, "Ooh, look at them ugly girls walking toward us. And the one with that orange yarn going through her hair looks like she's the queen of the ghetto."

"Jordan, not now," I say in a hushed tone. "She's crazy."

Hennessey says, "Trick, it's on now. I knew I was gonna run into you again, sooner or later."

I grab Jordan's hand and take off running with the two girls with her chasing behind us. Jordan and I run through the food court zigzagging through the crowd, trying to get to safety before they catch us.

"Get her, Quanda!" I hear someone scream. I think it's that Hennessey girl. But I can't be for certain. "Yeah, you betta run, you effen *thot!* Stay away from Malik!"

"Wait! Wait! Ohmygod, Kennedy! What is happening? Why are we being chased by these wild girls?"

I can hear the two girls chasing behind us, calling us names and laughing at the same time.

"You betta hope I don't ever catch up wit' you, *bish!* You can run but you can't hide!" I hear one of the girls yelling in back of us as we zigzag through the mall, toward the escalators. "I know what you look like!"

My heart is pounding in my chest so hard that I think I am on the verge of having a heart attack. Jordan and I are both out of breath as we duck into Carol's Daughter, a skincare store, on the second level.

I have never been more frightened in my life. The last thing I want is to be attacked by that Hennessey girl and her friends; especially not after seeing how they all jumped on Malik that night at the restaurant.

"Ohmygod! Who were those girls?" Jordan wants to know, breathing heavily. She bends over, placing her hands on her knees, trying to catch her breath.

"I don't know them," I say, clutching my chest. I take slow, steady breaths to calm my nerves some.

Her eyes pop open. "What? You don't know them? Then why in the heck are they chasing us?"

"The girl who had the yarn in her head is this girl Hennessey..."

Jordan's eyes buck. "Ghetto trash. Go on."

I sigh. "She kind of got mad when she ran into Malik at Applebee's and saw me sitting there with him."

"Wait." She puts a hand up to stop me. "Wait one minute. Who the heck is Malik?"

"Oh, he's this guy I met through Sasha who I kind of like."

She frowns. "Wait a second. The girl you work with who hates you? That Sasha?"

"She doesn't hate me, really. But yeah. Her."

"That girl is trouble."

"How can you say that?" I ask, walking over to the entrance leading out into the mall and peeking out to see if those girls are anywhere in sight. "You don't even know her."

She snorts, placing a hand up on her hip. "Oh. And now you do?"

I turn to face her. "I didn't say that. But that doesn't mean it's okay to say unkind things about her."

"Hello," a saleswoman says, walking over to us. "Can I help you young ladies find anything in particular?"

Jordan looks over at her. "Yes, please. The nearest police station."

The sales lady gives Jordan a confused look, glancing from her, then over to me. "Excuse me? Is everything all right?"

"Oh, don't mind her," I cut in. "She's a little melodramatic. We're browsing, thanks."

"More like hiding out," Jordan says, irritated. "We've just been chased through the mall by a pack of hood hyenas." She looks down at her four-inch wedge heels. "I can't believe I had to run for my life in these shoes. I could have broken my ankles being dragged like a rag doll."

I apologize. Tell her I'll treat her to a pedicure.

She rolls her eyes. "That's the least you can do after

dragging me out to this trifling mall. And cohorting with that Sasha trash."

"That's not nice, Jordan. She really isn't bad. She's actually a lot of fun."

Jordan blinks. "Mmph. Isn't that something. Now you're taking up for the girl. How classic."

I raise my brow. "What do you mean by that?"

She rolls her eyes, picking up a body lotion sampler and sniffing it. "It's sounding real Stockholmish to me."

I suck my teeth. "Ohmygod, Jordan. You can't compare my getting to know Sasha to Stockholm syndrome. One, because she hasn't kidnapped me, and, two, I wasn't her hostage."

She waves me on dismissively, then sets the lotion back on the table. "Yeah, you were only the victim of her abuse at that little job of yours. But whatever. Glad you could find it in your heart to be so forgiving, so soon."

I shake my head, then walk over to where she's standing. "There wasn't really anything to forgive."

"Mmph. I guess not. So when did you and the crazy girl become new best friends? And why am I just now hearing about it?"

"Jordan, relax. It's not that serious."

She grunts. "Oh, okay. I'll be sure to remember that the next time I'm being chased through a mall by a bunch of knife-wielding thuggettes."

I shake my head, walking toward the mall entrance. "Come on. Let's get out of here."

"With pleasure," she says, stomping off ahead of me. "I can't wait to call Hope and tell her all about this drama."

"Can you please not?" I quickly say.

She shoots me a look. "And why not?"

"I want to be the one to tell her."

She rolls her eyes. "Alright. If that's how you want to play it, I'll keep your little secret. For now." Her last words to me before speedwalking toward the parking garage and leaving me behind are, "So much for fun."

24

The voice inside my head tells me not to do it, but...
I can't help myself. Maybe I can. Okay, okay...I don't want to. Can you blame me? There's something about him that I can't shake. Even after that whole mall incident over a week ago, it's like I'm more drawn to him than ever before. I don't know what it is that has me wanting to know more about him. But I do. Badly.

Maybe because I know I'll be living on the edge.

Maybe because I know he comes with a lot of drama.

And excitement.

And mysteriousness.

I close my eyes, as Ariana Grande's "Tattooed Heart" plays low in the background. Without thought, I start humming softly.

"Yo, wat's dat you hummin'?" Malik wants to know. We'd been texting practically all day during my work shift and now—although I'm on punishment and can't leave the house—we've gone from texting back and forth to talking on the phone. I tell him who the artist is. "Oh, word? I ain't up on her. Sing me somethin'."

I laugh.

"Nah, real ish, baby. Let me hear you spit somethin'."

"I can't sing."

He laughs. "So. It'll be our secret, a'ight?"

I giggle. "Ooh, I like that. Our little secret."

"You already know. So wat's good? You gonna let me hear it or wat?"

"Ohgod. Are you serious? I sound horrible."

"C'mon. What, you want me to beg? I know you ain't tryna make me beg for it, are you? But I will if dats wat you want."

The way he says *it* . . . that he'll beg for *it* . . . if I want him to, makes me feel warm all over.

Mmmm. Do I want him to beg for it?

"So you want me to beg?" he says in a low, husky voice. It sounds as if he's smoking.

"No. You don't have to beg," I say in almost a whisper.

He blows out a breath. "Oh, word? A'ight then. Let me get dat then. Let me hear dat sexy voice sing in my ear."

I blush. Then take a deep breath, and sing a verse. Then end it with, "All I need is all your loving . . ."

"Oh, word? Dat's all you need?"

I swallow. "It's from the song. I wasn't speaking of me, per se."

"Yeah, I know. But I'm sayin' . . . who you givin' all ya lovin' to?"

"No one."

"Oh, word? So when's da last time you let someone hit dat?"

I blink. "Ohmygod! Never!"

"What, you still a virgin?"

My eyes pop open. And for some reason I am embarrassed to tell him that I am. Silence. I am relieved when he doesn't press me for the answer.

"I bet you mad tight 'n' real juicy, like fresh fruit."

The way he says that makes me flood with heat and excitement. And I know I should probably not let this go any further than it already has. That I should probably change the subject now before things get way out of control and I end up getting into something I'm not ready for. But I don't.

"You think you ready to let a man make you a woman?"

"Who says I'm not already a woman?" I say coyly. I know I'm flirting with danger, still...

"Nah, you still a woman-in-trainin', yo. But hang wit' me 'n' I'ma make you a full-fledge, card-carryin' one." He pauses. "Dat's if you think you ready."

"Boy, I was born ready."

He cracks up laughing. "Oh, I see you like to talk a good one, huh? But I'ma man, baby. I ain't one'a dem li'l boyz you 'n' ya li'l friendz chase 'round da playground. You steppin' into man territory now, babe. I got somethin' for you to play on, but it ain't no swing."

"Mmmhmm," I purr without thinking. I'm surprised at how flirtatious I am being. I feel sexy. "I know that."

"Word? So wat's good? You think you can handle all dis good lovin'?"

I blink. Press my thighs together. "I don't know."

"I'm sayin'...then there's only one way to find out."

My heart skips two extra beats.

"Yo, I wanna see you, ma," Malik says real low and sexy-like into the phone, causing every bit of my sensibilities to go out the window.

"I want to see you, too." I glance over at the clock. It's a little after eleven o'clock at night. We've been on the phone for almost twenty minutes. Malik isn't really a phone type of guy. He'd rather text. But the fact that he called me and isn't rushing off the phone tells me he must really be interested in me. The thought makes me smile. "I know how you don't like talking on the phone, but I'm glad you called me."

"True, true. But you an exception, babe. I'm feelin' you, yo."

My smile widens. "I'm feeling you, too, Malik."

He blows a breath into the phone, causing me to close my eyes. I imagine his lips moving as he speaks. He tells me he wants to take me into the city to go shopping then out to dinner this coming Saturday. That he then wants me to spend the night with him.

My heart flutters. And everything inside of me starts to vibrate.

"Dis ish is killin' me, ma. You got me goin' thru it. Hearin' ya sweet, sexy voice got my man all excited. I wanna taste dem pretty lips." He lets out another breath. "Yo, you sure there ain't no way you can get out? Just for an hour or so."

I glance over at the clock again.

I pull in a deep breath. "Come get me. I'll be standing at the corner waiting."

"Aah, dat's what I'm talkin' 'bout, baby." I can hear the smile in his voice. "You know I'ma 'bout to make you mine, right?"

I wonder if he can see me smiling from ear to ear right now. Or if he can hear how fast my heart is beating this very moment. I feel like I'm floating.

I give him the address to where the WaWa is. He tells me he'll meet me there in twenty minutes before we disconnect.

Hurriedly, I swing the sheet off of me and hop out of bed, excited. I race around my bedroom trying to find something cute to wear, mindful not to make too much noise. I go into the bathroom, wash my face, and pull my hair back into a ponytail. Ten minutes later, I am gliding on a coat of cherry lipgloss then climbing out of my window in a pair of fitted jeans and a black T-shirt with the words LOVE ME printed across my chest.

I shimmy my way down the side of the house, then make my way in the still of the night down the winding, lamplit streets, through the gates, then down the street to meet Malik.

Malik's struck a match. And now I'm playing with fire. The only question is, how far am I willing to go? And just how badly am I willing to get burnt?

25

"Kennedy! What are you doing sneaking into this house, huh? Do you see what time it is?"

Oh *nooo*, busted.

Unfortunately, I was left with no other choice but to use the spare key hidden in a small black key box tucked down in one of the flowerbeds. When I crawled back up to my window to get into my room, the window was shut and locked. *Locked!* I couldn't believe it. I was locked out of the house. I'd been caught.

"Have you lost your mind?" my mother questions, flipping on the foyer light as I slip into the house and attempt to tiptoe my way up to my bedroom at a quarter to three in the morning. "Sneaking back in here at this time of the night. Where have you been?"

"I w-w-was only gone for an hour or so."

She tilts her head. "Don't you dare stand there and lie to me, Kennedy. I went to check on you over three hours ago. And you were not in your room. So where were you? And who were you with?"

"I-I was with Jordan," I say. The lie rolls out of my mouth without much thought. "She was really upset. And she needed someone to talk to."

She glares at me. "And the two of you couldn't talk over the phone?"

"No. I mean, yes. But I needed to be there with her."

She eyes me suspiciously. "Well, why didn't Jordan just come over here, huh?"

"I thought you said I couldn't have company."

"No. I told you that you were *not* allowed to leave this house. And you did anyway. You defied me. Something you've never done before. So it must have been really important for you to sneak out of this house. So where were you? And don't you dare lie to me, Kennedy!"

"I'm not lying," I whine. "I was with Jordan. Hope got into a big fight with her parents. Then she ran away and said she was going to hurt herself."

Mom raises her brow, looks at me as if she's trying to decide whether she should believe me or not. She narrows her eyes. "You just said you were with Jordan. That she was upset. Now you're saying you were with Hope." She taps her slipper-clad foot, crossing her arms. "Which is it, Kennedy? Were you with Hope or was it Jordan?"

I swallow. "Both. They were both upset. First Jordan called me. Then she did a three-way call to Hope. She was crying hysterical. Talking real crazy, like she didn't want to live anymore. I got scared. And asked Jordan if she could pick me up so we could be with Hope. I had Jordan meet me down by the gates, then we drove over to where Hope was."

Mom eyes me. "If Hope was in such a state of crisis why

didn't you let me know, huh? Why didn't you ask me if it was okay for you to leave out of this house to go see about her, huh?"

I lower my eyes. Glance around the foyer. Fidget with the hem of my T-shirt. I will my knees from shaking. "I thought you would tell me I couldn't go. And I really wanted to be there for her, Mom. I know I was wrong for sneaking out, but this was important."

She stares at me, studying me. I can tell she's still trying to decide if she buys the bull crap I've just offered her as my reason for defying her. "Yeah, it must've been really urgent for you to climb out of your window like that."

"I'm sorry, Mom. It won't happen again."

"That's the second time you've had to say that," she says, looking me up and down. "First, you stay out all night and come home intoxicated. And now this. These behaviors are starting to look like a pattern. And I do not like it one bit. Do I need to call your father?"

I shake my head. "No, please. Don't call Daddy. There's no need to worry him about nothing. I promise you, it won't happen again."

"I hope not. And you're certain you are telling me the absolute truth? You were with Hope and Jordan? And not that Sasha girl?"

I nod. "Yes. I'm telling the truth. I promise you, I wasn't with Sasha." Sadly, this fact is the only truth to my night.

Mom's stare drops to my shirt. She frowns. "Why is your shirt on backwards?"

I blink. Pull at the neck and see that the tag is in front. "I was in such a rush to get to Jordan, I must have put it on without looking."

She opens her mouth to say something, then stops herself. I take that as my cue to say more, to fuel the lie even more. "I'd never heard Hope talk like that before, Mom." I shake my head for effect. "She sounded so broken. And it scared me. I'd never think she'd run away from home in a million years. But she did."

My mom's face softens. The ice in her eyes slowly starts to melt. "That seems so unlike Hope."

"I know. That's why I had to sneak out, Mom. And I'm sorry. But I couldn't chance not being there for her and something bad happened to her." I look away. "I'd never be able to forgive myself."

"Well, where is she? Is she okay now?"

"Yes. She's okay. At least she seemed to be. She's staying at her grandparents' house for now. She promised us she wouldn't do anything to hurt herself."

"Go up to your room. It's late. And I have to be up in less than two hours for work."

"Good night," I say, quickly turning for the staircase.

"Kennedy?"

I stop in my tracks. Keep my back to her. "Yes?"

"I've never had any reason to doubt you. *Please* don't give me a reason to now."

I'm not," I offer, silently relieved that I'm going to get away with sneaking back in. For the second time. I say a little prayer, holding back a sly grin.

"For your sake," Mom says, "I hope not."

26

"Hope, I need a big favor from you."

"Okay. What is it?"

"If my mom says anything to you about being glad that you're back home with your parents, I need you to just go along with it, okay?"

Hope raises a brow. "Why would she say something like that?"

"Well...I kind of told her that you had a big fight with your parents and ran away."

She shoots me an incredulous look. "You did *whaat?*"

"Sssh. Keep your voice down. If I wanted a live broadcast I would have just shouted it out."

"Are you kidding me right now? You told your mom that I ran away from home? Why on earth would you tell her something like that?"

"I'm sorry," I say apologetically. "I know I shouldn't have put you in the middle of it. But it was the first thing that came out of my mouth."

"Well, why would you need to go to that extreme?"

"Well, uh, I kind of, sort of, snuck out of the house and got caught."

Her eyes pop open. "You did *whaat?*"

"Will you keep your voice down," I say, putting a finger up to my lips. "All I need for you to do is go along with the whole fight with your parents and running away thing. She might not say anything, but just in case she does. Can you do that for me? Please."

She narrows her eyes. "And what exactly am I supposed to say to her? You know I'm not good with fabricating stories."

I suck my teeth. "I'm not asking you to invent a full-fledged news report. All you have to do, if she asks, is say you feel horrible about what happened and that you're glad you're home to work things out. That's it. End of story."

She shakes her head in disbelief. "I don't believe this."

"Will you do this for me, please?"

"Yeah, I guess. But don't think I like it one bit either."

I reach over and give her a big hug. "You're a lifesaver. I owe you one."

She narrows her eyes at me. "Oh, believe me. Yes, you do. Big time."

"Oh, and one more thing. Can you please not say anything to Jordan about this? I'd rather you keep this between us."

She blinks. "Why? I thought we didn't keep secrets from each other."

I shrug. "Well, we don't. Not always."

She tilts her head. "No. You mean, *you* don't, not always. I share everything with you and Jordan."

"I know you do. And I do, too. But just not this; not right now."

She gives me a long stare. "Oh, like how you didn't want Jordan to tell me about those wild banshee girls chasing y'all through the mall with butcher knives the other day?"

"Ohmygod! I promise you. That is sooo not what happened."

She shrugs. "Doesn't matter. Jordan told me you didn't want her to say anything to me about it so what do I care what really happened?"

I can tell her feelings were hurt by it. And now I feel bad. "It's not that I didn't want you to know. I just didn't want Jordan to be the one to tell you since it had to do with me. I wanted to be the one to tell you when all three of us were together."

She rolls her eyes up in her head. "Uh-huh. If you say so."

"I'm sorry, Hope."

"No, no. Don't apologize. It's fine. So, who were you out with?"

"Malik," I say casually as if he's someone I've known forever, and she's just as familiar with him.

She frowns. "Malik? Malik who? Wait a minute! Is he the same guy those girls were trying to kill you and Jordan over? *That* Malik?"

I frown. "They weren't trying to *kill* us. Besides, it wasn't Jordan they were after. They wanted me."

She blinks. "Why?"

"Because this girl Hennessey, who supposedly has a baby with him..."

"*Hennessey*? What kind of hot trash name is that? And

Jordan did say she was looking real hot trash, too. All of them."

"Yeah. And she has a really nasty attitude. Malik says she's real jealous and crazy."

"Ohmygod, Kennedy! Why would you want to be bothered with a boy who went out with something like that? What is wrong with you?"

I tell her nothing's wrong with me. That he never really dated her. They just fooled around—as in had sex multiple times, that is. She wants to know where Malik's from and how I met him. I give her a recap of how we met, leaving out certain details like the night he had that guy who tried to force himself on me beat up.

"I guess you must really like this boy if he has you sneaking out of the house like that."

I huff. "He didn't have me sneak out. I snuck out on my own."

She gives me a blank look. "Okay, if you say so. So what y'all do?"

I shrug. "Nothing really; we just drove around in his truck."

Well, of course that's not so. But I can't tell her that we ended up parked on a one-way street in front of an abandoned house. She'd lose it. And I know for sure she'd collapse if she knew I've smoked weed, too.

I was surprised when he offered me some as soon as I got in the smoke-filled car and strapped my seat belt on. He handed it to me. "Here," he said, eyeing me. "I'ma help you get ya mind right." He started laughing. "Nah, let me stop effen wit' you."

I took the blunt from him, remembering how I'd watched Blaze and Sasha and her friend smoke it. I took a pull. I'm not going to lie. I was real nervous being with Malik, but happy and excited at the same time. After about the fourth pull, I felt real relaxed. Like I could take on the world.

"Mygod, Kennedy, what has gotten into you?" Jordan says, shaking her head. "And I still can't believe how could you lie to your mother like that. And sneaking out of the house like that to be with some boy you barely even know. Have you no shame? Anything could have happened to you. What if that boy would have kidnapped you and held you for ransom? Or worse, raped and killed you?"

"Ohmygod, Hope! You're starting to sound like Jordan. Both of you need to stop watching all those *NCIS* episodes."

"Well, it's true." She shakes her head. "But what I want to know is, how long have you been sneaking out of your house?"

I shrug. "I've only done it twice before."

"What? Really? To be with that Malik boy?" I tell her no. Not the first time. Tell her about Hazel Eyes. She gives me a blank stare. "Hazel Eyes? What kind of name is that?"

I shake my head. "It's not his real name. It's what I call him."

"What's his name then?"

"Blaze."

She raises her eyebrows. "Like that's any better." She shakes her head. "All these boys with them ridiculous names. Geesh. You sure know how to pick 'em, don't you?" She doesn't give me a chance to respond. "And how did you meet this Hazel Blaze boy, anyway?"

"It's Hazel Eyes. And I met him one day at the mall. He came to my job with two of his friends."

"Let me guess. And he's one of those thug boys, too?"
She quickly puts a hand up. "On second thought. You
don't even have to say it. I already know."

I frown.

Her phone buzzes and she pulls it out of her bag, glancing at the screen. "Oh, my mom just text saying she's outside," she says, texting back.

"Oh, okay. Remember what I said, keep what I told you
between us."

She sighs. "Okay, I will. This time."

"Thanks."

"Just do me a favor," she says, getting up and slipping
her feet into her sandals.

I take a deep breath glance at the clock, then stand up
as well. "Yeah, what's that?"

She walks over and gives me a big hug. "Be careful."

I bite my bottom lip. The way she says it sends a chill
down my spine.

I shudder, laughing nervously. "Girl, you said that like
Dracula's out to get me, or something."

She shrugs. "He might be."

I wave her on, walking her out of my room. "You're
overreacting." She follows me down the stairs.

She turns her lips up and shakes her head. "Maybe."

I open the front door, waving out at Mrs. Taylor. She
sees me, and waves back.

"For real, Kennedy," Hope says, placing her hand on
the doorknob. "Be careful. I know you think you like that
Malik boy. But he sounds like he has a lot of drama going
on around him. Watch yourself. Okay?"

I open my mouth to tell her okay, but I end up nodding
instead.

"I'm serious, Kennedy. I don't think you know what you're getting yourself into."

I give her a half smile. "Don't worry. I'm not going to get myself into any trouble. I'm only having a little fun."

"I sure hope you know what you're doing," she says, shaking her head as she walks out the door. I shut it behind her, more excited than ever before to know everything there is to know about the sexy, dark chocolate boo named Malik.

27

Giving myself to him is like magic...

"You mine, Kennedy," Malik says in between the soft kisses he is planting along my neck, then on my collarbone. I feel myself heating up in ways I never thought possible. My heart is beating so fast I think I'm going to faint. I feel myself getting caught up in the way his lips glide along my skin; every so often he flicks his tongue against my flesh. The warm wetness causes tingly sensations to shoot through my body.

I have never wanted to be with anyone...like this. In Malik's arms, his body grinding against mine as Trey Songz's sexy voice floats around the room from the iPod docking station. He slips his arms around my waist.

"You mine, ya heard?"

I swallow. Look up into his face. I want to be his. Only his. I *am* his. And now I want him to have the one thing I've proudly held on to. The one thing I've waited to share with someone like him. But I have to be sure first. I know what's in my heart.

Love.

But a nagging voice in the back of my head keeps telling me that I should wait. That Malik isn't the one. That all the drama from the last few days is only going to get worse. But his hands, his lips, the way his eyes roam all over me mixed with what I already feel in my heart for him is all the reason I need to dismiss the nagging voice in my head.

I look up and gaze deep into Malik's beautiful brown eyes. "Am I really all yours?"

He presses his lips against mine, then lightly nips my bottom lip. "You mine, baby."

"But are you mine, Malik?"

He leans his head in and kisses me again. "No doubt. I'm all yours, babe."

The way he says "I'm all yours, babe" causes me to melt inside. I want him. And I want him to want me, too. Only me. I don't want to share him, or have his crazy exes and psycho baby mommas trying to fight me every time they see me; especially that Hennessey chick. She seems like she's the craziest of them all.

"What about your baby mother, Hennessey?"

He eyes me, raising a brow. "What about 'er? That bird was a bad mistake. A one-night stand I can't erase. All she is is the mother of my seed. That's it. I'm not beat for her. Word is bond."

I want to believe him.

"But…" *Are you still sleeping with her?*

"She doesn't matter, a'ight?" His mouth covers mine, not allowing me to finish. We kiss until I lose my train of thought, then he slowly pulls back. "No buts…this is me 'n' you, babe. This is our night. So don't make it 'bout that nutty broad or nobody else. It's me 'n' you, a'ight?"

I nod.

His lips curl into a sexy grin. "Am I ya man?"

"Li'l trick, puhleeze. You'll never be enuff for Malik. He'll always keep creepin' over for all'a dis thickness…"

I swallow.

"Tell her how you came over last night, Malik. Let dis li'l uppity heifer know how you hit it raw…let her know how ya head stay south for dis sweet treat…"

I feel the tears coming. I try to blink back the burning. I try to shake the taunting voice.

"He ain't ever gonna be yours, boo-boo, so you might as well take ya li'l siddity, high-yella self back up to da 'burbs where you belong…"

"I want you to be," I say breathlessly as his hands glide effortlessly over my curves.

"Then let me, ma."

He kisses me again.

I pull back. "But what about all those girls who keep threatening me?"

Malik speaks against my lips. "I tol' you, babe. Them birds ain't 'bout nuthin'. I ain't checkin' for none'a dem like dat, word is bond, yo. So stop sweatin' dat dumbness, a'ight?"

I blink back the faces of the girls chasing me through the mall. I swallow back every bit of my senses feeling Malik's excitement pressing up against me. He wasn't a boy. He was a grown man.

With his own car.

His own money.

And a kid.

And baby mother.

And a bunch of ex-girlfriends.

And lots and lots of experience being with girls sexually.

And probably more drama than what I've already experienced.

Still...

I like him.

I want him.

"He's nothing but trouble..."

"Ugh, you need to leave that boy alone, Kennedy..."

"He's poison, Kennedy."

Malik is kissing all over my neck again. Clouding my head with heat and need and want. My heart is pounding a mile a minute with each kiss. Then his lips are on mine again. Our tongues are doing a romantic dance to the smooth sound of Trey Songz belting out his latest love song, crooning the words to what I am feeling right now as Malik lifts my shirt up over my head, then unsnaps my bra, releasing my desires and inhibitions.

I take a deep breath. "Malik, don't hurt me." My lips quiver. "If you are going to be with other girls, tell me now."

I feel myself on the brink of tears.

"Nah, I tol' you. You da only one I'm checkin' for, babe. It's all you."

A lone tear slides down my face.

"I got you, ma." He stares into my eyes. "C'mon, babe. Don't cry. It's me 'n' you. Word to mother."

No other words are spoken as he lays me on his bed, removes the rest of my clothes, and then takes off his own. I drink his body in. Swallow, hard.

He climbs into his bed with me. "You sure 'bout dis?"

I nod.

He smiles, pulling me into his arms. "Am I ya man?"

I look up into his eyes. See the only guy who has ever made me feel like this. And for me, nothing else even matters. Not the roaches I see crawling along the wall and know are probably scrambling around my clothes trying to find a way inside of my pockets for a trip home with me, or the pile of dirty clothes he has piled high in the right corner of his bedroom. Not the fact that he has a kid with some crazy girl. Not the fact that he has ex-girlfriends who still call him and stalk him and threaten me and want him back. No. None of those things matter. Nothing else means more to me than being here, in Malik's arms, where I want to be.

"Yes," I finally whisper against his lips. "You're my man."

28

"Where have you been for the last three days, Kennedy? Do you have any idea how worried I've been? I've been calling all around town for you. And why has your phone been turned off, huh?" My mom looks frazzled. And I feel bad for having her worry about me. But it couldn't be helped. Well, that's not true. I could have come home. But I didn't want to. Malik didn't want me to, either. We were having too much fun together.

"So you couldn't locate me," I say snidely.

It was only supposed to be for a few hours. Our drive down to Atlantic City. Malik wanted to walk the board-walk, do some shopping at the outlets and The Pier Shops at Caesar's, then grab something to eat at one of the restaurants on the strip. I wanted to go to Buddakan, one of my favorite Asian restaurants. I'd only been to the one in the city, but wanted to try the one in AC also.

Malik protested at first, saying it wasn't real Chinese

food unless it was at a local Chinese spot or an all-you-can-eat buffet.

I laughed at that because he was so serious when he said it. But after several minutes of prodding, he acquiesced. And so we went.

For appetizers, I ordered the chicken and ginger dumplings with sesame dipping sauce. And Malik tried the king crab tempura with sweet and sour ponzu sauce. Then for the main course, I had the Alaskan king salmon with miso mustard and a sesame spinach salad. Malik said he didn't want anything. He was just going to sit and watch me eat.

He laughed. "My baby mad greedy. You tryna run my wallet real hard tonight, huh?"

I smiled. "Is that a problem?"

"Nah, baby. It's all good." He slowly licked his lips. "It's gonna cost you later, though."

I wiggled my eyebrows up and down. "Ooh, for real?"

He looked around the dimly lit restaurant, then leaned forward in his seat, resting his forearms up on the table. "No doubt."

By the time dessert came I could barely get a spoonful of my almond bread pudding into my mouth. I was so stuffed. And so was Malik.

"Yo, let's get a room 'n' chill a bit before we take dat long ride back up da parkway."

"Okay," I said, excited by the thought of lying in Malik's arms, cuddling. Catching a quick nap. Then driving back home.

The plan was that simple. And I would have been home right before my curfew. With my mom being none the wiser had things not gone awry.

Malik had gotten us a room at the Days Inn. And it wasn't

long before we were both butt-naked and he was doing things to my body I never imagined humanly possible. We ended up dozing off. But a few hours turned into the next morning. Then one day turned into two, then three.

Surprisingly, not once did Malik suggest I call home. Not that it was his place to. But out of courtesy, I called her anyway. The second day. I told her that I was okay and that I was out of town.

"Out of town where, Kennedy? With who?"

I hung up on her and shut off my phone before she had a chance to call back and try to spoil my fun.

Then reality set in. I knew I had to come back home eventually. That I would have to answer to her. And, more than likely be grounded until my twenty-first birthday.

But at least I called her.

She blinks. Her eyes roam over me from head to toe, taking in the True Religion teardrop-print skinny jeans and the beaded tank. She blinks again. Glances down at the six-hundred-and-fifty-dollar dollar six-inch Gucci sandals on my feet. Then her eyes land on the Louis Vuitton bag dangling from the crook of my arm.

"Where did you get those clothes and that expensive pocketbook from?"

I toss my hair. "Relax, Mom. I didn't steal them, if that's what you're getting at."

Her nose flares. A hand goes up on her hip. "*Relax*? You must want me to slap you into next week, talking to me like that.

"And don't you dare tell me another one of your lies that you were out with Hope and Jordan because I've spoken to both of their parents. Now you had better tell me what's really going on. Now!"

"I was with Sasha," I say nonchalantly.

"With *Sasha*, where?"

I huff. "Out."

"Out where, Kennedy?"

"It's no big deal," I say, rolling my eyes.

"What do you mean 'it's no big deal'? It's a big deal when you've been gone for three days! And it's totally unacceptable!"

I suck my teeth. "Nowhere."

"You must think you're real grown, don't you?"

"I'm almost grown," I say, real sassy.

Mom gives me an incredulous look. "Oh, no you're not! And *almost* doesn't count. Not in this house!"

"Fine!" I yell back at her. "I'll go stay somewhere else! I don't have to live here!"

The rest of the week I stay locked in my room, out of my mother's sight. She's not saying much to me. And I'm not saying much of anything to her, either. For what? I'm grounded. Well, so she thinks. I'm still sneaking out of the house. Not every night, though. Still...every chance I get I'm with Malik.

This time, instead of climbing out of my bedroom window, I'm sneaking out through the wine cellar door down in our basement. And I'm back in the house way before three A.M.

She really thinks she can keep me chained in this house. Stuck and bored. I don't think so.

29

I moan as Malik's tongue slowly slips into my mouth. His hand glides down the small of my back, then rests on my butt. He squeezes it, and I feel myself melting a thousand times over. No boy has ever made me feel the way Malik has.

He makes me feel... alive.

Wanted.

Special.

Loved.

Sexy.

He presses his body into mine and we meld into one. I can feel his excitement. And he can feel mine. I am so hungry for him. He's hungry for me. I don't know how much more of this tongue-dance I can take before I am going out of my mind.

His kiss becomes more intense. His tongue swirls against mine. Once, twice, again and again, he kisses me until I am feeling light-headed and dizzy.

Whoever thought a person could feel tell so much about another person from just a kiss. But this isn't just any kiss.

No. I'm being kissed by a boy...I mean, a man.

I love his expressive face when he's in deep in thought, or when he's laughing or angry or, like now, looking at me like I'm the most important person in his world.

I love his bad boy persona. Love his street grit. His take-charge commando ways.

Malik makes me feel like a woman. I feel grown. And like I'm ready to take on the world.

I love the way he wraps his arms around me and holds me tight. I feel so, so safe when he holds me. I love how he puts his almond-shaped eyes on mine, and smiles at me. Love the way his heart beats against mine. And how he tells me each beat is his love for me. I love that about him. I love...

Him.

All of him; every drop of bad boy blood that runs through his veins.

Malik is my drug.

I'm hooked on him.

He knows it.

I know it.

I love him.

I love him.

I love him.

Three weeks!

And I am in love!

How did it happen so fast?

I keep asking myself that question over and over. Yet, no matter how many times I mull it around in my head, I can't seem to come up with an exact moment that *it* (love) happened. It just did. Unexpectedly.

And boy, oh boy, I'm happy that it did.

Malik is the only guy I can ever see myself being with.

He has a good heart.

He's thoughtful. Generous. Caring.

He's my everything.

"I want you so bad," he murmurs against my lips as if he's reading my mind.

"I want you, too," I say back. He kisses me again. But just as things start to get hotter and steamier than they already are, one of his three cell phones start ringing.

He groans, pulling away. He tries to fix himself in his sweats. "See what you did?" He shakes his head and grins as he retrieves his ringing cell from off the dresser.

I swallow, touching the bare space his lips have now left on my own.

"Yo," he says into the phone.

I walk over to his bed, stepping over an ashtray overflowing with half-smoked blunts. I reach for last month's edition of *XXL* magazine lying on the floor beside the bed and sit.

"Nah, Chillin' wit' my girl, son. Yeah, yeah. You know how I do it, fam. Say what? Word? Yo, get the fu—" He cuts himself off. "Yo, babe..."

I look up from the magazine.

"I'ma 'bout to step out and finish up dis call, a'ight?"

"Okay."

He walks over to the bed, leans in and seizes my mouth with another kiss. A quick peck, but it is one that holds promise of what's to come when he returns from his phone call. One I can't wait to collect on.

I idly flip through the pages of the magazine before deciding I'm really not interested in reading anything about Kanye's paranoid rants. I like his music. But I think he's really crazy. Like maybe he hears voices or something kind of crazy. I toss the magazine over onto the bed, get up and pull my iPhone from out of my messenger bag to check my messages.

I have four text messages.

The first text is from Hope: UM, HELLO? CALL ME.

The second message is from Sasha: THERE'S A POOL PARTY 2MORROW IN UNION. U DOWN?

The third text is from Mom: I'M TAKING YOUR AUNT LISA OUT FOR HER BIRTHDAY. TRY TO BE HOME BY SIX. TTYL.

The last text is from Blaze: YOOOOO WATZ GUD? WEN WE LINKIN UP?

This is like his third or fourth text over the last few days wanting to *link up,* as he calls it. But I've been avoiding him. Now with Malik in my life, I don't have any room for any other guys in my life, especially since I promised Malik last night that I would cut off any boys who I knew liked me, that I used to date, or have gone out with. He said it was disrespectful. And all they'd be is a distraction from what we have. And I believed him. Not that I have a lot of guys I've dated. Still, I don't want any distractions.

And I don't want to ever disrespect Malik.

I quickly text Blaze back. HI. WE CAN'T. I HAVE A BF NOW.

Less than a minute later, he sends a text back. OH WORD? AIGHT DEN. GOOD LUCK WIT DAT.

I delete his text messages, then start cleaning up Malik's messy room. I start with the fifty pairs of sneakers that are scattered all over the floor, putting them back into their designated boxes. I empty out his ashtray, then gather all the empty Heineken beer bottles. Sixteen.

Ohmygod! How can anyone sleep in this slop?

"Girl, you real *stoopid*," someone says in back of me, startling me. I jump, turning in the direction of the voice. "You prolly da dumbest ho he's been wit' so far."

I blink. It's his sister, Mercedes, sneering at me. I'm not sure why they call her *Mercedes* since nothing seems exclusive about her current situation.

"Please don't call me that," I say calmly.

"Don't call you what? *Dumb?* Or *ho?*"

"Both."

She tsks. "Well, you are *dumb*. And by da time Malik finishes runnin' all up in you like he does da rest of 'em, a *dumb ho* is exactly what you gonna be."

"Well, I can't speak for anyone else, but I know I'm not going to be anyone's *ho.*"

She chortles. "Yeah, that's what dey all say 'til he gets 'em strung out on da *D.*"

I give her a confused look.

She huffs. "Da dingdong. Da wood. Oh, excuse me. I mean. Da penis."

I blink.

She's so crude.

She snorts. "Li'l girl, you don't know nuthin' 'bout nuthin'. All you are is some young, fresh piece of tail for my brother."

I take a deep breath, willing my heart to slow its rapid pace. I don't know why, but Malik's sister unnerved me. From the first day I met her I've tried to be nothing but nice to her, but my attempts are only met with glares and snide, nasty comments.

"Malik isn't going to do me like he's done any of those other girls. Your brother loves me."

She cracks up laughing. "*Your brother loves me*," she mocks. "He ain't ever gonna do me like he's done dem other hoes. Hahahaha." She shakes her head. "Just like I said, dumb."

I blink. And now I immediately feel stupid for letting that last part slip from my lips. "*Love?* My brother *loves* you? You think? Girly, bye. My brother loves anything wit' a big booty 'n' a smile. Why you think he has four baby *muhvers*?"

I blink.

Four baby mothers?! I thought he only had one baby mother. Four? No, she's lying. She has to be.

She must see the stunned look on my face.

"What, you ain't know? Oops." She covers her mouth. "Looks like the cat's out the bag."

"I already knew about his baby mothers," I lie.

She shifts her weight from one swollen foot to the other, staring at me as if she doesn't believe a word I've said. "Oh, really? Well, isn't that special. Then I guess you know raw punnany is da only thing my brother is gonna ever love. He doesn't know howta love anything other than what's between yo' legs, li'l girl. But you keep believin' whatever lies he tells you. You'll learn soon enough. That's my brotha 'n' I love him. And trust. I'll beat a *bish* down if she ever tries to play him. But I can tell you not really 'bout dis life so you need to stop pretendin' 'n' head on back 'cross town where you belong. But I know you ain't. So I'ma tell you dis to save you some heartache. Get out now before it's too late. All my brotha's gonna do is dog you out, sex you out, then toss you out like a used tampon. Just watch."

I swallow.

"Yo, Mercedes," Malik says, brushing by her as he finally walks back into the room, "what ya picklehead in here talkin' to my girl 'bout?"

I breathe a sigh of relief that he's come back in when he has. I don't know how much more of his sister's sneering I could have taken.

Thanks to her, my mood is ruined.

I am sooo ready to get out of here.

She narrows her eyes at me, then looks over at Malik. "Oh, we was just havin' us a li'l girl talk." She starts laughing, shaking her head. She turns to leave, then turns back. "Oh, you got yaselfa real winner right there. I can't wait for Big Sexy to meet dis one."

"Yo, go 'head wit' dat, Mercedes," Malik says, grabbing her by the arm and pushing her back from out of his door so he can shut it. "Get da eff up outta here wit' da dumb ish." He slams the door.

I can hear her laughing as she walks off.

I glance over to my right and notice three roaches scurrying along the wall.

Malik kicks off his sneakers, removes his T-shirt, then steps out of his jeans. He stretches out in the center of his bed in only his boxers and sweat socks. He grabs and pulls at his privates until he gets himself excited.

"Yo, take dem clothes off 'n' c'mon over here 'n' give ya man some lovin'." He pats the space on the bed beside him. "Ya man needs some special attention."

I swallow. "Who's Big Sexy?"

Malik frowned. "Yo, don't start askin' me a buncha silly questions, yo. She ain't nobody, a'ight." He keeps grabbing himself. "So chill, a'ight?"

I nod. "Okay."

He grins. "Me 'n' big man need you to come handle us, *now.*"

Reluctantly, I remove my clothes, leaving on my bra and panties. Then slowly I make my way over to him. Each step causes the voice in my head to get louder.

"*...All my brotha's gonna do is dog you out, sex you out, then toss you out...Just watch.*"

"*...Get out now before it's too late...*"

I climb into bed beside Malik.

It's already too late, I think as I close my eyes, letting Malik's lips and hands wander all over me.

I lose myself in his touch, his scent, his sweet kisses. He has become everything to me. It doesn't matter what Mercedes or anyone else says about Malik.

I love him.

30

"Keep it a hunnid wit' me. Why you wit' him?" Hazel Eyes wants to know, looking up from his tray. I agreed to meet him at the mall...to talk. And now he's sitting here across from me at the food court, questioning, drilling me about my relationship with Malik. Even though I had already told him that I didn't think we should hang out anymore, he insisted on knowing why. So I told him about Malik and me. And, honestly, it felt good to be able to talk openly about Malik, for once, to someone.

Hazel Eyes unwraps his grilled chicken cheese steak, then chomps into his sandwich, the smell of green peppers and onions mingling with meat and melted cheese swirling around my nostrils.

I take a slow sip of my Dr. Pepper, eyeing him as he slaughters his sub in big bites, causing grease and ketchup to coat his lips.

"Why am I with who?" I finally ask, feigning ignorance.

He looks up from his food and with a mouth full of sub.

His brows crease. "C'mon, Kennedy. Don't play me, yo. You know who I'm talkin' 'bout. Why you wit' dude? I mean, what's he got dat I don't, huh?"

"He's different."

"Different how?"

"Ohmygod! What is this, an inquisition?"

"Nah. I thought you was feelin' me; dat's all. I kinda thought we was buildin' on somethin'. But it's all good."

"I am...I mean, I *was,* feeling you. But then I met Malik. And I don't know. Things just clicked with us."

"Oh, word? Like how?" he says, stuffing fries into his mouth.

I shrug. "I just like him more, that's all."

He takes another big bite of his sandwich. Talking, then chewing, then swallowing, before rinsing it all down with two long swigs of Sprite. Finally he says, "What you like 'bout him, huh?"

I shift in my seat. Shift my eyes from his gaze, taking in what's going on around us. I keep an eye out for Jordan since I'm out here with her. I meet his gaze again.

"I don't know. I mean. It's hard to explain."

He twists his lips and nods, glancing at his Invicta watch. "I ain't got nowhere to be, so try." He takes a sip of his drink. Then belches. "My bad."

I shake my head.

"So you gonna give up all dis"—he sits back in his seat, spreading open his arms while making the muscles in his chest bounce—"for dat dude?"

I nod. And although I am certain of my decision, I feel horrible. But I'm not sure why. Yes, I do. It's because I was really starting to like him, too. But Malik won me over more. And now my heart is all wrapped up in him.

"I think I love him, Blaze," I admit softly.

"Didn't you just up and meet dude?"

"So," I say defensively. "Time is all relative. I know him enough to know how I feel about him."

He frowns. "But you don't even know dude. Riddle me dis, then I'ma leave it alone: You smokin' wit' him?"

"Yeah, a few times. Why?"

He nods his head. "How many times he got you sneakin' outta da house?"

"I beg your pardon." Indignation rises in my voice. "Malik doesn't have me doing anything I don't want to do."

"Yeah, but I bet he doesn't tell you not to, either."

"No. He doesn't. Still, that doesn't make him a bad influence either."

"Did I say that?"

I roll my eyes at him. "Well, no. But you implied it."

"Nah, I simply asked a question."

"Boy, bye! Fall back with that dumb ish," I say without thinking. I shock myself.

He grins and then runs his tongue across his lips.

"What? Why are you looking at me like that?"

He folds his arms across his chest and cocks his head sideways, taking me all in. "You changin', yo."

I give him a shocked look. "No I'm not. I'm still the same girl."

He shakes his head. "Nah, you different, ma." He narrows his eyes. "What, you let him hit dat?"

I swallow. Shift in my seat. "Why would you ask me something like that?"

"You just have dat look, yo. Dats all."

"What look?" I ask curiously.

"If you ain't lettin' him hit it, then it don't matter, does it?"

"No, but I still want to know what you mean by that."

"He hit dat yet?"

I frown, feeling uncomfortable. "That's none of your business."

He stares at me, grinning. "Yeah, you right."

I watch him finish up the rest of his fries, trying like heck to keep my gaze off his lips. I suddenly feel as if I'm cheating on Malik by having thoughts of how good Hazel Eyes' lips felt on me. Those are not thoughts I should still be having, right? I mean, we only fooled around twice. His lips are the last thing I should be daydreaming about, right?

Ohmygod! What in the heck am I doing here with this boy? What was I thinking agreeing to meet him here behind Malik's back?

I glance at my watch. It's a quarter to four. I push back my chair and stand. "Hey, I gotta get going. I'm supposed to meet my friend Jordan at four o'clock down in front of Sephora."

"Oh, a'ight," he says, scratching his chin and looking up at me.

"Okay, then. I'll see you around, I guess."

"No doubt. Be easy." I turn to leave, but he says something that stops me in my tracks. "That dude ain't right for you, Kennedy. I ain't 'bout kickin' no one's back in, feel me? But dude ain't gonna do nothin' but bring you down, yo."

I blink. "Why would you say that?"

"I'm just sayin'…be careful, babe." He tears his gaze away from mine and chomps heartily on the last bit of his sandwich.

I walk away without saying a word.

*   *   *

For the next three weeks, Malik and I become inseparable. I spend every day with him, sneaking off to be with
him, some—no, most—nights not even bothering to go
home. I've even quit my job just so I can have more time
with him. Well, actually, to be perfectly honest, Malik sug-
gested I quit. So I did. He said he didn't want to have to
share me with a job. That he'd give me whatever I made
every two weeks, plus an extra few hundred dollars.

My boo wants me all to himself.

Still...so much has happened in such a short period of
time.

My mom and I, all we do is fight now, almost every day.
Blaze no longer calls me. And it's really for the best, anyway. Then there's my strained relationship with Hope and
Jordan. Every since I told them in confidence about Malik
they've been against us being together. Well, moreso Jordan than Hope. Still, they both seem to have something
snide to say about it. So I don't spend as much time with
them anymore. Mostly because I get tired of them bash-
ing Malik, who they don't even know. And bad-mouthing
Sasha—who they've never met—like they're so perfect. I
feel like I shouldn't have to constantly defend my boyfriend,
or whom I want to hang out with, to them. Or to anyone, for
that matter.

With Hope and Jordan, I feel like I am constantly under
a microscope with them dissecting every little thing I say.
It's become too exhausting trying to get them to respect
my choices. So I've slowly distanced myself from them.

Besides, Malik feels it's for the best.

And I agree with him.

"Yo, I know they ya girlz 'n' all, but if they ain't tryna
have anything good to say, then you need'a cut 'em off.

Dey need to stop hatin' on ya man, yo. All dat negativity is for the birds, yo."

"You're right," I said, deciding right then and there to deal with them on a very limited basis. And I have been.

Malik stands behind me, hugging me. I can't lie. I won't lie. Malik's arms feel so good wrapped around me. I feel so wanted, so needed…so special.

"I can hold you in my arms forever, baby," he says, kissing the back of my neck. Then pauses. "Yo what you thinkin' 'bout, huh?"

I smile, glancing up at him over my shoulder. "You."

He grins. "Dats watz up, baby." His cell starts ringing. He plucks his phone from off his hip, glancing at the screen. "Yo waddup? Oh, word? When? Oh, a'ight, bet. No doubt, no doubt…I got you. A'ight, bet." He ends the call, then brings his attention back to me. "Check it, baby. I gotta make a quick run tonight."

My mood immediately turns sour. He promised to take me out to dinner tonight. I look at him. My body stiffens. "A run where?"

He frowns. "Yo, wat I tell you 'bout questionin' me, huh?"

"I'm only asking. I thought we were going to go into the city tonight; that's all. I was really looking forward to it."

"We was, but somethin' came up I gotta handle."

"Oh," I say, disappointed. "Well, what am I supposed to do while you're gone?"

He looks at me as if I've asked the dumbest question in the world. "Wait for me. What else?"

I frown. Try to break out of his embrace, but he is holding on tight. He turns me around to face him. "What, you mad now?"

"Nope." I turn away from him, walking toward the door.

He grabs me. "Where you goin'?"

"Home," I say, pouting.

He smirks. "Oh, word? And how you gettin' there?"

Oops. I hadn't thought about that.

I shrug. "I don't know. Walk."

He chuckles. But I don't see anything amusing. "Yo, stop. You ain't walkin' nowhere. And you ain't leavin'."

I suck my teeth and cross my arms. "I wanna go home."

He smiles, looking me up and down.

"Nah, not tonight. You lookin' 'n' smellin' too good to go home." He pulls me into his arms, then kisses me on my forehead, then the tip of my nose, then lightly on my lips. He presses himself into me. Then starts grinding real slow and nasty-like into me. I can feel his excitement growing. "I need you." He glances at his watch. "C'mon. Let's lay down real quick."

"Are you going to see some other girl?" I ask, feeling insecurity creep into my heart. I can't help but remember what his sister has said about him. Even though I know she was only saying those things to be messy and I've never told Malik everything she's said about him, her words linger in the back of my mind.

"Ain't no other girl, yo. It's me 'n' you, ya heard?"

I nod. "It better be."

Malik gently grabs my chin and turns my face toward him. "Da only girl I'm checkin' for, Kennedy, is you, baby. You know dat, right?"

I look into his eyes for any signs of deceit. There are none. My disposition softens. I nod. "Yes."

He grins. And then there's the sound of his pants being unzipped. "You my everything, baby; ya heard?"

I swallow and nod. "Yes."

The last thing I remember before removing all of my clothes and getting swept up in the heat of his hands and kisses is him saying, "Let's make a baby..."

31

"Girl, my period late," I hear Mercedes telling some-one on her cell as I walk into the kitchen to get something to drink. She's leaning over the sink, staring out of the window into the backyard.

She looks over her shoulder at me when she sees me going to the refrigerator. She sucks her teeth, straightening her body. "I don't need to take no test. I already know I am. My period is never late unless...uh-huh. Girl, who knows." She laughs. "I tol' dat nucca to pull out...girl, please. I was lit dat night 'n' besides it was feelin' too good."

She laughs again.

I pour myself some apple juice in a glass, trying to act like I'm not listening in on her conversation. I take a few slow sips.

Mercedes glances over at me, rolling her eyes. "Can I get some privacy? Unh-uh...Malik's li'l girlfriend he keeps leavin' over here. Mmph...don't even get me started."

She shoots another look at me, then rolls her eyes up in her head.

I press my lips tight, blinking my eyes real hard. *Why is she so dang hateful?*

I quickly drink the rest of my juice, then wash and dry the cup out, put it back, then go back into Malik's bedroom. As soon as I get ready to turn on the TV and lie across the bed, Malik texts me and says he's on his way home. He wants me to heat up his food in the refrigerator. Now I have to go back into the kitchen. I suck my teeth, going to the bathroom, first, to wash my hands, then back out into the kitchen, hoping Mercedes is nowhere in sight.

She is.

I take a deep breath. Brace myself.

I can feel her eyes on me as I flit around the kitchen, pulling down a plate from out of the cabinet, then rinsing it off before placing his takeout from Munchies—a Jamaican restaurant in South Orange—onto his plate and putting it in the toaster oven.

I turn to walk out, catch Mercedes staring at me.

"You really think you got da magic touch, don't you?"

"Huh?" I ask, confused. "What do you mean by that?"

She twists her lips up. "It means, you really think Malik's all into you, don't you?"

I shrug. "He says he is."

She laughs. "Nuccas say anything to anyone stupid enough to believe 'em."

I blink. "I don't think I'm stupid."

She laughs again. "You'se a lie. But dat's a matter of opinion."

"How many months are you?" I ask, trying to change

the subject. And I immediately regret having ever said a word to her.

"Why?" she says nastily.

I shrug. "I was only asking."

"No, you were just bein' nosy. Tryna be all up in my business. You really think you betta than me don't you?"

"No. Of course not," I say incredulously. "I don't think that about anyone."

"Yes you do!" she snaps. "But you ain't. Just because you come from a little change dat don't make you better than me."

"I know it doesn't."

She rolls her eyes. "Mmph, it sure doesn't. But keep actin' like it does 'n' see what happens."

I blink.

Then, without thinking about whether or not I should say it, without editing it in my mind first, I ask, "Do you know who the baby's father is?"

Her eyes darken. Her face hardens into an ugly stare. "*Bish*, yeah, I know who my baby *fahver* is. See. Dis why don't nobody 'round here like you. You too nosy 'n' stay tryna talk slick."

I think to tell her I didn't mean it like that. But before I can open my mouth to plead my case, her mother walks into the kitchen and says, "Mercedes, I know you ain't even pregnant, again? Is you?"

Mercedes shoots a dirty look over at me, then sucks her teeth. "You see, *thot*. You 'n' ya big mouth."

"I asked you a question," her mother says, glaring at her. "Is you knocked up again?"

Mercedes looks at her mother and nods.

Her mother rolls her eyes, shaking her head. "See, dis here don't make no sense. You just had a baby three months ago 'n' ya knocked up, again. Mmph. What you gonna do wit' four babies? I know you ain't even tryna have it, is you?"

Mercedes shrugs. "I don't know yet."

"Wat you mean you don't know yet, huh? You betta hope DYFS takes dis one, too, 'cause I ain't watchin' no kids."

I blink. *Three babies?* She's only twenty-one! Ohmygod! I thought she only had the little girl.

"I said I don't know," she snaps back at her mother. "Now get off my case about it. I'll let you know wat I'ma do when I know wat I'ma do."

I quietly ease out of the kitchen, leaving the two of them there to argue. I want no part of any of their family squabble.

Ten minutes later, I go back out to the kitchen to check on Malik's plate. Mercedes comes back into the kitchen wearing a smirk on her smug face. "Someone's here to see you."

I give her a confused look. "Someone's here to see who, *me?*"

She twists her lips up. "Umm, did I stutter? Who else do you see in da room? Yeah, *you.*"

"Who is it?"

She shoots me a dirty look. "Do I look like ya butler? You'll see when you get to da door."

I turn the oven off, then remove the food. "Okay, well let me wrap up Malik's plate, first." I pull out the aluminum foil from underneath the sink, wrap his plate up, place it back into the oven, then walk out into the living room.

I think I see her lips curl into a sly smirk.

32

"Hi. Are you looking for me?" I say guardedly, walking to the door. The brown-skinned girl at the door, with the clenched jaws and menacing scowl on her face, is unfamiliar to me. Her hair is pulled back into half a teeny ponytail. There isn't much hair gathered up into her red scrunchie sitting up on top of her head. Still, she wears it proudly with bangs slicked down over her forehead. A weave-piece, I think. She has one hand up on her hip. The other hangs to her side, balled up into a tight fist.

"You Kennedy, right?"

I nod. "Yes. That's me."

She narrows her eyes. "Then yeah, *bish*, I'm lookin' for *you*!"

For a split second, I think I hear someone in back of me giggle. But I can't be for certain. Yet I am not willing to take my eyes off the girl in front of me to see who's behind me.

"W-why?" I stammer, holding on tightly to the screen door handle.

"You know Sha?"

"Who?"

"Don't even front. You know who *Sha* is. *Shaheed.* The boy you were upstairs at dat party trickin' wit', then lied 'n' said he tried to rape you."

I blink. "I-I..."

My mind quickly scrambles back to that night. The only two people who I told were Malik and Sasha. I try to remember if I'd ever used the word *rape*. I don't remember.

My heart starts pounding.

"I never said he tried to rape me."

"*Bish*, yes you did! Don't lie; you dirty cockteaser!"

I blink. And then it comes back to me. What I'd said to Malik that night.

"H-h-he tried to rape me..."

Ohgod!

"I-I didn't mean that," I say quickly. I can't believe how much my voice cracks. "It's just that he wouldn't stop grabbing on me when I told him to stop."

"Yeah right, trick. And you wanted it."

I shake my head. "No, I didn't. I didn't even know him."

She scoffs. "You dumb *bish*! Then why you even go upstairs wit' him if you didn't know him, huh? Don't even try to act like you didn't know what time it was."

"I swear. I didn't know. I thought he only wanted to talk."

"Well, he didn't. And you know it. Then you gonna lie 'n' get him jumped."

"I didn't do that. I swear."

"Yes you did. And now you 'bout to see how it feels. So you need'a step outside so we can handle dis woman-to-woman."

I swallow.

I can't lie. I am desperately afraid. And I don't know why. I mean, I do know why. There's a tall, thick girl with big hands standing on the other side of the door sneering at me.

I haven't done anything to anyone, and especially not to her or the four other girls standing in back of her. But clearly, judging by her hostility toward me, she seems hell-bent on thinking that I have wronged her in some way.

And I can tell just by the way she's glaring at me that she isn't interested in hearing anything I have to say. And neither do any of her friends. They're not here to talk. She's here to kick my butt.

All of a sudden my eyes get watery.

And the only thing that stands between me and what I'm beginning to think, *feel,* is going to become my worst nightmare is flimsy mesh in a metal frame. I hold the door handle even tighter.

"Trick, I said come outside!"

I swallow.

She's now up on the tiny porch, one hand up on her hip; the other pointing at me through the screen like it's a gun. Her face is so close to the screen, I can feel her hot breath through the torn mesh.

I try not to look at her. Instead I focus on the scary black snake she has tattooed on the side of her neck.

And I feel like crying.

"Goddammit, Mercedes!" I hear Malik's mom yell in back of me. "Who is at my front door wit' all dat noise? You know I ain't for no ratchetness early in da day!"

"Dats some chicks from around da way for Malik's li'l

girlfriend," she says. She sounds amused. "Looks like she done got caught up in some drama."

"Say what? I know one thang, li'l Miss Uppity betta go on 'n' take dat mess away from my goddamn door. Tell her I said to go outside wit' dat mess! I don't know why Malik left her here anyway, like we some babysittin' service."

I cringe. And the next thing I know, I am stumbling out the door as it swings open and hits Snake Neck. I've been pushed from behind. I am caught totally off guard. So is Snake Neck. Before I can break away, or even scream for help, she lunges at me.

"Bish! I'ma kill you!"*

She grabs me by the shirt and punches me in the jaw. I am no street fighter. Heck, I'm not any kind of fighter. But this girl is. And she is out for blood.

I scream.

Her friends circle us, cheering her on.

"Beat her face in!" someone yells out.

Next thing I know I feel Snake Neck's razor-sharp fingernails clawing into my face, like she's trying to peel my skin off.

Instinct and desperation set in and my arms and hands take on a life of their own. I start swinging wildly. I wind-mill her up. My fingers clawing at her hair, my nails digging into her skin: there is no one here to help me and I am fighting for my life.

I hear people yelling, "Fight! Fight!"

But I am not sure who or where it's coming from.

I can't believe this is happening to me. All because of some boy who tried to have sex with me. All because Malik had him beat up. All because Sasha had to go off and leave me alone at some party I had no business being at.

Someone knees me.

Someone else punches me in the back of the head.

Ohmygod!

I am being jumped.

Someone else's hand wraps around my hair.

I am being yanked and punched and kicked.

I feel the tears burning my eyes and rolling down my face as I try to fight these girls off me. I struggle to hang on to Snake Neck's hair, struggle to not hit the ground, knowing that it will be over for me if I do.

I bite Snake Neck's arm. She yelps. Hits me upside the head. But I don't let go. I tighten my grip and try to rip a chunk of her arm out. Now she is screaming. And her friends are punching and kicking, harder and faster.

Snake Neck and I both hit the ground. I am on top of her. Her crew is now stomping and kicking me. My stomach and side and chest hurt.

"Yo, what da *fuqq*!" I hear someone yelling. "Get da *fuqq* up offa her!" Then I feel someone yanking bodies off of me.

It's Malik.

33

Speak now or forever hold you peace...
"I've been holding back from saying this," Jordan says, slipping out of her leather open-toed Giuseppe sandals, the ones her mom bought her at the beginning of summer from Barney's New York. "Because I don't want this to turn into an ugly argument."

I reach for the new Ni-Ni Simone book my mom bought me and left up on my dresser for me. I guess it's her way of trying to make up with me. For the last week we've been fighting constantly, especially after I came home over a week ago beat up and bruised up from when those girls jumped me.

She was pissed.

"I want you to tell me who those girls were. Then we're going down to file assault charges on them."

I wouldn't cooperate. I refused to tell her anything. And I didn't want her to press charges. Truth is, there wasn't anything to tell. I didn't know much of anything where any of those girls were concerned. No names. No addresses. Nothing.

Anyway, back to this book. My mom knows how much I love all of Ni-Ni Simone's books. I have her whole collection. But, as I sit here flipping through the pages, it feels like forever since I've picked up a book—*any* book—and read it.

Fact is, the last book I read was two weeks before the school semester ended, over a month and a half ago. Seems like so much has changed since then.

I look over at Jordan, closing the book. "You don't want *what* to turn into an argument?"

She lifts her feet up onto my bed. "How I feel about what you've been doing over the summer so far."

I frown. "What do you mean, *what* I've been doing so far?"

"You know, hanging out all the time, smoking, drinking..."

"Ohmygod! I only drank once."

"Yeah, and you got really drunk. I'm still really bothered by that. You could have died from alcohol poisoning or something."

I roll my eyes, sucking my teeth. "But I didn't. It wasn't that serious. So next."

"Well, it could have been," she says back. "How do you even know someone didn't put something in your cup?"

"Jordan, stop! You really need to lay off the *CSI* episodes. No one put anything in my drink..." *I hope no one did. No, of course not! Sasha wouldn't have done anything like that. She's not like that.*

"How do you know that? Did you see them make it in front of you?"

I raise my brow. "Well, no. But Sasha got it for me."

She gives me a blank stare.

"Look. Forget it. I don't want to rehash that. Yeah, I drank, got drunk, and threw up everywhere..." *And practically took all your clothes off.* "It happened once. And I haven't touched alcohol since. I'm never drinking again. I learned my lesson."

"I'm glad you did. But what if someone would have taken advantage of you? Anything could have happened to you."

That boy Shaheed's face pops into my head, his hands groping all over me. I shake the thought. "But no one's taken advantage of me. So stop saying that. And I don't appreciate you bringing all this up way after the fact. So moving on. What else?"

"Well, you don't have to get all snippy. I'm only sharing how I feel."

"I'm not getting snippy. I just don't feel like hearing shoulda, coulda, wouldas today. But whatever. What else you wanna get off your mind?"

"Honestly, Kennedy, I think you're getting in way too deep with this new crowd you're hanging with. I don't like that you sneak out and you're having sex with that boy. I feel like you're moving too quick. You don't even really know him."

"Ohmygod, Jordan! You say that like he's some random guy. He's *my* boyfriend."

"Yeah, one you have to keep secret from you parents. What kind of boyfriend is that?"

"See, I knew I should have never told you about any of that."

"That's what friends do. Confide in each other."

"Yeah. But they don't turn around and throw it back in your face, either."

"I'm not throwing it in your face. I'm simply stating how I feel. That's also what friends do when they care about each other. They share how they feel. I mean, I am allowed to feel how I feel, aren't I?"

I shrug. "You can feel however you want. I can't tell you how you should feel."

"Exactly. And, right now, I feel like your loyalty to Hope and me has changed."

"How do you mean, my loyalty's changed? I'm always loyal to both of you."

She gives me a look of disbelief. "Oh, really?"

"Wait. Is this about me ditching going to the mall to hang out with Sasha?"

"Well, yes. No. I mean, every since you started hanging out with that trashy Sasha girl and sneaking around with that drug slinger you've been acting real different," Jordan says softly.

"Ohmygod, I can't believe you'd say that."

"Well, it's how I feel."

"Well, first off, his name is Malik," I correct with attitude. "Secondly, he's not a *drug* slinger. And third of all, Sasha isn't trashy. So don't say anything negative about her 'cause you don't know her. All you ever do is judge."

"Ohmygod, Kennedy! I'm not judging anyone. Are you that dumb and blind? That boy is a drug dealer and you know it. So stopping lying to yourself."

"I'm not lying to myself."

"And that's a lie right there. That's all you've been doing is lying. Lying to your parents. Lying to Hope and me. Lying, lying, lying. But you go ahead and believe it. Maybe one day it might all become true. But for now, I don't care what lies come out of your mouth. Your little thug boy is a drug dealer and—"

"He is not! So stop saying that about him."

"Oh really? Then *what* is he then, huh, Kennedy? Because I know and *you* know he *isn't* a trust fund baby. And he *isn't* the owner of some Fortune Five Hundred company and he isn't working on Wall Street. And we *both* know he *isn't* a doctor or a lawyer. So if your high school dropout boyfriend isn't a drug dealer, then what is he? How does he afford that Range Rover and all that jewelry and all those fancy clothes he's been buying you, huh?"

"From his lawsuit," I blurt out.

Jordan gives a fake, restrained laugh. "And you believed that? Hahahaha! How special. What lawsuit, Kennedy?"

"That's none of your business!" I snap. "And I don't appreciate you trying to be all up in my man's business. Or mine!"

"Wellllll, *excuuuuuse* the heck out of me," she says defensively. "You want me out of your business. Fine. I'm out of it. But don't you dare pick up the phone and come crying to me when your man and your new bestie both drag you down into the gutters with them."

She's gone too far. I can tell I've hurt her feelings. But oh well. She's hurt mine as well.

I take a deep breath. Collect my thoughts. Check my emotions. Then say, "Listen, Jordan. I don't need this crap from you. I don't want to fight with you, okay?"

"Well, I don't want to fight with you either. But I don't like what that boy is doing to you. He's changing you. He's no good for you. And the only thing he's going to do is bring you down, Kennedy. You are worth so much more than what you're becoming."

I huff. "And *what* is it you actually *think* I'm becoming, Jordan?"

"I've already said it. Ghetto."

I blink. "Why? Because I don't wanna always talk proper. Because every now and then I wanna use slang words? That's not me trying to be anything."

"Yes, it is," she counters, giving me an incredulous look. "That's you trying to be"—she makes quotation marks with her fingers—"down. The way you're now dressing, the way you're talking, and even the way you're sitting here now with your lips all twisted up. You're trying to be something you're not."

"That is so not true," I retort indignantly. "Why don't you just stop hating on me?"

She grunts. *"Hating* on *you*? Is that what you call it, me being concerned about my friend hanging with the wrong crowd and going down the wrong path? That's *hating* to you? Really, Kennedy? How priceless. You're taking up for the same girl who just a few weeks back bullied you and treated you like crap. Now all of a sudden she's your hero." She rolls her eyes. "Mmmph. How epic."

Jordan sounds jealous to me. Maybe she is. Or am I being paranoid?

"I mean, I've been trying to be sympathetic to your obsessive need to frolic with that kind of element." She shakes her head. "But, it's getting increasingly more disturbing. Hope and I were talking about it last night and she agrees."

I blink. Somehow I feel betrayed. Hurt. That the two of

them have been talking about *me* behind my back like this. I thought they were my friends.

"*Ohmygod!*" I shriek. "*Bish*, bye! Are you effen serious? I can't believe you and Hope have been dogging me out behind my back."

"We haven't been *dogging* you. We've been discussing our concerns; that's all. It's like you're changing." Jordan pauses for a second, then adds, "And you're even acting real ghetto now."

I am taken aback. Literally floored that she would say something like this to me. That I'm acting ghetto. What the heck is *acting* ghetto?

"I'm acting ghetto, how?"

"Listen to yourself. You sound just like one of those section-eight girls. Acting all ghetto-fabulous."

"Are you effen kidding me? Ohmygod, Jordan! Have several seats! And go find your life! I can't believe you just said that. How am I acting ghetto-fabulous? Please explain."

She plants a hand on her hip, jerking her neck from side to side. "You're acting *ghet-to*...right now. Cursing and telling me to have *several seats*. That's that gutter-trash talk."

There's no need for her to be getting all snip-snappy with me. Shoot, she's lucky I still want to hang out with her lame butt. But if she can't respect my boo and my friendship with Sasha, then I'm going to have to cut her off.

I eye Jordan as she eases up from off my bed, then hooks the straps of her handbag into the crook of her arm.

"I miss my best friend," she says. "I can't do this with you, Kennedy."

I tilt my head. Give her a quizzical look. "You can't do what with me, Jordan?"

"This. Watching you become this stranger. I can't sit back and silently watch you ruin your life."

I frown. "I'm not ruining my life. I'm having fun. Something you should try having instead of always being so uptight and stuck-up."

She blinks. "Is that how you see me? Uptight and stuck-up?"

"It's the truth, Jordan. That's what you are. A joy-killer. My god, no wonder no one likes you."

Her eyes fill with hurt. Her bottom lip quivers.

I quickly regret ever saying those words. But it's too late. It's out now. And I can't take them back. "I-I'm sorry. I didn't mean it like that."

"Wow. Don't apologize for how you feel. You meant exactly what you said. That's probably the only honest thing you've said all summer."

"Jordan, I—"

She puts a hand up. Stops me from finishing my sentence. "The truth hurts. But I'll get over it. Just like I'll get over *you* and our friendship." I eye her as she removes her friendship bracelet. "This girl you've become isn't the girl I want to associate with any longer. Call me stuck-up. Call me uptight. Call me a joy-killer. Call me whatever you want." She pauses. I can tell she's holding back tears. "The only person I've *ever* cared about liking me is you."

I feel like I'm going to cry myself. I know where this is going. I can feel it in my bones. An aching. My chest tightens. We've had plenty of fights. But none that have ever felt like this one. Absolute. Final. Like there is no coming back from it.

I stand up, reach over and gently place my hand on her shoulder. We'd been friends, besties, sisters, for like forever. But, in a snap, words have suddenly changed that. I feel like I am about to lose a piece of myself.

"I'm so sorry."

A tear slides out from Jordan's eye as she stares at my hand. Neither of us says anything for a long, pained moment. She removes my hand from her shoulder. Lays her bracelet down across my nightstand before finally breaking the heavy silence between us.

Her lip quivers. "So am I," she says somberly, and walks out the door.

34

"Kennedy, where have you been?" My mom wants to know the second I step through the double doors. She greets me at the door with a dagger-like glare. Her face painted into a tight scowl.

"Out," I tell her, briskly walking through the foyer, tossing my house keys up on the round foyer table centered in the middle of the entryway.

"I know you were *out! Out where?!*" she snaps, hot on my heels. "You've been gone for almost twenty-four hours. How many times do we have to keep going through this, you leaving up out of this house and going missing for two and three days? And who was that you were sitting out in our driveway with in that Range Rover?"

It was Malik. But that's none of her business. He'd dropped me off before heading into the city to take care of something. Lately, it seems like that's all he does is *take care of something* in the city. But I try not to question him because he doesn't like it. He thinks it's disrespectful for a girl to question her man. I would never do that. And I don't ever want him to think I'm being disrespectful to him.

"You're to look pretty and be seen, yo. Not heard," he told me when I asked him the other day why he had to go into New York all the time. "I ain't effen wit' no broad who's gonna give me grief e'erytime I gotta make a move, ya heard? I dig you, real spit, baby. But you gotta stay in ya lane. Word to da mother. You need'a fall back or I'ma have to replace you, feel me?"

I blinked, caught totally off guard. My heart dropped. I couldn't believe he'd break up with me for asking him one simple question. I wasn't trying to be nosy, or get all up in his business. I truly just wanted to know. But to Malik my asking was "out of line," as he called it. So this time I kept my mouth shut when he mentioned where he was going. I didn't want to upset him. And I didn't want to ever be replaced.

Anyway, before letting me go inside, he'd reached over and given me a long passionate kiss, then told me how much he already missed me.

I couldn't help but blush.

I felt special.

He always makes me feel special. Like I'm his everything.

I know he's mine.

Still... I wish he didn't insist on me coming back here. To this house. With *her*. But ever since those girls came over to his house to fight me he says he doesn't want me left there alone. And he doesn't want me hanging with Sasha, either.

So I'm stuck here. And now I have to hear her mouth.

I don't know why he just couldn't take me with him!

"Kennedy, do you hear me talking to you?"

I ignore her, walking into the kitchen to grab a glass of cranberry-pomegranate juice. I fill my glass, then drink it down in four big gulps. I pour another glass.

So what if I've been gone since yesterday. I was out with Malik. We spent the whole day down at Six Flags, then went to grab something to eat at the Cheesecake Factory. Afterward, Malik brought me back to his place—well, his mom's apartment—and we smoked and cuddled. And kissed. And well, you probably already know what happened next.

"Do you hear me talking to you, young lady? I asked you a question. I'm getting tired of you thinking you can do whatever you like around here!"

I take a deep breath. "I heard you the first time. Dang. Get off my back."

"Then answer me, dammit. And don't you dare use that language or that tone in this house at me."

I shoot her a nasty look. "Oh, but it's okay for you to use it at me. I don't think so." I gulp down the last of my drink, then set my empty glass into the sink.

Mom slams a hand up on her hip. Her nose flares. "Don't you question me, young lady! I'm the parent! I'm the adult! Not you!"

I let out a disgusted grunt. "You're such a hypocrite."

"*Whaaaat?!* Oh you have really lost your mind!"

"I haven't lost anything," I snap. "I'm finally standing up for myself. I'm living my own life."

"Kennedy, what has gotten into you, huh?! You've never spoken to me like this. You leave up out of here and half the time don't let me know where you're going. Or you tell me you're going to be one place and then I find out you weren't even there. Your brothers never pulled half the stunts you're pulling."

"Well, get over it," I snap. "I'm not the perfect little goody two-shoes that my brothers were. It's not my fault they were a bunch of nerdy pricks! How about this: I don't wanna be the perfect daughter. I don't wanna follow your stupid house rules. I don't wanna be stuck in this prison camp. I wanna go out and have fun. I'm sixteen years old. I shouldn't have to have some dumb curfew or have you tryna control my every move. I'm sick of you!"

My mom's jaw drops. Then in one swift motion she is in my face, the palm of her hand slicing into my cheek.

Slap!

"Don't you ever—and I do mean ever—talk to me like that as long as you live. I brought you into this world, little girl. And I will snatch you out of it! I keep warning you! I will *not* have that talk in my house!" She yanks me by the arm. "Do you *understand* me?! You will not disrespect me! I am your mother. Not one of those skanky little girls you're trying so hard to be like! I will not tolerate it! *This* is *not* you, Kennedy!"

"You don't know *who* or *what* I am," I shoot back, yanking my arm from her. In all of my sixteen years of life, she's never hit me. I've never even experienced a spanking as a child. Time-outs and loss of privileges are the only forms of punishment ever dished out in our house. Until this very second.

She gives me a pained look. Then shakes her head in frustration. "You're right. I don't know you. Not anymore. All I know is, the girl that's standing in front of me wearing that godawful hoochie-momma outfit and hooker heels is not the daughter I've raised. And I will *not* allow this kind of dress in this house. Your breasts are practically popping out of that blouse and that little skirt you have on is barely covering your behind. It's not acceptable."

I know I should apologize, or even run out of the kitchen and simply slam my bedroom door, but I don't. The stinging in my cheek won't let me. The voice inside my head won't let me. They both tell me otherwise. Tell me to rebel.

And I do.

"You know what?" I say, putting my hands on my hips. "Screw you! I'm sick of you trying to ruin my life! You don't own me! I don't have to listen to you! I can wear what I want. I'm sixteen! And grown! I can do what the heck I want, when I—"

Slap!

"Oh no you can't! And you won't!" *Slap!* Her palm slams into the side of my face causing my ears to ring. And this time tears spring from my eyes as I grab hold of my face, stunned that I've been hit again. She glares at me. "*You* are *not* grown! Not here in my house! Not at sixteen! Not as long as your father and I take care of you, you're not! Now I don't know where you're getting your information from, but you've been sadly misinformed. At sixteen, young lady, you are nowhere near grown. You may *think* you are. But I am still responsible for you. You will do as you are told! Now get your smart-mouth behind upstairs, take off those street clothes and go wash your face! You're grounded!"

"I hate you!" I scream, stomping up the stairs.

35

"Screw her!" I mutter to myself, snatching open my dresser drawers and tossing everything into my designer duffle bag. "I don't have to take this crap from her. I'm outta here!" I rush into my walk-in closet and start yanking clothes off hangers and stuffing them into my bag. "Putting her hands on me like that! I hate her!"

I grab my phone and text Sasha, giving her the 4-1-1 and asking her to come get me. Five minutes after I send the text, my cell rings. It's her.

"She did what?"

"She slapped me," I repeat, walking over to my wall mirror and looking at the bruise she's left on the side of my face.

"For what?"

"Because she's such an evil witch," I say, pacing my floor. "All because I didn't come home."

"You ain't come home one night 'n' she's spazzin' on you like dat? Girl, you need to handle her. You prolly should call the police on her."

"No. I can't do that. She's still my mom."

She grunts. "Mmph. Whatever. Do you, boo. All I know is, your momz be buggin'."

"I know. All she wants to do is try to ruin my life. She acts like I'm out in the streets committing crimes or something. All I'm tryna do is have some fun before it's time to go back to school."

"Girl, you betta get yo' life! Ain't nobody got time for dat! You need to pack your ish 'n' get up outta dere! Mmph. I wish my momz would. I know you effed her up real good for dat, right?"

I blink. *Is this girl serious? First she says I should call the police on her. Now she's asking me if I hit her.*

Fighting my mom isn't something I've ever considered. I mean, talking back is one thing, but to fight her. No. That's going way too far. I don't care how pissed I get at her, I don't think I can ever hit her.

She starts laughing. "Oops. I forgot who I was talkin' to. Li'l Miss Scaredy-Cat. You know you an undercover Oreo. So you betta do what dem white girls do 'n' stomp her lights out."

I blink.

She keeps laughing. But I don't see anything funny. "You know dem rich white girlz you roll wit' down at dat fancy school you go to be whippin' da hot dog piss outta dey mommas. Then again, you prolly wouldn't. I know you ain't got it in you to go wit' da hands."

"She's my mom," I say defensively. "I can't hit her."

"Oh, but it's okay for her to put her hands on you, right? Girl, bye. Miss me wit' dat."

"I disrespected her," I counter. "I shouldn't have spoken to her like that."

She sucks her teeth. "And she disrespected *you*. Smacking you up. She shoulda kept her hands to herself. Girl, bye. Miss me wit' dat dumbness. Momz or not, she crossed da line puttin' her hands on you, boo. But whatever. She's your headache. Not mine. So what you gonna do now?"

"I don't know. I was hopin' you could come get me."

"When? Now?"

"Yeah. If you don't mind."

"Girl, I do mind. I'm gettin' ready to get my box beat up."

"Oh."

"Where's Malik?"

"He went into the city. And probably won't get back until late. I gotta get out of here."

"Well, did you call him?" I tell her no. Tell her she was the first person I called. "Well, I think you should holla at ya man 'n' see what he says."

I swallow. "Yeah. I guess you're right."

"Hit me later," she says just before the line goes dead.

I pull my cell from my ear and stare at it. *How rude!* It rings again, startling me. My stomach lurches as I glance at the screen.

Oh God!

I answer the call on the fourth ring. "Hello."

"Kennedy?"

"Yes, Daddy. It's me."

"I just got off the phone with your mother," he says calmly. "She's extremely upset. She says you've been sneaking out and becoming extremely disrespectful. Is this true?"

"D-daddy, I-I . . ."

"Answer the question, Kennedy. It's a yes or no."

I fall silent as tears roll down my face. Daddy has never

raised his voice to me, and whenever I've had to be disciplined he's always left it to my mom.

"Kennedy?"

"Yes. I'm here."

"Then say something. I need for you to tell me what in the heck is going on there. Because what I've heard so far, I am not liking."

"I don't care," I blurt out.

"Excuse me? Young lady, what did you say to me?"

"I said I don't care. I'm sick of being told what to do. I want to live my own life. I'm old enough to make my own decisions."

"Kennedy, sweetheart," Daddy says calmly. "What has gotten into you? This is not you. Your mother says you've been drinking and hanging out with a wrong crowd."

"Ohmygod! She's such a traitor. She promised me she wouldn't tell you about the drinking. It was only one time. I got drunk. And I didn't like it. It was no big deal."

"It is a big deal when you don't come home," he says, raising his voice. "Your mother is worried sick about you."

"Well, she can stop. I don't need her worrying about me. I can take care of myself."

"Wait a minute. Where is all this hostility and disrespect coming from?"

"I'm not being hostile. I'm just sick of Mom not trusting me. I'm old enough to make my own decisions."

"Listen, sweetheart, you're right. You can make some decisions for yourself. And your mom and I both need to be able to trust you to do what's right. I know that you may think you're old enough to know what's best for you, Kennedy. But right now, your drastic change in behavior says otherwise. I'm flying home Friday evening. I'll be home early Saturday morning. We'll talk about this then. Understand?"

I sigh. "Yes."

"Good. Now do me a favor and go apologize to your mother, then promise me you won't do..."

The line goes dead. I disconnect the call. I didn't want to hear anything else he had to say. I'm not apologizing to my mom. And I wasn't going to promise him anything. Malik promised to take me to this big party this weekend. And nothing, or no one, is going to stop me from going.

My cell rings back. It's Daddy calling again. I let the call roll into voice mail. When he calls back a third time, I hit IGNORE. There's nothing else to talk about. I've made up my mind. And he's made up his.

I call Malik. "Yo, whaddup?"

"I got into a big fight with my mom," I tell him. "She slapped me. And now I have to get out of here. What time are you coming back to Jersey?"

"Whoa, whoa...slow down. Run dat by me again." I repeat myself. "Why she go off like dat?"

I shake my head as if he can see me through the phone. "She's crazy. All I know is I have to get away from her."

"A'ight. Did you call Sasha?"

"Yeah, I did. But she didn't sound like she was interested in coming to get me. She told me to call you."

"Oh, a'ight. I gotta go uptown real quick, then should be headin' back dat way in a few. You think you can stay put until I can get there?"

I nod. "Yeah. I'll just stay in my room."

"A'ight, bet. I'ma text you when I'm on my way, a'ight?"

"Yes."

"You ain't gotta put up wit' dat ish, ya heard? I'ma get us a spot next week. In da meantime you can stay at my momz's crib."

I swallow. "Are you sure? I don't think she likes me."

"Yo, she ain't gotta like you. But she knows she betta respect you. I pay da bills up in dere, so she's gonna do wat I say."

"What about your sister?"

"I done already put my foot down for what went on wit' dem broadz comin' through to get at you. So she ain't gonna give you no grief. She ain't tryna have me take it to her neck again. Don't worry 'bout packin' nothin'. I'ma take you shoppin' tomorrow."

"Okay."

Three hours later, Malik finally texts back to say he's twenty minutes away. I know if he comes to the house there's a chance—no, it's a definite—that my mom will call the police on him. I don't want that. I tell him to meet me at the WaWa down the street.

I won't be needing this, I think, tossing my packed bag into my closet. As I prepare to creep down the stairs, I am greeted by mom with, "Kennedy, what is this?"

I blink. My mom is standing in front of me holding up the two blunts I'd hidden in the inside panel of my pocketbook. "I know you did *not* bring drugs up in this house! Have you lost your mind, huh, Kennedy? Answer me!"

I blink again. I can't believe she went through my stuff!

"Don't stand there looking at me crazy! You better open your mouth and tell me something, girl! Now!"

I can't help but roll my eyes.

She scowls. "Is there something wrong with your eyes?

Because I know you didn't just roll them at me. Now I asked you a question? What. Is. This?"

"I don't believe you!" I yell. "I don't have to tell you nothing! You have no right going through my personal things! Do I go through your stuff? No!"

"*Excuuuse* you?! I have *every* right"—she stomps a foot—"to go through your things when your behavior warrants it. And, lately, I do not like what I am seeing. And now I see why. How long have you been smoking this mess, huh?"

"That's none of your business," I snap. "Why can't you stop being a joy-killer and just stay the heck out of my life?"

"*Every*thing you do is my business, little girl! *You* have no life unless I say you do! And for the rest of the summer the *only* joy you'll see will be punishment!"

"You can't do this to me!" I scream at her.

"Oh, I most certainly can. Now get your ass back upstairs! I don't know who this new crowd is you're hanging with, but it stops today. Do you understand me?"

"You can't tell me what to do!" I try to brush by her. "I don't have to listen to you!"

She snatches my arm. "Girl, you had better watch your tone with me! You have no business bringing drugs into this house! And I will not stand for it!"

"*Ohmygod!*" I shriek, snatching my arm back. "Get a grip! It's only marijuana! You're acting like it's some hard-core drug or something! It was hidden inside of my pocket-book. Not out in the open. So what's the big deal?!"

"The big deal is, it's illegal! And you brought it into this house! I don't care where you had it hidden. If the police found this"—she shakes the plastic baggie in my face—"on *you* you'd be arrested! Is that what you want? To be carted off to jail?"

Tears spew from my eyes.

"No, I want you to stay outta my life! You're gonna have to let go and stop tryna ruin my life!"

She raises her hand to strike me, but quickly stops herself. "I'm warning you, Kennedy! So help me God! I will smack the piss out of you! *You* will *not* speak to me that way! I am your mother! I will never let go of trying to guide you in the right direction. And right now, I'm trying to stop *you* from making some horrible mistakes. The last thing I want is seeing you hooked up with the wrong crowd. All it takes is one time being at the *wrong* place at the *wrong* time with the *wrong* crowd and you could end up a jail cell, or worse."

"I'm already in jail!" I scream at her. "So it can't get any worse than it already is. Anyplace would be better than being here with *you*!"

I brush by her, practically knocking her over. I run down the stairs and out the front door, cursing and hollering at the top of my lungs, without looking back.

I hear my mom running behind me, calling out for me. "Kennedy! Kennedy! Get back here! Do you hear me?! You get back in this house, right now, or I'm calling the police!"

I keep running and running until my chest aches and my lungs burn. My mind is made up.

I'm never going back there again!

36

Malik makes me feel safe. Simple as that. He makes me feel special. And wanted. And, with everything that has happened over the last week, Malik is all I need to get by, to survive. I haven't spoken to (or heard from) my mother since our fight. And I don't want to.

I don't even know if she's tried reaching me on my cell because I threw it in a fit of anger and broke it. Malik had to purchase me a new phone. Now I don't have any of my contacts. And I haven't been on Facebook to see if she's looking for me.

Knowing her, she is.

A part of me feels so bad. And knows that I am probably in deep trouble.

Then there's the other part of me that just doesn't care. Not right now, anyway.

Sasha was right when she said I needed to get my life. Well, guess what? That's exactly what I've been doing. Getting. My. Life. I have been having nothing but fun. Going to parties. Going to clubs. Shopping. And spending every waking moment with Malik.

He's been so supportive. He even got us an efficiency room two towns over because he said we needed our own space. Truth is, I overheard his mother telling him when he came back at two o'clock in the morning to pick me up that she didn't want me staying in her apartment. "She too young 'n' too hot in the tail. And she ain't gonna be nothin' but trouble. You need'a git you somebody yo' own age. And leave dat li'l girl alone."

"Ma, you need to go 'head wit' dat dumb ish," I heard Malik tell her. "Kennedy ain't gonna bring me no heat. Her momz threw her out 'n' I ain't tryna see my girl out on da streets."

His mother grunted. "Mmph. You need to call DYFS 'n' let dem deal wit' 'er."

"Chill, ma. Ain't nobody callin' DYFS on nobody. It's all good. We outta here, a'ight? I already got us a spot."

"*What?* What you mean, you got y'all a spot? You still gonna pay this rent 'n' make sure me 'n' Mercedes got money to live off of?" I heard him tell her that he had everything covered, then the last thing I heard her say is, "I can't believe you gonna turn ya back on ya own family for that li'l uppity girl."

"Yo, sexy, what you over there thinkin' 'bout?" Malik nudges me, taking his eyes off the road ahead of him. "You a'ight?"

I nod, looking over at him. "Yeah. I'm okay."

"Oh, a'ight. Just checkin' on my baby. You seem like you kinda lost in thought."

I shake my head. "No, not really."

Truth is, my mind has been reeling back and forth between my fight with Jordan and the haunting words of Mercedes. Last night, as usual, I was left alone at Malik's mother's while he went out to make "a run" into the city with two of his friends. And, once again, his sister with her ole messy, mean self felt the need to corner me in the kitchen when I'd come out to grab something to drink out of the fridge.

"I keep telling you, silly girl, all my brotha's gonna do is use you up. Screw you up. And have you somewhere rockin' in a corner tryna slice ya wrists."

I blinked, then scrunched my face up at her. "Why are you telling me this? Malik's your brother."

She snapped, "I know who da *fuqq* he is. Do I look stupid to you?"

"No, not at all." *But you sound crazy*, I thought as I stood there staring at her. "I'm just wondering why you would say mean things about him; that's all."

She scowled. "Say *mean* things 'bout him? Girl, bye. I ain't said nothin' mean 'bout my brotha. But you too stuck on dumb to see dat I'm tryna school ya."

She rubbed her swollen belly, then pulled a chair out from the table and sat. "Sweetie, all you ever gonna be to Malik is a young piece until he finishes runnin' all up in you 'n' guttin' you out."

I cringed.

"Mercedes!" her mother yelled from the living room. "Leave dat girl alone!"

She snorted. "I ain't botherin' her. I'm tryna school her."

"Well, don't school her! Leave her be! I don't feel like hearin' Malik's mouff 'cause you effen wit' dat girl of his. If she wanna be drunk in love over him, let her. She gonna have ta find out da hard way, like the rest of 'em; that's all."

Like the rest of them, I thought, wondering what she meant by that. When I asked Mercedes what her mother had meant, she simply smirked and said, "You'll find out soon enough."

I'm not sure what I'm supposed to find out, but what I do know is, I need to know this: "Umm, how many kids do you have?" I finally ask Malik, shifting my body to face him.

He takes his eyes off the road for a split second to look over at me.

"I mean, I know you have a baby with that girl Hennessey."

"Dat ain't my baby, yo."

I raise a brow. "Say what? I thought you said she was your baby mother."

"Nah, I never tol' you no ish like dat."

I blink. I am certain that he told me that that night she showed up at the restaurant. I could have sworn he did. Okay, maybe he didn't.

"But I keep hearing you have other kids with other girls, too."

Malik's face turns up into a scowl. "Who tol' you dis?"

"Your sister."

"Dis *thot*," he mutters, shakin' his head. "Listen. I got two kids, a'ight. A four-year-old and three-year-old. They both down south wit' dey momz."

I give him a confused look. "So Hennessy's baby isn't yours, but you have two kids with someone else?"

"Yeah. Both my BM's live in Atlanta."

Both my BM's?

"But what about Hennessey's baby?"

He reaches into the ashtray and retrieves a half-smoked blunt, slipping it between his lips. He presses the lighter, then a few seconds later lights the weed-stuffed cigar. Smoke quickly fills the interior of his truck.

"I already tol' you. It ain't mine. She keep tryna put it on me, but I ain't beat. I know wat time it is. She tryna get a come up, but it ain't gonna be on my dime. I mean, yeah, I smashed, but it wasn't 'bout nothin'. Dat broad's a freak. She let all my manz 'n' dey boyz run all up in her."

He says this as if what he's telling me is not that serious.

His sister Mercedes's voice haunts me. *". . . You prolly da dumbest ho he's been wit' so far . . . raw punnany is da only thing my brother is gonna ever love. He doesn't know howta love anything other than what's between yo' legs, li'l girl . . ."*

I cringe at the idea of knowing that he's had unprotected sex with her, knowing she was sleeping around with other guys.

"And you're sure her baby isn't yours?"

He shoots me a look. "What I just say. Let it go. We got it in, a'ight. I ain't strap up. It is what it is."

I raise my eyebrow. "Look. Just forget I even asked," I say, folding my arms.

"A'ight then. Stop stressin' over dumb ish, yo." He shakes his head. "You young broadz real wet behind da ears, yo."

I shift uncomfortably, blinking. "Well, maybe you should get with someone whose ears aren't so wet then since you feel like that. I won't ask you anything else." I turn my body and stare out the window.

I hear Malik sigh. He reaches over and lightly grabs my knee. "Yo, c'mon, baby. I didn't mean it like dat." His voice softens. "It's just dat da past is in da past 'n' I don't want us to have to live in it, a'ight. Henney's baby ain't mine.

But I give her a few dollars here 'n' there 'cause I feel kinda bad for her. But dat don't mean I'm tryna claim her baby as my seed, yo."

I don't say anything. I keep my gaze locked out into the darkness watching the buildings as they pass by.

He gently squeezes my knee. "I'm where I wanna be wit' who I wanna be wit'."

I turn my head to look at him, then go back to looking out the window. Thinking. Wondering. Hoping. Desperately wanting to believe that I am—that I will always be—enough for him.

Silence fills the space between us.

What if Blaze was right? What if Malik really isn't right for me? Then what? I feel like I have given up so much of myself to be with him that I can't imagine being without him. And I can't imagine it not being right.

The truck stops at a stoplight.

Malik lights another blunt, takes a pull from it, then hands it to me. "Here."

He pulls off when the light turns green. I take a deep pull from the blunt and release the smoke through my nose, then hand it back to him. It doesn't take long before I am feeling the effects of the marijuana. I am feeling much more relaxed. I settle back into my seat, laying my head back against the headrest.

Malik reaches over and grabs my hand. "Yo, we good, baby?"

I glance over at him through half-slits and nod. Then lean over and kiss him when we stop at another light.

He laughs. "Yo, my baby lit, huh?"

I nod, grinning.

A car in back of him honks its horn. Malik speeds off.

Then reaches over and takes my hand again. He brings it up to his lips and kisses it. I close my eyes, lean my head back against the headrest again and smile once I feel warmth and wetness of Malik's mouth as he sucks each of my fingers.

"Mmm...you taste so...sweet."

I smile.

And for the next three weeks, Malik and I become inseparable.

37

Saturday night.
The place is packed.

The music is loud.

Marijuana smoke fills the air as guys walk around hold-ing bottles of Ciroc and Hennessey in one hand while holding blunts up to their lips with their other hand. There's a group of girls passing blunts between them, while others are grinding up on guys on the dance floor.

The inside of my stomach trembles. And I don't know why. Something doesn't feel right. But I can't put my fin-ger on it.

"Yo, Malik, my nucca, wutz good, yo?" someone yells over the music. I look to the right of me and spot a tall, brown-skinned guy sitting between two cute girls with really big boobs wearing skimpy outfits. He stands up, spreading his arms open. He's wearing a neck full of jewelry. He's real tall. Taller than Malik. And really, really cute. He kind of puts me in the mind of Kendrick Lamar a little, but a cuter version of him.

"Yo, whaddup, Que." He rushes over and the two embrace in a brotherly hug, giving each other that pound-handshake-thingy they all do. "Long time no see. Where you been, yo?"

"Layin' low, my nucca. Watz good wit' you." He glances sideways at me, and grins. "I see you still pullin' da honeys, yo. You sharin'?"

Malik laughs. "Nah. Not this one, my dude. It ain't dat type'a party."

I shift my weight from one foot to the other, feeling slightly uncomfortable with the way Malik's friend is looking at me.

Malik turns to me. "Kennedy, this my manz, Que. Que, this my girl Kennedy."

"Yo, word?" He smiles. "Watz good, ma? You got a twin?"

I give him a half smile, shaking my head. "Sorry. I don't."

Malik wraps his arm around me, kissing me on the side of my head. "Nah, my baby's one of a kind, yo."

"I can dig it." He glances over his shoulder. "Yo, let me get back to these two broadz before they start gettin' restless."

"No doubt, playa," Malik says, giving him another one of those fist and shoulder bumps.

"Yo, you need'a come holla at me a li'l later, a'ight? I got some bidnesss I wanna holla at you 'bout."

"A'ight, No doubt. I got you."

I eye his friend on the sly, then ask him who he is. And how he knows him. Malik shoots me a look. Then catches himself from saying something when a dark-skinned girl wearing her hair pulled back into a tight ponytail that hangs down past her butt swishes her hips over toward us. She's wearing a pair of white booty shorts and a silver glittery, low-cut bra. I glance down at her feet and wonder how in the heck she's able to walk in those super-high platform heels.

"Heeeeey, Malik," she coos over the music, ignoring the fact that Malik has his arm draped around me.

"Yo, watz good, Tasha. How you?"

She bats her fake lashes. "I'm good. Real good." She licks her lips, then smirks. "But you already know dat."

My body stiffens.

"Yo, dis my girl, Kennedy. Kennedy, dis Tasha."

She cuts her eye at me and gives me the once-over. I open my mouth to speak and she rudely twists her lips up and turns her gaze back over to Malik. "I ain't seen you in a minute, boo. What you been up to? How my girl Mercedes doin'?"

"Crazy," Malik says, laughing as he glances around the party. "But, yo, let me get movin'. I'll holla."

"Yeah, you do dat." She shoots me a dirty look, then says, "I know you still got my number. Use it." She walks off. Her hips sway full speed as she moves through the crowd.

Jay-Z's "Open Letter" starts playing and Malik bobs his head from side to side. "Yo, let's dance." Before I can object, he's pulling me onto the dance floor with him. Several songs later we are passing a fat blunt back and forth. And whatever nervous energy I had earlier is now gone. I'm feeling good.

Beyoncé's "Drunk In Love" starts playing and I pull

Malik onto the dance floor. Whatever he had in that marijuana has me feeling like I can fly. I turn my back to Malik and he wraps his arms around me. I lift my hands up over my head, close my eyes, and get lost in the music as he grinds on me.

Out of the corner of my eye, I see a tall, stocky guy with shoulder-length dreads and half-sleeve tattoos stalking over in our direction, but I don't give it any thought. I keep dancing, blocking everything out until the guy jumps up in Malik's face.

Words are exchanged.

Malik pushes me out of the way.

Then all I see are punches being thrown.

I look on at the scene in fear, confused, as other guys start rushing to the dance floor fighting.

I get knocked to the floor, and scream.

38

Pandemonium.

That's the only way to explain what is unfolding right before my very eyes.

Gunshots!

Loud.

People are screaming at the top of their lungs, scrambling for safety. Ducking bullets. Dropping to the floor and rolling for cover.

We are all terrified.

"Ohmygod, *Malik!*" I shriek. "What's happening?" He snatches me by the hand and is practically dragging me. I know I said I wanted to have a thrilling summer. But this goes way beyond my definition of excitement. The crowd stampedes out the back and side emergency exits. We all pour out of the building, scattering.

Malik and I run up two blocks, then finally slow down. I try catching my breath.

"W-w-what is going on? What h-happened in there?"

"Listen, babe. Not now, a'ight. I need you to focus."

"*Focus?!*" I scream hysterically, yanking my arm from him. "Are you kidding me? A bunch of gunfire broke out in the middle of a club. And I barely made it out alive! We could have been killed. How—"

"Yo!" he snaps, pulling out his keys and disarming his alarm. "Chill wit' da questions, a'ight? I need'a think!"

I swallow.

He opens the driver's side door, tells me to get in, then hands me the key to his truck. "Stay here. You hear me? And if anything starts looking crazy be ready to peel off. You hear me?"

"Y-y-yes. But w-where are you going?"

"Back to handle…" Malik stops in midsentence and glances over his shoulder just as a black Suburban with tinted windows rolled halfway down with its headlights out approaches us. The first things I see are two black guns being held out the front and rear windows, aimed directly at us. "Yo, get down!"

But it's too late. I duck down and scream as the gunmen open fire, shooting up the side of the truck.

Ohmygod! Ohmygod! Ohhhhmyyygod! I'm going to get killed!

I hear tires screeching, then more gunshots being fired. Fearfully, I peek to see what's happening. I am a shaken mess.

Through tears, I witness Malik pulling a gun from his waistband, aiming at the speeding SUV and firing shots. He takes off running behind the truck. I've never seen him, or anyone—except Raynard Price, a guy who ran track and went to school with my brother Kent—run so fast. He hits the back of the truck, causing it to swerve then slam into a parked car.

My heart is beating rapidly. This is all a terrible nightmare.

Just when I think it can't, won't, get any worse, there are more gunshots being fired. At Malik!

And then...

He hits the ground.

"Nooooo!" I scream, swinging open the door and hopping out of the truck, leaving the door wide open. I run to where he is. I run down the street. "Malik! Malik!"

There is blood everywhere.

He's been shot.

Ohmygodohymygodohmygod!

"Ohmygod! Malik! Are you okay?"

Sirens blare in the distance.

"I'm fine. Aaah, s*hiiiiit*! Punks clipped me in the leg 'n' shoulder, dat's all."

"Ohmygod! I have to get you to a hospital."

"Kennedy! I need you to focus! *Uhhh!* There's no time for that!" He starts breathing heavy. "I need you to take this gun, and go back to the truck and get a black book bag from outta the backseat. It's on the floor."

"Okay." I am crying uncontrollably.

Sirens squeal louder as they get closer to the scene.

"Uhhh...I need you to get dat bag 'n' get outta here. Don't look inside. You hear me? Call Sasha 'n' give her da bag.

"But what about you?"

"I'm cool. Just go."

"I can't leave you like this!"

"Look, baby, I got dis. Get outta here, a'ight? Now!"

He hands me the gun. Without a thought, I take it and run back toward the truck. I am shaking violently.

I can see the flashing red and blue lights. I open the backseat door, find the book bag and open it, stuffing the gun inside, then start running in the opposite direction. Seconds after this, police are everywhere. I don't know how many show up after the first eight squad cars I count. A sea of blue uniforms hops out of cruisers. Weapons are drawn. Everything is happening so fast.

"Police! Stop where you are!"

Ohmygod! Are they talking to me? I haven't done any-thing wrong.

"Police!"

My knees shake. "What's going on?"

"Drop the bag!"

Ohmygod, they are talking to me!

"Please. Don't shoot. It's all a big misunderstanding. Someone started shooting at my boyfriend. Then he started chasing them. And then he got shot. Please. You have to call an ambulance. My boyfriend's is bleeding pretty bad."

"Ma'am. This is your last warning! Put you hands where we can see them. Now!"

I do as they say. Next thing I know I am being swarmed by police. Then tackled to the ground. There's a knee in my back. I am being handcuffed, then violently yanked up.

Ohmygod! Where's Malik?

I glance over to where I left him lying. He isn't there.

"You are under arrest..."

Oh, nooo!

He's gone!

"You have the right to remain silent..."

Ohmygodohmygodohmygod! What have I gotten my-self into?

39

If I ever thought there wasn't such a thing as a hell on earth, I was sadly mistaken. There is a hell on earth! And it's this place! The Lorna P. Johnson Youth Detention Center. Metal doors clanking open and closed. Nasty steel seatless toilets. Metal bed frames bolted to concrete walls. Thin mattresses. Cheap bedsheets that cut like sandpaper. Pig slop served on thick, clunky plastic trays.

I have been fingerprinted. Have had my mug shot taken. And have basically been treated like a criminal. Like I am guilty.

I'm not guilty!

I haven't done anything!

This isn't what my life is. Or was supposed to be like. Fingerprints and face mugs. And charges of crimes I didn't commit. But somehow it's what it's become. This isn't how I planned my summer to turn out. But somehow, in the blink of an eye, this is what it has come to. And now what's left of my summer is ruined!

I'm locked up! I'm sitting here in a drab navy blue uniform with the words LORNA P. JOHNSON YDC stamped across the left side of my chest in small block letters and a pair of slip-on canvas type sneakers that hurt the bottom of my feet.

I am surrounded by other teens that had a penchant for making bad choices. Some of them were repeat offenders. Some of them were here on violent charges. And some of the girls here are scary. Rough-looking. Disrespectful. Nasty. Trifling. Vicious. And crazy. And all they want to do is pick fights with each other, including with me.

It's crazy here!

Being called filthy names. Being threatened. Having to constantly watch my back. It's all too much to bear.

I'm starting to feel like the walls are closing in on me. I have to get out of here before I lose my mind.

I thought being arrested, handcuffed, then shoved into the backseat of a police car was humiliating. But nothing prepared me for (or compared to) being in this hellhole. From getting processed at intake to getting strip-searched. I'd never felt so violated in my whole entire life, standing butt-naked and being told to bend over and pull open my butt cheeks while some strange woman looked on.

I take a deep breath, willing my emotions in check while removing the receiver from the base of the phone and dialing.

Please pick up! Please!

"Yo?"

"Hey," I say softly, relieved and happy to finally hear Malik's voice. I had been trying to reach him for the last four days to no avail. I'd even left several messages for him with Sasha. But even she's acting funny now.

"Look, Kennedy," she said nastily when I called her last night. "You're going to have to chill with all these calls. I gave him your messages."

"And what'd he say?" I asked anxiously.

She sighed. "He said a'ight."

"That's it?"

"Yeah, basically."

"Is he in the hospital?"

"No. Somebody he knows is a nurse. She handled things."

"Oh." I was relieved to hear he was okay. But saddened that she hadn't expressed that he was deeply hurt by my arrest. "Did he at least ask you how I was doing?"

She huffed. "Look. Not really."

Hurt washed over me. He hadn't even thought enough about me to ask her if I was okay. I couldn't believe it. And I couldn't believe she was acting like I was inconveniencing her.

"Well, look, girl. You can write me if you want, but I don't take calls from jailbirds, unless you my man. No shade."

"Oh, okay. I understand." My feelings were hurt. But I kept it to myself. I felt like I had no one. "I'll let you go then."

"Cool. Keep ya head up, girl." And with that said, I heard the dial tone.

"Who dis?" Malik roars into the phone, bringing me out of my mindless fog.

I blink. "It's me. Kennedy. Oh, wow. You've forgotten who I am that fast?" I say, half joking. "Have I been re-placed already?"

I clutch the phone tightly.

He lets out a chuckle. "Oh, nah-nah. Just didn't think

you'd be callin' me straight through; that's all. I thought your calls were collect."

"They are. But the social worker let me call you since I can't make collect calls to cell phones and I haven't been able to reach you any other way. Did you get my letter?"

"Oh, a'ight. Yeah. I got it. Good lookin' out, babe. I been meanin' to hit you back. But you know how it is."

"No. I don't know how it is, out there anyway. I'm in here stressing, Malik."

"I feel you, babe. I'm stressin', too, yo. Shit's been mad hectic. I just got outta da hospital."

I blink. "When?"

"Yesterday."

I frown. "Sasha told me you didn't go to the hospital. I thought some nurse you know took care of everything."

"Oh, yeah. She did. But I still had to go to the hospital."

I swallow. I can't believe I'm hearing all of this. That he was in the hospital, even though Sasha said he wasn't. That he's too busy to take a few minutes out of his time to write me back. I'm the one locked up for something that he should be locked up for. And this is the thanks I get. I thought I was so important to him.

Something doesn't add up.

His story.

I don't know what to believe.

"You could at least write me back, Malik." I feel myself getting teary-eyed. "I feel like I'm in this alone." I start crying. "I don't even have a way of talking to you. Didn't Sasha give you my messages?"

"Nah," he says. "I ain't seen her in a minute."

I frown. "She told me she gave you my messages."

"Yo, eff dat broad, yo. She stay lyin'."

"Well, I don't know if she's lying or not. She had no reason to lie to me. She said she told you that I wanted to talk to you. Now you saying she didn't. Obviously somebody's lying."

"Oh, word? So you callin' ya man a liar? Is dat how you doin' it, huh?"

"I don't know what I'm calling you. All I know is, I'm not feeling like you're here for me. And I don't feel like you're my man. I feel abandoned in here."

"Yo, c'mon, Kennedy. Chill. I got you, babe. Word is bond. I'ma handle that letter later tonight for you, a'ight? I'ma hit you wit' a few dollas, too, a'ight? You know you my heart, boo. I ain't gonna leave you stranded, ma. Ever."

I sigh, reaching for a tissue on the social worker's desk, then blowing my nose. "Money isn't allowed in here, Malik. I'm in a youth detention center, remember?"

"Oh, right, right. My bad. So you good? You need some books or sumthin'?"

My nose flares. "No, I'm not good, Malik. I'm locked up. I want to come home. I hate it here." More tears swell in my eyes, then rapidly fall unchecked. "I can't do this, Malik. I think I'm going crazy. This place is horrible. The food is disgusting." I glance over at the social worker. She's playing a game of solitaire on her computer, pretending to not be listening in on my conversation. "I feel like I'm going crazy," I whisper into the phone. "These girls in here are trifling. Always looking for a fight."

"I feel you, babe. You gotta keep ya head up, though. Stay focused, you feel me?"

I sniffle. Wipe my tears with the arm of my sleeve. "I'm trying. But it's hard. I just want to get out of here."

"When's ya court date?"

I tell him it's in two days. Ask him if he can come to court. My heart drops when he tells me no. "I would if I could, babe. You know that, right?"

"Then why can't you come?"

"I have warrants, yo. I ain't 'bout to chance havin' dem mofos run down on me if I come through."

"I'm scared." I feel myself starting to hyperventilate. "I can't do this, Malik."

"All you gotta do, babe, is play ya position, ya heard? Just sit tight and ride it out. This is your first time. You don't have any priors. And you're a minor. They'll go easy on you."

"Are you *frickin'* kidding me! I shriek. "I don't want them to *go easy* on me. I want them to release me. I want out of here! I didn't do anything! That gun wasn't mine and neither were those drugs. And you know it!"

"Whoa, whoa. Slow down. You sayin' too much."

"No I'm not. Obviously I'm not saying enough because I'm in here. And *you're* out there. Living la vida loca. You have to come to court and tell them what really happened. *Please*, Malik, you have to come get me out of this place. You can't let me sit in here and rot."

"Oh, word? So now you tryna dry-snitch on ya man, is that it? You tryna talk all reckless in front of them social workers, is dat how you doin' it, yo? You tryna hem me up, is dat it?"

I frown. "I'm not *dry-snitching*. Or trying to get you hemmed up or whatever that means. All I'm *asking* you to do is tell the truth. That's all. I shouldn't have to be locked up for helping *you*."

My plea is met with a deafening silence.

"Hello? Malik? You still there?"

"Yeah, uh, I'm here. Look, I gotta go handle somethin' real quick. Let me hit you back a li'l later, a'ight?"

Is he serious? I stare at the phone in disbelief. I blink. "You can't *hit* me back, Malik. I don't have the luxury of making calls whenever I want. I'm locked up! Remember?"

"Oh, true. A'ight, well, see if you can hit me up later. I gotta go make this run. I love you, a'ight?"

"Bye, Malik."

I hang up, glancing at the timer. I've wasted eight minutes of my ten-minute phone call on nothing. I dial home. The phone rings for what seems like forever before someone finally answers. My heart skips a beat.

"Hello?"

"Hello? Mom?" I burst into tears. "I'm so sorry for everything. You have to get me out of here, please."

"Who is this?"

I blink. *What the heck is wrong with everyone acting like they don't know my voice?*

"It's me. Kennedy, Mom."

"And where are you calling me from?"

I choke back a scream. "In...in the d-d-detention center."

"That's what I thought. No, sweetie. This isn't the Kennedy I know. This is some imposter calling here. Because the Kennedy *I* gave birth to wouldn't be calling *me* from some detention center. No. She'd be home with her family. The Kennedy I know wouldn't have cursed me out, or been sneaking out of the house, or telling me to stay out of her life. The Kennedy I gave birth to would have never run away, or brought drugs into this house. No, not my child."

Tears sprout from my eyes. "Mom, please. I know I screwed up. Can you please..."

"Oh, no. Don't 'mom, please' me, Miss I'm Grown. Remember, you chose the streets over your family. You told me to stay out of your life, remember? Now you want to call here, crying. Now you need me, huh. Well, guess what, Miss I'm Grown? You don't get to pick and choose when you want your family in your life, or me as your mother."

I scream and cry and can barely breathe. I am crying hysterically. Hearing the hurt and disappointment in her voice is killing me. I wish I could take everything I said back. Wish I could undo what I'd already done. But I can't. And I don't know how to make it better.

"I know, Mom. *Plllease*. Don't say that. I was wrong."

"That's too bad," she says evenly. Distant. "Now what do you want, Kennedy?"

"Are you going to come to court for me?"

"No. Let the streets be there for you. You made your bed, now lie in it."

The line goes dead.

And I'm left being lifted up from the floor like a rag doll by two COs then dragged back to my cell. All I remember hearing is the door clanking shut.

And I am alone.

40

My hands and feet in shackles, two guards—one male, the other female—escort me into the elevator up to the second floor where juvenile court proceedings are handled. It is my retention hearing. Whatever that means. My attorney explained it to me when he came down to the holding cell to speak with me. But everything he was saying went over my head. This is all confusing to me. Aside from watching Court TV, I know nothing about a retention hearing. Or being in a real courtroom. And what's most frightening is knowing that right at this very moment my entire fate is in the hands of someone else. I feel so helpless not knowing what's going to happen to me.

My stomach quakes with anxiety as we enter the courtroom and I am seated at a wooden table. My hands remain cuffed. Every few seconds, I glance over my shoulder to see who comes to court for me.

A few short minutes later I hear large wooden doors behind me open. I glance over my shoulder. It's Daddy dressed in a navy blue suit. He looks so worn out. He's flown in from Dubai, has had to take a leave of absence from work, just to be here for my court date.

I feel so horrible.

My mom is ignoring me.

My brothers are all pissed at me.

Jordan and Hope aren't speaking to me.

Sasha is all of sudden acting as if she can't be so bothered with me.

And the only thing Malik seems to care about is me keeping my mouth shut.

I have no one.

I half hoped, half expected, to see my mom walking in behind Daddy. I am disappointed when she doesn't. I mean. I am happy to see Daddy. I am. Really. I am a Daddy's girl. Still...

"All rise!" The bailiff says in a singsong voice, opening the back courtroom door. In walks a short, brown-skinhed lady. She looks nothing like what everyone said. She's pretty. And seems nice enough. I try to gauge her mood. But I can't. She's wearing no expression on her face.

The courtroom falls silent as she briskly makes her way toward the bench, her black judge's robe swooshing behind her as she climbs up the stairs to the bench and sits.

"Court is now in session!" The bailiff barks. "The Honorable Julia Lee Anderson presiding. All electronic devices are to be turned off now. Please be seated."

Judge Anderson glances around the courtroom. "Good morning." She clears her throat, placing her reading glasses on. "We are here on the matter of the juvenile Kennedy Simms. Docket number JV-dash-one-three-three-four-seven-

two-thousand-and-thirteen. This is a retention hearing."
She looks up from her papers. "I see we have representa-
tion from the state. And counsel here for the defendant.
Counselors, please identify yourselves for the record."

The prosecutor stands up. A white woman. Blonde
hair, pulled back into a sleek ponytail. Sparkling blue eyes.
Milky white skin. Thin. She looks like she should be on a
runway instead standing in front of a judge in a courtroom. She's all business as she says, "Emily Swanson for
the state, Your Honor."

My attorney stands. "James Ford for the defendant."

The judge nods her head, then scans my file, glancing up
and peering at me over the rim of her glasses. She is giving
me dirty looks. Maybe it's my imagination. Maybe not.

She gets right down to business.

"You've been charged with the following: two counts possession of a weapon, specifically a .38-caliber tear gas pen
gun containing a rifle bullet and a semi-automatic pistol..."

I choke back a scream.

Those weren't my guns!

"...possession of the narcotic painkiller oxycodone, possession of the prescription anti-anxiety drug Xanax, and
possession of cocaine."

Those weren't my drugs!

The judge looks up at me. "Do you understand the
crimes you are being charged with, young lady?"

"Yes, ma'am," I say meekly. "But I didn't do anything.
They weren't mine."

She tilts her head. Gives me a blank stare. "Were they
not in your possession when the police arrested you?"

I swallow. "Yes. But..."

She cuts me off. "Then you *did* do something. And now

you've gotten yourself caught up in the middle of a big mess."

I lower my head. I already know what she's thinking. It's what my attorney already told me down in the cage. I mean, holding cell. Like my attorney basically said: It was on my person. I was the one holding the backpack. I was the one with the guns and drugs that were inside.

I am guilty as charged.

She lets out a grunt, shaking her head. "I don't know what in the world is wrong with you young girls today, wanting to be all fast and grown. Disrespecting your parents. Choosing the streets over your family." The judge flips through my folder, then looks up over her wire-rimmed glasses and slams the folder shut. She points a wagging finger at me. "You, young lady, obviously come from a good home; with two parents who apparently love you and want nothing but the best for you. And they've probably spoiled you rotten, I'm sure.

"But obviously you want to squander everything they've done for you. You want to be in the streets. You want to play hood wife to some hoodlum. Well, guess what, young lady? You can play Bonnie if you want. The streets don't give two cents and a wooden nickel about you. And neither does Clyde, or Bobby, or Raheem, or Mustafa. But since you want to ride dirty for his cause, then you'll have to suffer the consequences..."

Please, God! Where are you when I need you?

"I'm going to order a urinalysis and substance abuse evaluation. I suspect her urine may come back positive and I'd like to have that in writing if that is in fact the case."

My heart stops. *Oh, my God. She's going to crucify me.*

Her glare is burning into my flesh. All of a sudden, I break out into a sweat. And feel myself start to shake from the inside out.

She eyes me. "You want to be some gun-slinging thug-mami, don't you?"

I shake my head. "No, ma'am."

"Oh, yes you do." She glances over at the bailiff. He shakes his head. "You're a beautiful young lady. But those looks aren't going to get you anywhere in life unless you learn to use your brain. Sadly, intelligence doesn't guarantee common sense. So if you think for one minute those looks are going to get you out of this mess you're currently in, you are sadly mistaken.

"Judging by the crimes you are being accused of committing, it's apparent to this court that you would rather be out in the streets with the thugs, living a life of crime, hanging with a bunch of fast hoochie-mommas instead of being the respectable young lady your parents have raised you to be. There are rules put in place at home and in life for a particular reason. Do you know why there are rules, young lady?"

I nod.

"You are to open your mouth and speak when I speak to you. A head nod does not suffice, do I make myself clear?"

I swallow, hard. "Yes, Your Honor."

"Good. Now answer the question. Do you know why there are rules in place?"

"Yes."

"Why?"

"So that there is order and structure. And to help guide us to do the right thing."

The judge peers over her wire-rimmed frames; she studies me for what seems like forever, then narrows her eyes at me. Her burning glare causes me to squirm in my seat.

"Do you know the difference between ignorance and stupidity, young lady?" I nod my head, and am immediately scolded again. "I've warned you once. You open your mouth and speak. I won't tell you again. Do I make myself clear?"

"Yes, ma'am." I speak. Tell her my understanding of the difference between ignorance and stupidity. That ignorance is not having information, of not knowing. That stupidity is having the information, having an awareness of what's needed to get something done, but choosing to do nothing with it.

"And did you not *know* what was expected of you by your parents?"

"Yes, Your Honor."

"And do you not *know* what the law expects of you?"

I nod my head. "Yes, Your Honor, I do."

She scowls at me. "Yet, you *chose* to disobey both your parents and the law. Is that correct?"

I swallow. "Yes, I mean, no, ma'am," I say almost in a whisper.

"What is it? Yes or no? Did you or did you not disobey your parents' rules?"

"Yes."

"And did you not disregard the law?"

I swallow. "Yes."

"And that makes you what?"

I swallow back the thick lump in the back of my throat. *Stupid, stupid, stupid!* I can't bear to say it aloud. I am so screwed. The truth, the realization, is too painful for me to deal with right now.

My attorney stands to address the court. "Your Honor. If I can interject for a brief minute..."

She looks up from my file. "Make it quick, counselor."

"My client is a straight-A student with no priors. And, though she's made some foolish mistakes, she's a good kid. We ask that she be allowed home on house arrest until her next court hearing. Mr. Simms, the juvenile's father, is here also on behalf of my client. And he's prepared to take her home today."

The judge peers over the rim of her glasses, again. "Mr. Simms, is this true?"

Daddy stands.

Please, God! I beg you...

"That is correct, Your Honor. If the court is prepared to release my daughter then we are more than willing to have her home, with conditions of course. Perhaps under some sort of house arrest..."

Yes, please. House arrest. You can keep me under lock and key until my eighteenth birthday. Just let me go home.

I look over at Daddy with pleading eyes. He gives me a pained look. Then asks the judge if he can address the court again. I do not even realize that I've stopped breathing until I hear him say, "My wife and I are very concerned with our daughter's recent behaviors. I'm not sure what has gotten into her. In a matter of weeks, between the drinking and lying and doing God knows what else, she's turned into someone my wife and I barely recognize."

I start sobbing.

"Save the tears," the judge snaps unsympathetically.

"You'll have plenty of time for crying back at the detention center, where you will sit until your next court hearing."

"Ohgodnoooo! Why can't I go home? I didn't do anything. I want to go home."

The judge scoffs. "Well, guess what, young lady? It doesn't matter what you want. And you've already proven that it doesn't matter what your parents want, because if it did, you wouldn't be sitting here in my courtroom, taking up my time."

Oh no, oh no...please don't...

The judge looks at me long and hard, causing me to break out in a sweat.

Doomsday.

The beginning of my end.

"Disappointing." She shakes her head. "Just sad. It's obvious you come from a good home, young lady, but that isn't good enough for you. It isn't hood enough for you. And the fact that you have a clear understanding of right from wrong speaks volumes, young lady." The judge narrows her eyes at me. "It says that you think you can do whatever you want, whenever you want with no regard to how your choices will affect other people around you, particularly your parents..."

No, no, no, no, nooooooo!

Daddy, pleeeeeease say something.

"No I don't," I cry out. "I want my life back! I want to be home with my family! I'm going to go crazy in that hellhole! Daddy, *plllllease*! You can't let them do this to me! Don't let them keep me!"

Judge Anderson brings her gavel down on the bench. "Order in the court! Young lady, your outburst will not be tolerated in my courtroom. Another outburst like that and

I will have you thrown out of my courtroom. Do I make myself clear?"

I glare at the judge through tear-filled eyes. My jaw is twitching. I feel like I am on the verge of having a nervous breakdown.

After a few tense seconds, the judge breaks our stare down, looking over at my attorney. "Counselor, I'd advise you to—"

"I don't need him to advise me! I want to go home! Pllleeeease! You can't keep me locked up like this." I raise my shackled hands. "Like some animal."

The judge slams her gavel down, again. "Order in the court! Sheriffs, get her out of my courtroom before I hold in her in contempt! You had a home, young lady. But you chose the streets over your home. You would rather be in the streets with the thugs and hoochie-mommas. Now your home for the next two weeks will be in my house. The Lorna P. Johnson Youth Detention Center. I have found sufficient evidence for probable cause in which case, juvenile to be remanded. Get her out of here, *NOW!* Next case…"

I let out a blood-curdling scream.

Just like that.

It is over for me.

I am being dragged out of the courtroom, yelling and crying out hysterically.

41

"Stuck up, trick!"

"Yo, word is bond, Kreesha, you should take it straight to her face."

"Yeah, you right, I should. But she don't want none'a dis knuckle work right here." She holds her fists up and starts punching and swinging up into the air.

I shift my weight on the steel bench in the dayroom. *Please, God...you have to get me out of here. These girls in here are crazy! I don't know how much more of this place I can take.*

I keep my eyes locked on the television mounted up on the wall as I say my prayer in my head. Every so often I glance over at the stainless steel table this Kreesha girl and her groupies are sitting at.

"That stank *bish* thinks she's better than us. Over there sittin' all up under da COs like that's gonna stop sumthin'. Pfft. Please."

"A'ight, Wilkens," the female CO sitting at the table with

me says sternly, looking up from her crossword puzzle. "That's enough out of you."

Kreesha sucks her teeth. "Yeah, whatever. You can't babysit that *thot* forever."

I press my lips tightly together and tap my foot determined to not let her get to me. I keep my eyes on her in case she decides to sneak me. I'm learning fast here. Never sleep. Never keep your back facing the door. Always face forward so you can see everything coming and going around you. I don't want to fight her. Truth is, I think her friends will jump in if I do. Still, she keeps taunting me. And I'm getting tired of her and her cronies bullying me.

"Mmph. Isn't that the same stink *bish* who was effen ya cousin Hennessey's baby daddy?"

Hennessey.

I cringe when I hear that name. Now I knew why she looked so familiar to me. She was one of the girls who were with that Hennessey girl at the restaurant that day when she came in causing a bunch of commotion.

Ohmygod! This is crazy!

"Yeah, that's her. Now she in here 'n' I bet you her so-called man is back at Henney's house right now knockin' it down."

Her friends all high-five each other, laughing.

The Kreesha girl asks one of the COs if she can get up to get a drink of water from the fountain. She gets up from her seat, then heads for the water fountain. On her way back to her seat she makes a fast beeline over to where I am, jumping in my face. "*Bish*, facts," she says through clenched teeth. "If you even think 'bout snitchin' on my cousin's man, I'ma bash ya eye sockets in..."

My heart drops. I look over in the direction of the

guards. They all seem preoccupied playing games on their
phones or texting or doing whatever it is they aren't supposed to be doing while on the clock. I think to write a
grievance, but quickly dismiss the idea. The last thing I
need is problems with them, too.

No one likes a snitch.

Malik's voice plays in my head. *"I need you to ride dis
one out for me, baby, ya heard?"* That's what he told me
last night when I called him from the social worker's office.

"Malik, I can't. I-I..."

"You love me, right?"

"Y-yes. But..."

"Am I ya man?"

Tears started falling from my eyes. "I don't know. I
hope so."

"Yo, c'mon, don't do that, Kennedy. You know I'm ya
man, yo. It's me 'n' you. Don't I always have ya back?"

"Yes."

"Then a'ight. You already know what it is. I'd do it
for you."

"Then get me out of here, Malik! This place is driving
me crazy! This food! These nasty girls! I can't stand being
caged in like some animal."

"Babe, listen. I hear you. I know what it's like, feel me?"

"No, I'm not feeling you. I'm not feeling anything
you're saying. The only thing I'm feeling, Malik, is alone.
I'm feeling like you don't care what happens to me as long
as it isn't you."

"Here you go again wit' dis ish. You know I care 'bout
what happens to you. Don't I pick up e'ery time you call?"

"It's not enough, Malik."

"Yo, check it. All you gotta do is keep tellin' 'em it ain't yours. They have no proof, yo."

"Yes, they do. I was the one holding the bag. Your bag."

"Yo, chill-chill. You doin' too much. You know dat bag wasn't mine. You was mad twisted dat night, babe. Remember how ish popped off? Dude threw his bag down on da ground when he heard Five-oh comin'. Remember? I tol' you not to touch it, but you did anyway. You was on one dat night, babe."

I blinked. I couldn't believe he was really trying to make me second-guess what really happened that night. Yeah, I had a few drinks. And, yeah, I smoked that blunt with him, but I was still very cognizant of what was going on around me.

Wasn't I?

Yeah. I was.

That was/is Malik's bag. And those were *his* guns and *his* drugs. Not mine. And not anyone else's. *His.*

"I know what happened that night, Malik," I whispered into the phone. "And I know exactly what you told me."

"Oh, so now you wanna snitch on ya man, is dat it?"

"No, Malik. I want you to tell da truth."

"Yo, real spit, baby. You gonna have ta chalk it up to da game. Da truth is, you were da one holdin' dat bag. You wanna rock wit' a baller, then you need'a know how to bounce wit' da ball. It's on you, baby. Now what you gonna do? 'Cause if you really love me like you say you do, then ain't no way you tryna see ya man get bagged."

"Malik, please," I begged. "Don't do this to me. Don't I mean anything to you?"

"Yo, you my world, baby. But you got my head all effed up. I can't believe you tryna snitch, yo. You my heart,

Kennedy; dat's on e'erything. But I ain't rockin' wit' no rat, yo. You wanna move cheese then do you. But you do know what dey do to snitches, right?"

I swallowed, hard. My heart pounded in my chest.

"They wake up wit' stitches..."

I scream when Kreesha's fist crashes into my face.

42

"CO?" I call out, raising my hand. It's Wednesday night. And all of the South Wing residents are in the dayroom, either watching TV, playing cards or some sort of board game, reading a book, or huddled at a table talking about whatever it is they talk about. Things I am not privy to. As usual, I am sitting away from the rest of the girls in here.

Alone.

Even after that girl jumped me, they all still blame *me* for her getting put in lock-up. Ad Seg. Or whatever it's called. The point is, *she* attacked *me*. Not the other way around. And, yet, I'm being treated like the villain.

Whatever!

"What is it, Simms?" Officer Linden says. She's a brown-skinned lady with big brown eyes and big thick lips with bad acne and a nasty attitude. She hates her job. I only know this because I overheard her once talking to another CO saying how all this was is a high-paying babysitting job.

How she hated coming to work and having to deal with "these disrespectful kids."

I feel sorry for her.

I feel sorry for me.

"Can I have a pencil and four sheets of paper, please? And three envelopes?"

She lets out a disgusted sigh, getting up from the steel table she's sitting at, the one closest to the door. She walks out into the hallway, then a few seconds later she returns with a new notepad.

She gives me permission to walk over to her table. She writes my name down on a sheet of paper, then hands me a numbered pencil, several sheets of paper, and envelopes. I thank her.

All she does is grunt. Then adds, "Don't bother me for the rest of my shift."

I remind myself to pray for her tonight when I am praying for myself.

I turn to walk back to the table I was sitting at and there's a boy sitting there. I blink. It's the same boy who is always winking and licking his lips at me.

Hasaan, I think.

Boys and girls aren't allowed to sit together unless there's a CO sitting there with them. He knows this. I glance around the dayroom for another vacant table. There are none.

He grins knowingly.

Lucky for me one of the COs notices that he's moved from his table to mine without permission and yells at him. "Banks, who told you to move?! Get back over where you were sitting!"

He curses the CO out, tells him to suck his privates. The next thing I know, there are COs hopping up from their seats, tackling him down to the floor, then dragging him out of the dayroom.

And this becomes the excitement for the night.

"Yo, dat's effed up," someone says when everything finally settles. It's a guy's voice. I don't turn to see who it is. I don't care. "Franklin 'n' da rest of da COs in here be on some BS, yo. They ain't even have ta do my boy dirty like dat."

CO Linden barks, "Lewis, shut your trap. Or you'll be next."

He sucks his teeth loudly. Then mutters something under his breath before going back to his card game.

"I can't stand that stuck-up *bish*," I hear one of the female residents say. She says it loud enough for me to hear it. And I know she's talking about me. They're *always* talking about me. "She stays tryna get someone in trouble. Dat's why nobody likes her now. Kreesha shoulda knocked both her eye sockets out."

Her friends laugh.

I take a seat at the table, ignoring her comments.

I have to get out of here.

God, please get me out of here. I beg of you!

I stare at the blank sheet of paper, take a deep breath, then pick up the pencil and start writing.

Dear Mom,
  How are you? I hope you are doing OK. I know you are still very angry with me. I know how upset and disappointed you are in me. I'm disappointed in me. I know I've hurt you. And I am so very sorry

for that. I hope that one day you can forgive me. You haven't stopped loving me, have you? I know I've said and done some bad things, disrespectful things. But you wouldn't really disown me, would you? I couldn't handle that if you did. I think I'd die.

I'm OK, I guess. I mean, I guess it could be worse. No. It can't get any worse than this. This is hell for me, Mom. But I am trying my hardest to make the best out of it by following the rules here. Something I know I should have been doing while I was home. I thought your rules were stupid rules. But they weren't. These rules here are crazy. I take back everything I've ever said about your rules being stupid. The only thing stupid was me not listening to you. I'd give anything to have to follow you and Daddy's house rules again.

Mom, I don't know what I was thinking. I only wanted to have some fun. I wanted my summer to be different from all the others. All I wanted was some excitement. I didn't think I'd get caught up in a bunch of drama. You were right, though. And now I wish I would have listened to you. But it's too late now. The damage is already done. I am here. At the mercy of a judge.

Stuck.

And scared.

The girls here are vicious. They all want to fight me. They've threatened to slice my face open. And stab me in my neck. I am afraid to go to sleep at night, even though the COs have put me in a room by myself. At night, it is the scariest here. I don't sleep. I can't sleep. I am too afraid to. I don't know how much more of this I can take. Sometimes I think about dying. Not that I want to hurt myself because I don't. It's just that I'm already dying inside. The longer I stay in here, the more of me withers away. I've lost everything.

But I know I have no one to blame but myself. I am the one who put myself here. It's my fault. And whatever happens to me in court or in here I know I brought on myself.

I just wanted to write you and let you know how much I miss you. And love you. I am so sorry for being disrespectful to you and for breaking curfew and sneaking out of the house and bringing drugs into our house. I should have never done those things. Please give me another chance to make it right. I'd do anything to be home, in my own bed. Being here has shown me how much I've taken my life, my freedom, and my family for granted. You never really know just how good you have it until it's taken away from you. You and Daddy have always wanted what's best for me. I know that now. I was too stupid to see it before.

I love <u>you</u> so much, Mom. Please, please, please come see ME. Or write me back. <u>Please</u>!!!!

Love,
Kennedy

When I am done, I reread the letter to my mom, then fold it and seal it inside an envelope. My next letter is to Jordan.

Dear Jordan,

I know you are mad at me. And there's a chance that you might not even open this letter or read it. But I had to write you anyway. I had to say I am so, so, so sorry. You were right! There's so much I want to say to you. All Malik did was use me. And now he wants me to rot in jail and take the blame for something that I had nothing to do with. The only two things I'm guilty of are: falling for a guy who was never any good for me, and dissing my two best friends. Malik never really cared anything about me. I know that now. And Sasha was never a real friend. She was just a girl I hung out with and went to parties with. She didn't care about me. She was jealous of me. I feel so stupid. Can you <u>please</u> find it in your heart to forgive me? I was such a fool! I'm so sorry for hurting you. I was wrong for putting Sasha and Malik before you and Hope. I see that now. You were so right about everything. I really hope it isn't too late to make it right between us. I miss my best friend!!! ☹ I am so alone in here. And I'm scared, Jordan. Please write me back. If you choose not to, I understand.

Friends forever (I hope),
xoxo
Kennedy
P.S. Next week I will be on honors level and I will be able to have visits from friends. Two friends can visit. The visiting time is on Saturdays at 10:30 in the morning. Please, please, please, please come see me.

I neatly fold her letter, then slip it inside an envelope and seal it. I do not know what will become of either letter once they are mailed. The only thing I can do now is wait. And hope. And pray.

I feel all of my emotions rushing over me.

And then there's an aching in my heart.

Malik.

Tears spring up from my eyes, but I fight them back, unwilling to break down in front of everyone in the dayroom. I'd given him every part of me. Did things with him that I never thought I'd ever do with anyone.

I gave up my virginity to him.

Because that's what he wanted.

Because that's what I *thought* I wanted.

Because I loved him.

I put myself out there.

Made myself vulnerable.

Because I thought he loved me.

But it's all a lie. Everything. I was so stupid. His sister, Mercedes, was right. His baby mother was right. Hope and Jordan were right. My mom was right. Everyone else knew, saw it, except for me.

But I got caught up. Caught up in his lies. Caught up in his touch, in his kisses, in his promises. I got caught up in wanting to believe that I was the girl of his dreams.

And now I am here.

And he is out there.

Free.

Doing God knows what.

Perhaps ruining the next girl's life.

I lay my head down on my folded arms resting on the

table. I am so helpless. The feeling that I am alone starts to overwhelm me.

"Snitches get stitches..."

"Don't you love me...?"

"I'ma need you to ride dis out for me..."

"You gonna have ta chalk it up to da game, baby..."

"You my heart, Kennedy; dat's on e'erything. But I ain't rockin' wit' no rat, yo."

The realization, the gravity of my situation, weighs heavy on me. I can't breathe. I feel myself starting to hyperventilate.

"...He doesn't know howta love anything other than what's between yo' legs, li'l girl..."

I start heaving.

I think I am having an anxiety attack.

I clutch my chest. Then without warning, unmoved by the stares on me, I cry my eyes out.

43

Another week flies by, and I am still here, rotting away. Confused. Torn. Hurt. Sad. Dejected. You name it, I'm feeling it.

I still haven't heard back from Jordan. And my mom is still refusing to talk to me. My whole life is a mess! And to top it all off, I don't know what is going on with my case. Or when my next court date is. I haven't spoken to my attorney since my last court hearing. And I've left him several messages, begging him to please come see me.

My dad is the only who has come to see me since I've been here. And as happy as I am to see him, our visits are always strained. He sits across from me looking so, so helpless. So conflicted. Then when it's time for visiting to end, he stands up and wraps his arms around me telling me how much he loves me. Then I have to sit back down in a hard plastic chair and watch him walk out the door. Sometimes I'd rather he not even bother coming here.

Seeing him leave—knowing I can't leave with him is so painful.

I know it hurts him as well.

And I have no one to blame but myself.

For being so stupid!

"Kennedy, you have to tell them whose guns and drugs they were in that bookbag," Daddy insisted last night when he'd come to see me.

I turned my gaze from his, casting my eyes down to my feet. "I can't," I whispered.

"What do you mean, you *can't*? Why not?"

"Daddy, I can't be a snitch. I just can't. Nobody wants to be known as a rat."

Yeah, snitches get stitches...

He raised his brows. "So you're more concerned about what the *streets* are going to think of you for doing what you need to in order to save your own butt?"

"Daddy, I have to be loyal."

He gives me an incredulous look. "To whom? The streets? A bunch of reckless street thugs? What about the loyalty to your family? To the ones who have always been there for you, huh? You mean to tell me you're willing to throw your whole life away protecting some thug?"

"Daddy, he's not a bad person."

"Then who is he? He sure isn't all that good, either. Any boy encouraging you to disrespect your mother, break curfew, and run away is nothing but bad news in my book. I want to know who he is so I can have a few words with him."

I blinked back tears. "Daddy, please. I can't tell you who he is."

"He's a coward, that's who he is," Daddy snarled, narrowing his eyes. "A punk. A worthless piece of—" He catches himself, shaking his head. "Your brothers all want to come home and handle him out in the woods like real men do. But they all have too much to lose. We all do. And so do you. What has gotten into you, Kennedy, huh? This girl you've become isn't the daughter your mother and I raised you to be."

I shifted in my seat, lowering my head. He was right. This isn't who I am. Or who they raised me to be. I wasn't surprised at his irritation, though. But seeing the hurt in his eyes killed me. I know that it's been building up inside of him, this anger. And I'm sure he wanted to yell, scream, and threaten me as well. And under different circumstances, he probably would, even though he's never raised his voice at me before.

Daddy shook his head, confused. "What has gotten into you, Kennedy?"

"I love him, Daddy."

He frowned. "Sweetheart, what you think you feel for that scum of the earth may feel like love to you. But trust me. Anyone who is willing to let you take the fall for him isn't worth loving."

Daddy's words stung. He was right. And even though I know everything he said was true, there's still a part of me that doesn't want to believe it.

I swipe tears away as I dial Malik's number. One of the afternoon social workers is nice enough to allow me to use the office phone. And I am thankful.

Malik answers on the fourth ring. "Yo." His voice booms through the phone. "Watz gucci, yo?"

"Malik. It's me. Kennedy."

"Oh, a'ight," he says nonchalantly. "Watz good? You a'ight?"

I glance over at the social worker sitting at her desk, writing in charts. I lower my voice. "No, I'm not all right. I'm scared, Malik."

"Oh, word? Don't be."

"How can you say that? That's easier said than done. You're not the one sitting here being charged with stuff that isn't yours. Why can't you write the judge a letter and tell them that it's yours?"

"Whoa! Whoa! Whoa! Hol' up...you talkin' mad reckless right now. I don't know what you're talkin' 'bout, yo."

"*Whaaaat?!*" I snap. "Are you freakin' kidding me?"

He sighs heavily. "Nah. I ain't 'bout to go down for some ish dat ain't mine. Dat's all you, yo."

"What do you mean it isn't yours? It was in *your* truck where *you* told me to go get it!"

"Nah, you buggin'. You wanna be 'bout dat life, then you need'a woman-up 'n' eat dat, yo."

"Malik, I've given up everything for you."

He lets out a sarcastic laugh. "Ha! Yeah, right. Don't hit me wit' dat ish, yo. You wanted to be all fast 'n' grown for yaself. I ain't have jack to do wit' dat. You gave up ya life 'cause dat's what you wanted to do. Now deal wit' it."

My heart sinks.

No, there's no way I heard him right. There has to be a bad connection. Or I am hearing things.

"W-what did you just say?" I ask, trying to make sure I heard him correctly. I hold my breath. Wait.

He repeats himself. "I said you gotta wear dat, babe."

I can't lie. My heart literally drops to my lap and explodes into a thousand pieces. This time I know I've heard him correctly, but I still want to believe, hold on to the possibility that somehow there's a mistake.

There is none.

And I am floored!

"How can you do this to me?!" I scream. The social worker taps her desk, giving me a look to lower my voice. "I'm sorry," I say, covering the receiver, then lowering my voice. "Malik, I'm in here because of you."

"What? Hol' up, yo. You in that joint 'cause of yaself."

"No! I'm in here because you gave me your gun and told me to go back to your truck, get the bookbag in the backseat, then put the gun inside. You told me to—"

"Get da *fuqq* outta here, yo. You buggin', for real for real. Ain't nobody put a gun to ya head to tell ya to do what you did."

Tears flood my eyes. "Ohmygod! How can you do this to me?!"

"Nah, love. Like I said, you did it to yaself. Next time know how ta move."

I stare at the phone, flabbergasted.

"Malik, *please*...don't do this to me, *please*...I thought you loved me!"

"Look. I'ma holla atchu later. You on some ole other ish right now."

And before I can open my mouth to get a word in, Daddy's words come back to haunt me just as the line goes dead.

"Anyone who is willing to let you take the fall for him isn't worth loving..."

A few seconds later, I am being dragged out of the social worker's office back to my cell, kicking and screaming hysterically. It takes three COs to get me back into my cell.

They place me on the bed, facedown. Tell me to stay still, but I am too busy crying to listen to anything they have to say.

I am distraught.

The COs are finally able to retreat from my room, slamming the steel door shut. I hop up from my bed, pacing the small space like a wounded animal. I squeal. Yelp. Howl.

"I can't believe that mofo! That…that…lowlife! I should have never let myself get involved with him! Aaaaaaah! Let me out of here!" I scream, banging on the door. I am caged in, like, like some savage. I start pounding and kicking the door. But it is no use. No matter how hard I kick and bang on the door, the door isn't budging. It isn't going to open. All it's doing is hurting my hand.

"Simms, knock it off!" a CO shouts.

I keep banging and screaming.

"I said stop making all that noise or I'm going to drop your levels and place you on IP."

"I don't care about room restriction," I cry out. "Leave me alone! I don't have any reason to stay on honors level! I want to go hoooooooome! Pleeeeeaaaase, let me out of h-h-heeeeere…"

I know I said I wanted a little taste of the wild side, a little slice of the hood pie. But I was so wrong. I take it all back. I don't want any of it. I want my life back.

I fall out on my little thin bed on its metal frame and cry and scream into my pillow until my throat burns and my eyes swell shut.

44

Three days after my phone conversation with Malik, and then my emotional meltdown, I am finally out of my room—I mean, cell. It doesn't mean much, however. Being out. I'm still here. I still feel caged in. Still feel trapped. Still feel stuck. Still feel like everything around me is moving in slow motion. But it's not. Everything is moving fast. Except for this case. Except for me getting out of this hell that I've somehow gotten myself into.

One of the social workers had the audacity to tell me that I needed to try to adapt. To stop fighting what I can't change. To accept that this, being here—locked up—is my reality... for today.

And yesterday.

And tomorrow.

And the day after that.

Well, guess what? I will never adapt to this way of being. I can't, won't, accept being in this place. Ever. I don't belong here. I belong home.

I should have never gotten involved with Malik! I wouldn't be in this mess if it weren't for him.
No, I wouldn't be in this mess if it weren't for me!
I'm such a fool!

"The prosecutor wants to offer you a plea agreement," my attorney says, interrupting my thoughts as he looks up from his legal-size notepad. He's finally decided to come to the detention center and show his face. "To discuss my case," he said when I walked into one of the spare offices used as a conference room. Whatever! Three whole days before my court date! Really?

It's Friday. I have court on Monday. My life depends on him getting me out of here. And this is the best he can do? I give him a confused look. "A plea agreement for what? I haven't done anything. Why can't they give me bail so I can go home?"

"Kennedy," he says, calmly, "there's no bail for juveniles in the state of New Jersey."

I huff, folding my arms across my chest. "Figures. Then why won't they release me on my own recognizance? Can't they do that?"

He gives me a sad look. "Kennedy, there's no easy way to say this. The ballistics report came back. There's a body on one of the guns..."

My eyes pop open. I cover my mouth. *Ohgodohgodohgod...I think I'm going to be sick!* I blink several times. Try to steady my rapidly beating heart. I can't believe what I've heard. A body?

"W-what do you mean, there's a body?" He tells me that one of the guns was used to commit a murder. That the prosecutor now wants to proceed with a hearing to waive me up as an adult, which means I could be facing trial as an adult and sentenced to at least fifteen years if I'm found guilty and convicted.

I can't believe what I am hearing. This has to be a bad dream I'm having. I know if I can just open my eyes everything will be back to normal. I blink back tears, then blink again. The tears start falling and I wipe them away with my hand as quickly as they fall.

"Can they really do that?"

He nods.

I don't know anything about a body, or a murder. I sob, begging and pleading for him to help me get out of this mess. "I didn't shoot or kill anyone. I swear I didn't. You have to believe me. I can't spend my life in prison! I don't want be waived up! Please! You have to help me get out of this!"

"Kennedy, the only person who can help you get out of this now is you. The prosecutor wants a name, and you can more than likely walk out of here with two years probation; if that."

Snitches get stiches…

"If you even think about snitchin' on my cousin's man, I'ma bust ya eye sockets out…"

I shudder in my seat.

"I-I-I can't." I start wailing all over again. "I didn't do anything!" He reaches into his briefcase and hands me some tissue, then gives me a few moments to pull myself together. Without looking at him, I ask, "Can't we take it to trial? I know the jury will believe me."

"Kennedy. I need you to look at me." I look up. He shakes his head. "There's no jury in juvenile court. If we take this to trial, all testimony is brought before the judge who will then decide your fate. And believe me. If you're found guilty, Judge Anderson is going to make an example out of you. She'll sentence you to the maximum."

I swallow.

"But I didn't do anything," I plead.

"In the court's eyes, you did."

"This is BS! I thought I was innocent until proven guilty?"

He sighs. "That is true. However, you were in possession of the backpack containing two guns and drugs, that's already been established."

"But they weren't mine," I cry out. "Why won't you believe me?"

"It's not a matter of whether or not I believe you. At this point, it'll be all up to the judge."

That lady hates me! I knew she was out to get me the minute she laid eyes on me!

I can't think straight. I am too numb to think.

I need to talk to Malik again.

"You gonna have'ta chalk it up to da game, baby..."

"Kennedy, I can't tell you what to do. I can only advise you. And as your lawyer, I'm telling you it's time you start trying to save yourself. So unless you want to be considered a suspect in a murder investigation, I suggest you think long and hard on what your next move is going to be."

"You gave up ya life 'cause dat's what you wanted to do. Now deal wit' it."

"My advice, Kennedy. Give 'em a name. And take the deal."

I swallow. "I c-can't."

He stares at me, then slowly shakes his head. "Whoever it is you are trying to protect, I hope they're worth your freedom."

Right at that moment, the CO sticks his head into the tiny conference room and tells us our time's up. I didn't want it to be over. I still had more questions, like what will happen to Malik if I tell on him? What will happen to me if they can't charge him with anything? If I give the prosecutor his name, will I have to do any jail time or will I really just get probation?

All of these questions float around in my head as my attorney gathers his things and heads out the door. The CO walks me out of the room. As I am being escorted back to the dayroom, all I keep hearing in my head is, *"Anyone who is willing to let you take the fall for him isn't worth loving."*

45

"The subscriber you are trying to reach has a phone number that is no longer in service..."

I blink.

"Oh, no. This can't be right," I mutter to myself, hanging up and dialing the number again, this time pressing each number slowly. Again, I get the same recorded message.

I feel my heart sinking fast. I dial the number again. Same thing.

"The subscriber you are trying to reach has a phone number that is no longer in service..."

I choke back a scream, clutching my chest. I try Sasha's number. She answers the phone on the third ring. "Hello?"

"Sasha. It's me. Kennedy."

"Oh, hey," she says, not sounding too happy to hear from me. "What can I do for you?"

I am taken aback by her tone.

I swallow. "I'm trying to get in touch with Malik. But

there's something wrong with his number. I have court Monday and it's really important I speak with him."

She grunts. "Good luck wit' dat."

I steady my breathing. "Huh? What do you mean?"

She pops gum in my ear. "Girl, look. I hate to be da one to serve you ya papers, but it's like dis: Malik ain't checkin' for you, boo. And neither am I. He said you too soft. I tol' him from da rip you was baby soft like cotton, but he ain't wanna listen. But now he see it for himself."

Tears rim my eyes. "Is that what he told you?"

"Uh, duh...who else you think said it? All he really wanted to do is hit dat, anyway. And you was so hard up for some of dat hood D dat you let him, too, didn't you?" She starts laughing. "You a sucka, Special K. So you gonna need to make dis ya last call to me. Got it?"

"Ohmygod! I don't believe you're saying all this to me! I thought we were friends."

She laughs. "Girl, miss me wit' dat. You thought wrong. We ain't never been friends. You were just somethin' to do, boo. You just some li'l spoiled rich girl who wanted so desperately to be down for da hood so I was tryna break you in; dat's all. I tol' Malik when he asked me 'bout you dat you were a wanna-be down chick. You was a bet, boo."

"A bet?" I say more to myself in disbelief than to her. I swallow to keep my voice from sounding shaky. It takes me a moment to open my mouth and get the question out. But as painful as it might be, I have to know what she's talking about. "W-what kind of bet?"

She hesitates for a moment, then says, "Dat he could turn you out."

My stomach tightens involuntarily. I feel myself getting sick.

"...Get out now before it's too late. All my brotha's gonna do is dog you out, sex you out, then toss you out like a used tampon. Just watch."

Hot tears splash out of my eyes.

My stomach twists and churns.

And then...I vomit.

All over the social worker's desk. All over the floor. Thick puke shoots out of my mouth like an erupting volcano, angry and violent.

My only thought is, *how could I have been so stupid?*

It's Monday morning. I've waited three whole torturous days; two hundred and fifty-nine thousand and two hundred seconds, four thousand and three hundred and twenty minutes, for this day to finally come.

I would be lying if I said I'm not a nervous mess to see Judge Anderson again.

After my phone call to Sasha last Friday, I felt like I'd been stabbed a thousand times over. I spent my entire weekend in my cell, balled up in a corner, rocking and staring off into space. I think I am losing my mind.

Really.

I feel so empty.

Drained.

All I have been doing is crying. And praying. That's all I can do. And, honestly, the only thing that saved me from trying to hurt myself is that I finally got to talk to my mom when I called the house last night.

She picked up. And as soon as I heard her voice, I broke down in tears, begging for her forgiveness. "Mommy, I'm so s-s-s-sorry f-f-f-for e-e-veryt-t-thing I said to you. I s-s-should have never disrespected you. I'm s-s-s-sooo sorry. I wanna come home. I never meant to say all those mean, nasty things to you. I-I was wrong f-f-f-for lying to you and sneaking out of the house. I know y-y-you hate me, Mom! I hate me! I've been such a fool! D-did y-y-you get my letter?"

I sobbed and cried and carried on so bad that the CO threatened to terminate my call if I didn't calm down. They are so frickin' heartless!

"Kennedy," my mom said calmly. "Yes. I got it. And I chose not to write you back. Why? Because I will not become pen pals with my now delinquent daughter who chose to be disrespectful and to run the streets doing God knows what."

I sniffle.

"You are my child. I could never hate you. I love you. But I am deeply hurt by your choices. And I'm saddened by the outcome. But you will have to stand by your choices. It's your life. Not mine. It hurts me knowing that my only daughter is locked up like some criminal. But I have to remember that you are the one who put yourself there. Not me. Not your father. *You.* I am always going to love you because I carried you in my womb and brought you into this world. But I will never, ever, entertain this mess you've gotten yourself into. Your father will be there for you. But I will not. All I've done is prayed on it. And I stand by my words."

Her words cut me deep. But she was right. I did this to myself. I allowed myself to get caught up in something I wasn't ready for. And now I have to suffer the consequences.

"I-I-I-I have court tomorrow. Will you be there, please?"

She blows a breath into the phone. "I don't know."

Two COs escort me in through the side door of the

courtroom. I spot my dad. And mom. My heart leaps. She actually came. But her body language makes it very clear: "I don't want to be here." I quickly cast my eyes downward to avoid her angry, hurt glare.

Still...I am happy she's here.

I am on pins and needles as I take my seat. Every so often I glance over my shoulder at my parents. Dad looks weary. Like he hasn't slept in weeks. Mom sits stone-still. Her expression is cold and hard. But her eyes are swollen and red. She's been crying.

I did this to them.

"All rise!" the officer calls out.

As soon as the judge sweeps in, her robe swishing in back of her, she takes the bench. Glances around the courtroom then says, "I have a full calendar so let's get right down to business, shall we?" She looks over at my attorney. "Counselor for the defendant, are you ready to proceed?"

He adjusts his navy blue tie and stands. "Yes, Your Honor."

The judge shoots a scathing look over at me. "Miss Simms, do you understand the severity of your charges?"

I nod. "Yes, Your Honor."

"And you understand the purpose of today's court proceedings?"

"Yes."

"Then why has the prosecutor informed me that you are not willing to cooperate with a plea agreement?" She peers over the rim of her glasses. "Counselor, have you not advised your client of the state's desire for a waiver hearing to adult court?"

"Yes, Your Honor. My client's been advised."

I hear my mom in back of me, sobbing. I turn to look at her.

"Young lady, turn back around. Face forward. Don't worry about what's going on in back of you. What you need to be focused on is what's happening right in front of you."

The voices of Malik and Mercedes and Jordan and my dad and my attorney start playing over and over in my head.

"...unless you want to be considered a suspect in a murder investigation, I suggest you think long and hard on what your next move is going to be."

"...I hate to be da one to serve you ya papers, but it's like dis: Malik ain't checkin' for you, boo."

"Understand this, young lady, your stupidity is what's going to get you a prison sentence with double digits behind it, do you understand what I am saying to you? Your atrocious disregard for the law. And your ridiculous loyalty to some low-life is..."

"Whoever it is you are trying to protect, I hope they're worth your freedom."

"Im'a need you to ride dis out for me..."

"Anyone who is willing to let you take the fall for him isn't worth loving."

"You young girls are so desperate and starved for the wrong kind of attention. Here you have two parents who love you and provide you with the best of everything and that isn't good enough. You silly girls will soon learn the hard way that the streets don't give a hoot about you. And those boys hanging on the block instead of in the classroom with their pants hanging down off their butts are nothing but trouble. Whoever you are protecting has done nothing but use you..."

"It was a bet..."

"And you're so blinded by what you think is love that you're willing to throw your whole life away for *nothing*. Girls like you come a dime a dozen. And just like he's manipulated you, he'll manipulate the next girl. The only difference is, he's out there. And you're the one willing to do prison time for him..."

I swallow.

I can't get waived up as an adult! I can't do some long prison term. I'm not built for that. Mercedes and Sasha were right. I'm not about that life. I never was.

I just want to go home.

Snitches get stiches...

I don't care!

I lean over and whisper in my lawyer's ear. "I'll take the plea. His name is Malik. Malik Evans."

Epilogue

A month later...

"Simms," the CO calls out, walking into the dayroom. "Let's go. You have a visitor."

Ohmygod! They came! Jordan and Hope really came to see me!

My heart skips with the excitement of being able to finally see my two besties after so many weeks.

I finally received two letters from Jordan. And we've spoken on the phone twice. I've apologized profusely. And she says she's forgiven me for the error of my ways. I know she was serious, but I couldn't help but laugh at the way she said it, all business-like. "I just hope you've learned your lesson. And know not to ever put some boy or some hoochie before your real friends."

"Yes, yes!" I said with tears filling my eyes. "I promise you. I have. I've been such a fool."

"Uh, yes, you have. But who's keeping track?"

I laughed. "I've missed our friendship so much. I've missed you!"

"Ditto," she said, then started asking me a thousand questions about what it's like being here. I told her I'd tell her all about it in my letter to her. Before we hung up, she promised to come see me during visits either today or tomorrow. She also told me how badly I hurt her when I chose Sasha, and Malik, and the streets, over her and Hope.

"But all is forgiven."

I hope so.

I miss my friends.

I miss my family.

I miss my life.

I miss my freedom.

I've accepted a plea agreement. And pled guilty to lesser charges of possession. Under the terms of my agreement, my attorney is hoping the judge grants me two years' probation since this is my first offense. Oh, and substance abuse treatment since my urine came back positive for marijuana. I don't need to smoke that stuff anyway, so it's fine. I told my attorney and the prosecutor everything about that night of the shooting. Told them the names of everyone I ever remembered Malik associating with. Even told them about what he'd done to that boy Shaheed after he tried to force himself on me.

And, truthfully, I felt relieved not having to hold all that in any longer. Sadly, I would have taken the weight for Malik. And what's even more frightening is knowing that had he not turned his back on me, I would have kept protecting him. And he really would have let me.

Daddy was right. He's a coward.

Anyway, I heard they raided his mother's apartment

and she and Mercedes were both arrested. And now Malik's on the run. But now he's the prime suspect for that murder. And when they find him, he'll get what he has coming to him.

Hopefully.

I get up from the steel stool I've been sitting on for the last three hours, anxious to get inside the visiting area. The CO waits for the officer behind the thick Plexiglas in the control center to push the button for the door. There's a loud buzz and the door finally clicks open. I step through the door, glancing around the room for Jordan and Hope.

They aren't here.

I am speechless.

It's Hazel Eyes.

He stands up, grinning. I walk over to him, shocked to see him. All eyes are on him. He's wearing a white Gucci T-shirt with a pair of loose-fitting designer jeans that hang slightly off his narrow hips, but not enough to show his underwear. A Gucci belt keeps them from falling down. He looks so...*fine!*

He opens up his arms and gives me a hug. I fall into his embrace, breathing him in. And I can't deny it. It feels good having his arms wrapped round me. A sense of calm rushes over me. I am happy to see him. And I tell him so. He hugs me tighter. And we stand like this for longer than we should because the CO has to tell us to take our seats.

I roll my eyes up in my head, annoyed that our moment has been snatched away.

"So what's good wit'chu?" he wants to know, taking his seat directly across from me. "How you holdin' up?"

I glance around the visiting area.

I do not belong here. I should not be here.

I want to tell him that I'm barely holding on. That there are days when I am ready to let go of the proverbial rope. That there are times when I really feel like giving up.

I pull in a breath, then slowly exhale.

"I'm holding on as best I can."

He takes me in with his sparkling hazel eyes. "This is crazy, ma." He shakes his head. "Seein' you in here like dis."

"So much for that whole good girl theory," I say lightly. I half chuckle.

"Nah, you still a good girl. You just did some bad things. But dat ain't you, Kennedy. You better than dis life. Always have been."

I smile.

"I'm sayin', though, you too fine to be up in here. This ain't a good look for you."

"I know." I shrug. "There's nothing I can do about it now." Subconsciously, I fidget with the hem of my shirt. The way he is sitting here looking at me as if he's trying to see through me makes me I am suddenly feeling exposed. Naked.

Hazel Eyes seems different. In a way I wonder why I hadn't noticed it before now.

"Yo, I know you gonna do wat you feel you gotta do, but you can't go out like dis. I know whatever they say you did, you didn't do it."

I give him a strange look. "And how do you know that?"

He slowly shakes his head at me. "I already told you. 'Cause you're one'a da good girls."

I huff. "Yeah, right. Look at me. You do see where I'm at, right?"

"Doesn't matter. You still gotta chance to make it right 'n' get back on track."

"Can we please change the subject? I really don't want to talk about this."

"Oh, a'ight. Cool." He sits back in his seat, folding his arms across his chest and opening his legs. He shuts them. Then opens them again.

We sit silently for a moment.

"What's ya favorite color?"

"Huh?" I say, giving him a confused look.

He smiles. "I'm changin' da subject, remember?"

I nod.

"So what's ya favorite color?"

"Are you serious?"

"Yeah."

I shake my head at him. Tell him it's pink.

He smiles. "Pink, huh? That figures."

"Why?"

"Because it's all girly."

I pretend to be offended. "Whatever," I say, laughing. Something I haven't done in like...forever. And it feels good, really good. "I am a girl, silly."

"True, true. A real pretty one at that."

I shift in my seat. Swallow. Butterflies start to flutter in my stomach and I don't know why.

"A'ight. So what's ya sign?"

"Virgo."

"Oh, a'ight. You got any pets?"

I laugh. "Ohmygod. How am I going to have pets when I'm locked up?"

He shakes his head. "I meant at home. Do you have any pets at home?"

"Are you really going to do this, here?"

He smirks. "Do what? Try to get to know you?"

"Oh. Is that what you're doing? I thought you was just changing the subject."

"Yeah, dat too. But, I'm sayin'...we really didn't get da chance to really build like I wanted."

I look away from him.

"Yo, just because you dumped me for ole boy, dat doesn't mean I still wasn't feelin' you."

"I didn't dump you," I say softly. "We were never a couple."

"Yeah, but we coulda been."

Maybe we should have been and I wouldn't be caught up in all this mess.

I see sadness in his eyes. Or at least that's what I think I see. Maybe it's what I want to see. Who knows? All I know is, I am so alone in this place.

And sad.

I want to tell him this. But I don't.

He reaches over and grabs my hand. Then squeezes it before the CO tells him, "No touching."

He quickly pulls his hand back, and I feel robbed of his touch.

I swallow. Lean in, then whisper, "I'm scared."

He nods knowingly. "I know you are, ma. But you ain't gotta do dis alone, a'ight?"

I blink back tears, nodding.

"Thanks, Blaze," I finally say, fighting back the urge to cry.

He grins. "Nah, it's KeyShaun. I'm no longer blazin'."

I give him a surprised look. "Oh. For real? Why?"

Hazel Eyes, I mean Blaze...no, KeyShaun...gives me an intense look. He gazes at me with eyes full of sincerity and says, "I got my eye on dis li'l hottie from da 'burbs so I'm tryna change my ways. You know I'm givin' up dem bad ways for da good girl."

He winks at me.

I shift in my seat. Sadness washes over me. "I'm going to be sentenced next week. There's a chance I may not be coming home."

"Yo, it's all good. I'ma be here for you. I'ma write you e'ery week. And I'ma be up here to see you e'ery weekend until you get out, a'ight?"

I start to feel overwhelmed with emotions. I don't know if I can trust him. But I don't have any reason not to. I just don't want to get used to him being here for me, then abandoning me, like Malik did.

He must sense my skepticism. "Listen. I ain't dude, a'ight? I'm not gonna hurt you. Or try'n play you. I'm gonna be here wit' you. Word to mother. I got you."

All I can do is smile, and think, *no matter what happens, I'll be okay.*

And for the first time in a very long time, I feel hopeful.

Finally, under dark swollen clouds, I am being led from the holding cell up to Juvenile Court. Today is the day. The day of reckoning. Judgment day. It's been two months since my last court appearance. And today is my sentencing.

I take a deep breath as the correction officers lead me into the courtroom for what I hope to be the last time. I've been praying like crazy, hoping for the best, but expecting the worse.

Still...I am scared to death.

I see my parents. They are both sitting in the first row directly in back of me. Daddy has his arm draped around my mom. She pulls in her bottom lip, blinking back tears. Daddy gives me a pained smile.

I smile back as I take my seat at the wooden table beside my lawyer. I look across the room at the prosecutor, Ms. Swanson. She has her hair parted on the side, and pulled back into a chignon updo. She is flipping through her notepad, scribbling notes.

All about me, I'm sure.

I lower my head and say a prayer. My heart starts pounding as soon as we're instructed to stand and the judge whisks into the courtroom and takes her seat on the bench. She wastes no time. She glances down at her folder, then looks up and scowls at me.

The prosecutor and my attorney go back and forth talking language that only lawyers and judges understand. I start zoning out. Nothing they are saying makes sense to me. At the end of everything, all I hear is my name, "Kennedy Simms..."

Please, God...

I close my eyes and cross my fingers as the judge rambles on about how I allowed my choices to destroy my life. And how I allowed myself to get caught up with the wrong crowd. And caught up with a boy who meant me no good. And that she is going to make an example out of me.

I swallow.

"Therefore, I hereby sentence you..."

My heart crashes against my chest.

"To three years in a juvenile correctional facility..."

My knees buckle.

I scream. *"Nooooooooooooooooo! Pleeeeeeeeeease!! Nooooooooo!"*

The last thing I hear before everything fades to black is my mother cry out as the judge bangs her gavel.

And I faint.

CAUGHT UP

Amir Abrams

ABOUT THIS GUIDE

The following questions are intended to
enhance your group's reading of
CAUGHT UP.

Discussion Questions

1.) Kennedy is a "good girl" who appears to have it all, but she seems willing to risk it all for a good time in the hood. Like Kennedy, there are lots of "good girls" from suburban areas who seem to have a fascination with the "hood" life and with dating "bad boys." Why do you think this is so? Are you fascinated with "bad boys"? If so, why?

2.) What do you think of Kennedy's friends, Hope and Jordan? They both have very strong negative beliefs about boys from the hood. Do you feel/think any of what they believe is valid?

3.) Why are so many young dudes from the hood viewed as high school dropouts, disrespectful, weed-smoking, pants-sagging "thugs" who either end up in jail, strung out on drugs, or dead? Do you believe/feel there is any truth to these stereotypes? Why or why not?

4.) Kennedy seems to have problems with her parents' rules. Do you think parents have the right to monitor who their children interact with/date, or where they hang out? Why or why not?

5.) Have you ever lied to your parents about whom you were with, where you were, and what you were doing? If so, why? Have you ever snuck out of the house? If so, were you ever caught? What were the consequences for defying your parents' rules?

6.) What are your thoughts about Malik and Blaze? They are both from the hood and have urban swag Kennedy is attracted to, but they have seemingly different personalities. Why do you think Kennedy chose Malik over Blaze?

7.) Kennedy seems to dislike being referred to as a "good girl" by Blaze and feels as though it's a bad thing. What are your thoughts on the whole good-girl/guy versus bad-girl/guy mentality? Are you a good girl/boy who's attracted to bad boys/girls or vice versa?

8.) What are your thoughts on Sasha? Do you think she set Kennedy up? Could she have possibly put something in Kennedy's drink the first time they partied together? Why do you think Sasha befriended Kennedy in the first place?

9.) They say love is blind, and it seems that Kennedy was extremely naïve and too trusting. Do you know girls like her? How many girls do you know who cut off their friends and disobey their parents in order to be with a boy and/or a new set of friends? Has this ever happened to you? What did you do?

10.) It's obvious Malik's sister, Mercedes, doesn't like Kennedy, yet she felt it her place to "school" her about her brother. Why do you think she does this? Do you think she's wrong for telling Kennedy those things about him? If so, why? Do you think

Mercedes is behind that girl coming to the house and fighting Kennedy?

11.) After everything that happens, Blaze still wants to be with Kennedy and still sees her as a good girl. What are your thoughts on that? Do you think Kennedy will learn her lesson from everything she's gone through? Why or why not?

Pretty little lies gone viral have left Hollywood High's elite Pampered Princesses reeling. Now their secrets are in 24/7 overdrive—and only one diva can be victorious in...

Hollywood High
Lights, Love & Lip Gloss

1

Rich

2 a.m.

I will not be played.
Or ignored.

And especially by some broke side jawn.

Never!

I don't care if he is six-feet-and hey-hey-hollah-back-li'l-daddy fine.

Or how much I scribble, doodle, and marry my first name to his last name.

He will never be allowed to come at me crazy.

Not Rich Gabrielle Montgomery.

Not this blue-blooded, caramel—thick in the hips, small in the waist, and fly in the face—bust-'em-down princess.

Psst.

Puhlease.

Swerve!

And yeah, once upon a time everything was Care Bear sweet: rainbows, unicorns, and fairy tales. He was feeling me and I was kind enough to let him to think we'd be happily ever after.

But. Suddenly.

He turned on me.

Real sucker move.

And so what if I keyed up his car.

Tossed a brick through his windshield.

Kicked a dent in his driver's-side door.

Made a scene at his apartment building and his nosy neighbor called the police on me.

Still...

Who did he think he was? Did he forget he was some gutter-rat east coast transplant?

He better stay in his freakin' lane.

I've been good to him!

I replaced the windshield and had all the brick particles swept from the parking lot.

The next day, I topped myself and replaced the entire car with a brand new black Maserati with a red bow on top.

The ungrateful thot sent the car back. Bow still intact.

I've done it all.

And how does he repay me?

With dead silence.

I don't think so.

I don't have to take that!

And if I have to sit here in my gleaming silver Spider, in this dusty Manhattan Beach apartment complex, and wait another three hours for Justice to get home, I will.

4 a.m.

I should leave.
Go home.
Call my boyfriend, Knox.
And forget Justice.
If he can't appreciate a mature, sixteen-year-old woman like me, then screw him.
No. I can't leave.
I have to make this right.
No I don't.
Yes. I do.

5 a.m.

Where is he?

6 a.m.

There he is.
But where is he coming from?
Was he with some chick?
My eyes followed a black Honda Accord with a dimpled driver's door as it pulled into the half-empty parking lot and parked in the spot marked 203.
The red sun eased its way into the sky as I pulled in and pushed out three deep breaths, doing all I could to stop the butterflies from racing through my stomach.
I should go home. Right now.
After all, he is not my man.
My man is at his college dorm, thinking about me.
I chewed on the corner of my bottom lip. Swallowed.

And eyed from the brick two-story and U-shaped garden-style complex Justice lived in to the small beach across the street where an overdressed homeless woman leaned over the wooden barrier and stared at the surfers riding the rough waves.

"Are you stalking me?"

I sucked in a breath and held it.

Justice.

I oozed air out the side of my mouth and turned to look out my window. There he was: ice grilling me. Top lip curled up, brown gaze narrowed and burning through me.

Say something! Do something!

"Can I umm...talk to you?" I opened my door and stepped out. "For a minute? Please." I pulled in the left corner of my bottom lip and bit into it.

"Nah. You can't say ish to me, son. What you can, though, is stop stalkin' me 'n' go get you some help. Thirsty. Loony bird. If I didn't call you, it was for a reason. Deal wit' it. Now get back in ya whip 'n' peel off."

Oh. No. He. Didn't! This scrub is outta control!

"For real? Slow down, Low Down. When did you become the president? You don't dismiss me. This is a public lot. I ain't leavin'. And you will listen to me. Now, I have not been waiting here for seven hours for you to come out the side of your neck and call me a freakin' stalker. You don't get to disrespect me. And loony bird? Really? Seems you've taken your vocabulary to new heights; now maybe we can work on your losin' career. And yeah, maybe I've been waiting here all night. But the last thing I am is some loony bird."

Justice arched a brow.

"Or thirsty."

"Whatever." He tossed two fingers in the air, turned his back to me, and walked away.

Unwanted tears beat against the backs of my eyes. But I refused to cry. "Know what, I'm not about to sweat you," I shouted, my trembling voice echoed through the early morning breeze. "I'm out here trying to talk to you. Trying to apologize to you. Trying to tell you that I miss you! That all I do is think about you! But instead of you being under-standing, you're being a jerk!"

Justice continued walking. Just as he reached the stairs, I ran behind him. Grabbed his hand. "Why are you doing this?"

He snatched his hand away, spun around, and mushed me in the center of my forehead. "I'm sick of your ish, ma. Word is bond. You don't come runnin' up on me." He took three steps closer to me. And we stood breasts to chest, my lips to the base of his neck.

"Justice—!"

"Shut up!" His eyes dropped eight inches.

I need to go. I took a step back and turned to walk away. He reached for my hand and quickly turned me back toward him. Pulled me into his chest.

The scent of his Obsession cologne made love to my nose and I wanted to melt beneath his large hands that he rested on my hips.

He tsked. "Yo, you selfish, you know that, right?" He lifted my chin, taking a soft bite out of it. "Word is bond. What's really good witchu?" He tilted his head and gazed at me. "Just when I start to treat you like no one else mat-ters, you turn around 'n' play me. Leavin' me Yeah Boo let-ters 'n' money on the nightstand, like I'm some clown mofo. I don't have time for that. And then you get mad 'n' eff up my ride, like that ish is cute. You lucky I ain't knockin' you out for that, for real for real. Yo, you a real savage for that."

I sucked my teeth, feeling the light ocean breeze kiss my face. "I was pissed off!"

He released his hold on my hips. "Oh word? So every time you get pissed you gon' jump off the cliff? Is that it? Yo', you crazy if you think I'ma put up wit' that." He paused and shook his head in disbelief. "Yo, I gotta go. I'm outta here." He took a step to the side of me.

"Wait, don't go!" I stepped into his path. "Justice, please!"

He flicked his right hand, as if he were flinging water from his fingertips. "Leave."

I ran back into his path, practically tripping over my feet. "Would you listen to me?!" Tears poured down my cheeks. "Dang, I'm sorry! What else do you want me to do?!"

"Nothing."

I threw my hands up in defeat. "I keep calling you and calling you! And calling you!"

"And stalkin' me. Playin' yaself. Comin' over here bangin' on my door like you crazy, then keyin' up my whip. What kinda ish you on, yo?"

I felt like somebody had taken a blade to my throat.

Play myself?

Never.

He had me confused. "I don't deserve—"

"You deserve exactly what ya greasy hand called for. You really tried to play me, yo. You got the game jacked, yo. I ain't no soft dude, real talk. I will take it to ya face." He paused and looked me over. "Then you had ya dude roll up on me and sneak me? Word? Are you serious? That ish got me real hot, yo. " He paused again. "I shoulda burned a bullet in his chest for that punk move." His dark eyes narrowed. "You lucky I ain't knock ya teeth out."

Was I having an out-of-body experience? No boy had ever spoken to me like this. Ever. I was stunned. Shocked. Confused. Desperate. Scared…

I didn't know if I was quiet because I couldn't think of anything to say or because I felt a tinge of fear that told me I needed to shut up. The bottom of my stomach felt like it had fallen to my feet. I watched him take three steps toward me and I wondered was this the end.

He yanked me by my right arm. "Let me tell you somethin'. I don't know what you standin' there thinkin' 'bout or what's 'bout to come outta ya mouth, but it better not be nothin' slick." He paused and I swallowed. "Otherwise, you gon' be pickin' yaself up from this concrete. Or better yet, the evenin' news will be 'bout you floatin' face down in the ocean."

"I-I-I-I," I stuttered, doing all I could to collect my thoughts. "If you would just listen to me! I didn't have anybody sneak you. I didn't do that!"

His eyes peered into mine. "Well somebody hit me from behind! Now who was it?! Who?!"

Without a second thought. Without concern. Without regard or a moment of hesitation I pushed out, "London!"

That's right. London.

That crazy thot.

My ex-bestie.

Another one who turned on me. Tried to take hate to new heights by inviting me out to Club Tantrum and attacking me. For no rhyme or reason.

"London?" Justice repeated in disbelief. I could tell by

the look he gave me that what I'd said took him aback. He frowned. "Are you serious? London?"

"Yes, London! She's the real thirsty loony bird. Real crazy! She even jumped me at the other night! I know you had to see the blogs."

"What the..." He quickly caught himself. "Do I look like the type of dude checkin' blogs?" He pushed his index finger into my right temple, forcing my neck to slant to the left. "Now say somethin' else, stupid."

My kneecaps knocked, my heart pounded, and my throat tightened.

I should leave. This was a bad idea. Apparently, he can't appreciate me standing here, trying to woman up and handle our situation.

"Do you hear me talkin' to you, yo?!" he screamed in my face. "I said, what you mean it was London?"

I hesitated. "She just came from nowhere. You and I were standing there talking and the next thing I knew you hit the ground and there was London hovered over you with nunchuks in her hand!"

I searched his eyes to see if he believed me. The truth was it wasn't London. It was Spencer, my real, loyal, ride-or-die bestie. She'd snuck him. Hit him in the back of his head. And when he didn't move, Spencer and I got scared, took off, and left him for dead.

But none of that was the point. London deserved to wear this one. Especially since I was done with her. "I'm telling you it was London! She came from nowhere. You hit the ground and she was there with a bat in her hand!"

"London?" he repeated, shaking his head. "I thought she was over in Italy somewhere."

"Lies! She was never in Milan. That lunatic was home all

along, curled up in the bed! And I just knew she killed you! I just knew it!" Timely tears poured down my cheeks. "I'm sorry that I left you. I am. I was sooooo scared. I didn't know what to do. I called the hospitals! I called the morgues. I was even willing to pay for your funeral. I'm just so sorry. And when you were on that ground, motionless, I tried to shake you and you wouldn't move. London took off! I heard sirens. I got scared and I just ran!"

I boldly took a step toward him and pressed my wet cheeks into his chest. "You gotta believe me, Justice. I just knew you were dead. I really did and I didn't know what to do. I thought the police were coming. And I didn't want them to think it was me who killed you so I ran too! It was stupid." I stammered. "I-I-I left my car. Everything! It was crazy! I just got caught up in the moment! I thought you were hurt. I thought you were dead! You weren't moving! You should've seen the look in her eyes! That girl's crazy!"

I wept into his chest and he wrapped his arms around me and squeezed.

I batted my wet lashes. "Baby, did you do something to that girl?" I asked.

"Oh, so now I'm ya baby?" he asked in disbelief.

"Yes, Justice. Yes. Of course you're my baby."

"Really?"

"Yes. But why does London hate you so much? Did the two of you used to be a couple or something? I thought you were only friends."

"Yeah, we used to be friends. All that's dead now." He wiped my wet cheeks with the backs of his thumbs. "Now, back to you." He lifted my chin and placed a finger against my lips. "The next time you come outta pocket, tryna slick-talk me, I'ma slap ya mouth up." He tapped my lips lightly and I kissed the backs of his fingers. He snatched his finger away. "Nah, I don't think so. You still in the dog-house wit' me. Now what you gonna do to get outta it?"

"What do you want me to do?" I whined. "I'll do whatever."

"What you think I want you to do?"

I slid my arms around his thick neck and whispered against his chin. "I can show you better than I can tell you. Can I come inside?"

"Yeah." He ran his hands over the outline of body. "Right after you call ya man." He pulled his cell phone out of his back pocket. "And dead it."

My heart dropped. "Whaaaaaat? Clutching pearls!" My eyes popped open and I felt my breath being snatched.

"Ya, you heard me. Call that punk now." He pushed the phone toward me.

I took a step back and he took a step forward.

"You said you'll do anything, right? So do it. You said I'm ya baby. Then prove it. 'Cause, real ish, yo... I'm second to none."

"You being second to none and me breaking up with Knox, my soul mate, my future husband and future baby daddy, are two different things. He has nothing to do with this."

"Oh word?"

"Word. No. He. Does. Not." I shook my head and placed a hand up on my hip. "You need to learn to play your roll as a side piece 'cause you are all out of control. Appreciate the time I'm spending with you instead of standing here and thinking about my man. Like really? Who does that?"

Justice popped me on the mouth, just enough for it to

sting but not enough for it to hurt. "Let me be real clear wit' you: You ain't gettin' upstairs. We ain't kickin' it. I ain't effen witchu 'til you dead it wit' dude. Got it? Now poof. Outta here." He forcefully turned me around, practically yanked me back to my car, snatched open the door, and pushed me inside.